"TELL ME WHAT REALLY HAPPENED."

Letting out an explosive breath, he pulled me to my feet and we stood there, looking into one another's face like figures frozen in a moment of time.

"Please, Tara, believe me," he whispered hoarsely, "what happened cannot be changed now. Let it go." His hard mouth descended angrily on mine, as if to force my acquiescence. There was no tenderness in the arms that held me in an iron embrace. Hard, muscular sinews pressed against me and the hands splayed across my back held me with vinelike firmness.

I could not move away from the desire surging between us, engulfing my senses. I had longed for his embrace, turned restlessly in my bed dreaming of kisses and caresses that would carry me into the swells of passion, and there were no defenses I could summon now that fantasy had become reality.

LEONA KARR

OBSESSION

With love,
to my own handsome heroes,
Clark, Leonard, Jeff, and Marty

Book Margins, Inc.

A BMI Edition

Published by special arrangement with Dorchester Publishing Co., Inc.

Printed in the United States of America.

OBSESSION

1

Heavy air laden with moisture floated across San Francisco Bay and shrouded the theater district, where we had our lodgings that September morning in 1869. Gray clouds moving across the sun's face were almost opaque, like a heavy veil masking a dreary face. Ghostly wisps of fog hung low to the ground and swirled over the cobbled streets as carriages, hacks, drays, and horse-drawn trolley cars vied for passage through the bustling downtown area. Even at nine-thirty in the morning tinny music floated out of gambling houses and saloons and raucous laughter could be heard above the din. Merchants scurried to open their sidewalk stands as they peered anxiously at the pewter sky and set umbrellas into position over their merchandise. Muffled calls of vendors and newspaper urchins along Kearny Street blended with the sharp sounds of iron wheels and horses' shoes clattering through pools of water left from last night's rain. The capricious wind had a touch of malice in its chilly gusts as it swept off the ruffled waters of the Pacific Ocean and San Francisco Bay. I shivered as we walked to our appointment with Tyrone Langston at the Imperial Theater.

There was no reason for me to go with Budd and Jessie to the interview except that I couldn't stay in the rented room I shared with Nell. I knew she was expecting a "gentleman caller," and a seventeen-year-old girl hanging around would have been *persona non grata*. These romantic tete-a-tetes of Nell's had been a part of my life for as long as I could remember. As soon as our little theater troupe settled its baggage, some admiring swain would appear on the scene and soon I would be obliged to melt away into the wood-work until the romantic liaison was over . . . or we moved on to the next variety hall.

I can't remember being annoyed or put out by this arrangement. After all, Nell Trevor was as close to a mother as I'd ever had. In New York, in the early 1840s, even though they were no relation, Nell and my mother, Nola Townsend, had been billed as the Trevor Sisters. I'd seen old pictures of the Trevor Sisters, arm in arm, smiling and showing their ankles in a teasing fashion. After my mother's death, when I was still a child, Nell's over-flowing affection and her impulsive mothering came in spurts as I grew up. A flamboyant, natural redhead, now almost forty and pleasingly plump, Nell still retained a kind of lascivious, bold beauty. Her racy conversation, twinkling green eyes, and musical peals of light laughter were enchanting. I loved her dearly and took her excessive flaunting of social convention without question. She was my beloved Nell and so I took myself out on the cold, windy streets of San Francisco and hugged myself as I walked along the boardwalk,

8

looking longingly at the horse-drawn trolley cars as they passed.

The fare was only a few cents, but Jessie had deemed that the walk would do us good, and refused to take any coins out of the strapped box that hoarded the troupe's earnings. None of us questioned Jessie's miserly ways, nor protested the fact that every coin and gold nugget tossed upon the stage was quickly confiscated and all wages quickly commandeered and then reluctantly doled out when necessity dictated—and the term *necessity* had to meet Jessie's interpretation of the word. This tiny, formidable woman, tightly corseted in brown bombazine, was the only one of our group who was not a performer, and all management and financial affairs were held by tight reins in her small but steely hands. She wouldn't admit her age, but I guessed it to be close to fifty.

Budd and Jessie Rafferty were substitutes for the family I had never had. My father and mother, Richard and Nola Townsend, had been a part of the same theatrical group that landed on hard times in New York just about the time the gold rush was beckoning dreamers to make the perilous journey by land and water to the west coast. The troupe decided to come to a boisterous San Francisco, which promised to be a mecca for players willing to travel the circuit into the goldfields in 1852. It was reported that miners were eager for any kind of entertainment and generous with any new-found wealth.

The long trip by way of Panama took a toll on my mother's health and finally resulted in her death when I was only two. Nola Townsend had been slender and fair, which accounts for my own flaxen-colored hair and slight build, but I've been told that my deep-set, gray-blue eyes came from my father . . . and perhaps his willful disposition as well.

Apparently, he was a handsome rogue who viewed the theater as a lark, without much devotion to the art of acting. After the death of my mother he took off for Australia with some scheme of making a fortune in the country "down under." Unfortunately the old, weathered schooner he had taken ran into bad weather, and although some survivors were rescued after spending many days adrift, my father was not one of them.

I don't suppose my life changed much after I was orphaned by his death. By then, Jessie and Nell were surrogate mothers and tall, brawny, good-natured Budd Rafferty, younger than Jessie by about ten years, was always there to toss me in the air and make me giggle by trying to count my ribs. This likeable Irish comic was responsible for my debut on stage at the age of three, although no one had planned it that way. I was a plump child with a mass of natural curls bobbing on my head, growing up in the midst of the paraphernalia of costumes, wigs, and props. One evening, when the troupe was playing in boisterous Nevada City, I was amusing myself backstage as usual when I found a soldier's cap and toy gun in a trunk. With the innocence of a child, I promptly put it on and wandered out on stage to show Budd. At the moment he was in the middle of his drunken Irishman routine.

The audience roared instantly at the appearance of a grinning little blond girl wearing a soldier's hat and pointing a popgun. Being the showman that he is, Budd quickly recovered his surprise at my stage entrance and capitalized on the situation, giving me a smart salute. They said I laughed deeply and gave him one back. Then he marched around the stage with me in his wake, mimicking his long steps, as he sang some ditty with a rollicking air. Everything he did, I did, and I even joined in on the familiar song. More coins and nuggets than ever fell upon the stage that night, which Jessie collected in one of her shoes. These men were far from their own homes and children, and a lively, curly-headed girl found instant acceptance in their hearts.

And so began my theatrical career. I was billed as "Wee Tara Townsend, entertainer extraordinaire." Often I wore boy's clothes, did a fancy Irish jig, and played the banjo. Budd elaborated on our impromptu soldier routine and discovered that my talent lay in mimicry. I could impersonate the old, the fat, a clown or a snooty lady, all with a comic touch that delighted audiences. During those years we never played the fashionable theaters, but traveled from one crude mining camp to another, performing wherever there was room on stages made of a pair of sawhorses and planks with a flannel blanket for a curtain; in feed stores amid sacks and mining implements, barrooms, with gambling tables shoved to one side, and even in open tents with the high Sierra winds blowing through them. In Sacramento and San Francisco we had to be content with crude facilities like the upstairs of a billiard parlor, where an impromptu stage had been set up. I was carefully guarded by my surrogate family and was never allowed to make contact with any of the audience at any of our engagements. They quickly swept me on stage before these raucous crowds and off again. We kept on the move like gypsies, often traveling at night to the next place where we might put on a show.

Jessie kept me dressed in little girl's clothes long beyond the time when most girls lowered their skirts and put up their hair. I passed for eight when I was really twelve, but time caught up with me when I reached my teens. I filled out nicely and became too tall to mask as a youngster any longer. The last few years I played some minor parts, but, unfortunately, like all child stars my zenith had been reached. Apparently I had not inherited any great talent from either my mother or father and San Francisco audiences were wanting Shakespeare, comic farces, and melodramas beyond my ability.

Our tour of the mining camps had been less profitable than usual this year. Too many theatrical troops were making the circuit from Sacramento to Nevada City. That was why we had lost nearly all our company; only five of us remained. Besides Nell, Budd, Jessie, and myself, the only remaining member of the Rafferty Players was Farley Naylor, a gentle, hard-working Australian, somewhere in his thirties. He had loyally stuck it out through the hard times and his lean, ruddy face readily spread in a reassuring smile even when our best efforts did not bring in enough coins to buy his pipe tobacco.

Budd and Jessie were on their way to talk to Tyrone Langston. The owner and director of the Imperial Theater was signing on some new talent for the coming season and Budd was hoping that there might be a place for the remaining Rafferty Players in his new productions.

As we walked along Kearny Street, Budd put his brawny arm around my shivering shoulders. "If Langston signs us on, Tara, honey, sure we'll be getting you that new coat you've been needing."

Jessie snorted. Her currant-black eyes gave us both a disparaging look. "There's plenty of wear left in that wool cape Nell had a couple of seasons ago. I heard her say the other day that she was going to toss it in Tara's direction." Jessie's prim little mouth was set in a no-nonsense line.

Budd gave me his crooked grin, and one eyelid

lowered in a preceptible wink. "Seems to me there'd be enough cloth in one of Nell's cast-offs to be wrapping around Tara three times over. Besides, I'm thinking she might be liking something suitable for a young lady." His kind eyes flickered over the faded green plaid bodice and skirt that Jessie had rescued from a discarded costume basket. It had been worn in a Highland skit a few seasons back, and Jessie added an inset of grosgrain down the front to accommodate my full breasts and rounded hips. The skirt was off the ground by at least three inches, and Jessie had been eyeing it as if debating the economy of adding a band to it in order to extend its use for one more season. I wore a simple scarf over my head instead of a bonnet and no gloves.

At the moment I was less concerned about the fashionable aspect of my attire and more aware of the lack of warmth the dress provided against the chill of the dank breeze seeping into me bone deep. I hugged myself and tried to bite some warmth into my chilled lips. I was glad that the Imperial Theater was only a few blocks away. I had never been inside it. When our little troupe played San Francisco we were lucky to get a run in one of the variety playhouses. More than once we settled for an upstairs meeting hall or the back room of a saloon and counted ourselves lucky. Budd was the only real talent in the group, and it was because of his delightful sense of comedy and timing that Tyrone Langston was even considering hiring the Rafferty Players . . . but if Langston wanted Budd, he'd have to take the rest of us as well.

I think Budd would have taken off his coat and put it around my shoulders if he hadn't been dressed to make the best impression on Mr. Langston. The long frock coat, striped trousers, stiff collar, and white linen had seen many hours on stage, and Jessie had dug in the costume wicker basket in order to dress her husband properly for the interview. He was to represent the Rafferty Players, accompanied by Jessie, of course, because no business deal had ever been finalized without her grim nod of approval. I was just tagging along as I had been doing for several years now. My days of bringing in a steady flow of coins and nuggets had passed. My theatrical talents seemed limited, and efforts to bridge the triumphs of childhood to a mature actress had left me in some kind of limbo, and I had little ambition to be anything but a small part of the productions our troupe was able to perform. That this resignation and acceptance was to be wrenched away from me on that dull, gray day was bewildering even as I look back on it and realize that my whole life would have been changed if Nell hadn't had a male caller that afternoon.

I suppose there was nothing mystically grand about the square stone building that housed the Imperial Theater, but that morning it seemed to rise through the mist like some kind of royal residence, with Tyrone Langston its undisputed monarch.

"Of course, it's his gambling hall that's made him wealthy," said Jessie, as if trying to lessen the anxiety Budd was feeling about meeting San Francisco's wealthy actor, director, and property owner. "Langston came to California ten or twelve years ago, dead broke like the rest of us."

"He didn't stay that way long," Budd mused.

"Only because he saw men for the fools that they are . . . drinking and gambling their wealth away as fast as they get it." A begrudging admiration was in Jessie's tone even as her nose quivered distastefully. "He built the Golden Nugget and gave Frisco's gamblers and lucky prospectors a chance to make him

14

a rich man."

"Well, I'm thinking you can't fault him for that," Budd answered as we crossed the street. "He can't be more than thirty . . ."

"And filling up his pockets with both hands," Jessie added with her usual crispness as she eyed two large buildings dominating the street.

Next to the Imperial Theater was the gambling house, the Golden Nugget, which had started Ty Langston on his road to wealth. I thought Budd walked by it a little reluctantly, as if thinking a few beers even this early in the day would gird up his courage for the interview ahead. Jessie purposefully kept up her firm stride and led us to the imposing front doors of the Imperial Theater, a handsome gray building of cut stone with regal arches over the doorways.

Accustomed to side entrances in back alleys, I think we all felt presumptuous entering the front door of this legitimate theater. The three of us stood for a moment in the carpeted foyer of red and gold, shimmering in the crystal light of wall sconces and glistening chandeliers, as if we expected momentarily to be discovered and instructed to go around to the side door. Budd had automatically swept off his derby and was turning it nervously in his hands. It was Jessie who moved forward, with Budd and me in her wake.

As a quick-moving young man came down the steps of a curving staircase mounted against one wall, Jessie's crisp voice cut through the hushed silence as she addressed him. "Sir, we are looking for Mr. Langston's office."

"Upstairs . . . end of the corridor." His Mediterranean or Slavic features matched dark, curly hair tumbling around his face. He had the darkest eyes and eyebrows I had ever seen, and there was a hint of the artist about him. I wondered if he had just been interviewed. He seemed too small and slight to have much stage presence. Without pausing for further conversation, he rounded the carved newel post and disappeared through a doorway on the main floor without giving us another glance.

Jessie and Budd started to mount the carpeted staircase, but I held back. "I'll wait for you here."

They nodded in agreement. We all knew that my presence would not add anything to the interview. "Good luck," I called softly after them as they mounted the carpeted stairs and disappeared in the upper corridor.

Nervously, I wandered around the foyer, drinking in the elegance of its huge chandeliers and deep red carpeting. Gilded frames, hanging by long, gold cords, graced the red flocked walls, and I slowly made my way around, looking at hand-tinted photographs of Ty Langston in several of his roles.

I was not aware at first that something peculiar was happening to my breathing as my eyes met his in a series of Shakespearean productions. Then a sudden quickening of my heartbeat told me that I was reacting to the intensity of each portrayal. I knew that on stage he must command the audience with every gesture and word. One photograph showed him portraying a white-haired King Lear, his deep-set eyes dark and crazed. Another highlighted that bold forehead furrowed and his dark eyebrows drawn together with the mental agony of Macbeth. As I stared at it, I felt myself caught up in the anguish of a man consumed by ambition, and his torment was mine.

I turned away, and my eyes met his in the role of young Romeo. My foolish heart suddenly lurched. Thick, brown hair traced with chestnut highlights fell in casual waves around a vigorous, startling, bold, yet sensitive face. There was a twinkle of the rogue in that handsome visage, as if he knew the bewildering reaction his picture was having upon me. I could almost hear him laugh. My own lips curved as I responded to the invitation of his eyes and felt heat easing up into my throat. Under a purple velvet cap and large plume, he held me with a lover's gaze, and for an absurd moment I fantasized that I was the beloved Juliet who had set his blood on fire. I could almost hear endearments issuing from that full, rich mouth. My gaze traveled over the graceful curve of his neck and chin, and lingered on strong cheek bones that were slightly shadowed. The muscle in one cheek seemed to quiver in response to my stare. I took a step backward, as if the assault upon my senses was a huge wave spilling over me, dragging me under with bewildering intensity.

With a force of will, I turned away. Those eyes seemed to follow me across the foyer, through the curtained doorway, and into the theater proper. There was a warning in the air as tangible as the flickering gas lamps along the walls. I had never been one to give myself up to visions of ghostly specters or superstitions, but the back of my neck tingled as if a hand had been laid upon me. Even as I mentally chided myself for such foolishness, I could not chase the premonition from me . . . nor could I identify it. A peculiar sense of urgency was upon me as I moved down the dark center aisle toward the bare stage, where muted light was shining out from the wings.

I slowed my steps and looked up at the beautifully embossed ceiling, gilded and painted, accenting elaborate roccoco designs. Elegant boxes with swags of heavy wine drapery lined the sides and there were select seats in the dress circle and parquet on the main floor with a long balcony stretching across the rear of the auditorium. I feared with sinking despair that it would never be the home of the Rafferty Players. It was too grand, too much above the bawdy playhouses that dotted the mining camps, and too demanding of a dramatic repertoire that might be beyond the talents of our troupe. It certainly wasn't the place for a child protegee who had outgrown her talent and appeal. If Budd wasn't saddled with the rest of our mediocre troupe, he might make it here, I thought rather sadly.

I suddenly felt at home in these surroundings. A musty, close air tingled my nostrils with familiarity. This hushed, waiting, possessive silence claimed the heart and soul of anyone who dared venture out upon a stage. I knew that breathless moment of anticipation just before the curtain was raised. Even the cheap variety houses echoed before a performance with shuffling feet, raucous cheers, and the rumbling of the creature known as *audience*.

As I mounted the few steps at the side of the stage and pushed through a heavily draped archway, my excitement heightened. This might be the only chance I would ever have to see a legitimate theater, with dressing rooms that weren't closets or crowded halls, to view scenery that was more than painted canvas.

I expected to find several stagehands backstage who would be willing to show me around. Although I had developed shyness toward the public in general, I was always at ease with anyone connected with the wild, unpredictable entertainment business, and enjoyed talking to hard-working grips as they handled changes of scenery and props. I was surprised and disappointed to find the cluttered area beyond the wings deserted.

Stepping around ropes, barrels, baskets, and stacks

of frames, my footsteps echoed on the wide, dusty boards as I wandered about. A narrow back door caught my attention. Curious, I tried to open it, but it was locked.

Lifting my skirts, I went down a steep staircase, grateful for the amber light of several gas wall lamps. A hall branched out in two directions at the bottom of the stairs. I arbitrarily turned one way and found the green room, a long, narrow room, painted white, with notices of rules and fines posted on the wall. Some props, discarded costume baskets, chairs, wooden and upholstered, dainty settees, and a variety of tables. All looked well-worn, and I could visualize players gathered before rehearsals and performances, scattered about the room, talking, laughing, and quietly rehearsing lines.

I entertained a moment of wishful thinking that when the next season opened we would all be here, Nell, Budd, Farley, and, of course, Tara Townsend. Just what role I would be playing I couldn't quite visualize. Perhaps it was this foolish daydreaming as well as the chill left in my body from our walk that made me pause in the middle of the green room and pick up a dark green cape left lying on top of a wicker basket filled with clothes. My fingers caressed its deep, rich pile with pleasurable strokes. I raised it to my cheek and pressed my skin against its luxurious warmth.

Impulsively, I took off my head scarf and settled the long, elegant cape on my shoulders, pulling the hood up on my head. Its warmth brought forth a delicious sigh. If only I could have a winter wrap like this one, I thought. How elegant I felt. How womanly . . . how utterly feminine! Wisps of blond hair fell untidily around my face as I bent over a basket to touch the soft velvet folds of a blue gown.

At that moment I heard a movement in the doorway behind me, but before I could turn, I was assaulted by a deep and resonant voice. "Maureen . . . Maureen!" There were so many emotions threaded in that name that for a moment I couldn't react.

Imploring hands touched my shoulders and spun me around. Before his face registered disbelief, deep-set eyes met mine with the same lover's gaze and sensuous curve of the lips that had sent my heart plummeting when I gazed at his photograph. "You're . . . you're not Maureen." Disappointment flickered at the corners of his mouth and his eyes shuttered, as if to protect vulnerability. I could not read his thoughts. His face had closed against me.

At that moment I wanted to deny my own identity and be the woman he sought. I wanted to bring back that flush of tenderness in his eyes. I wanted his touch to be gentle and caressing, not the harsh grip he maintained on my shoulders.

The hood fell from my head, pulling my pinned hair down with it. "I . . . I was cold," I managed to say, not knowing how to explain the cloak around my head and shoulders.

His hands dropped away, but the heat of his touch remained on my skin. The face I had already memorized from his photographs was just inches from mine. A spicy, masculine scent, no doubt left by a barber's tonic, teased my nostrils. His attire was impeccable. He wore a fine maroon coat and white linen with starched collar and cuffs. A soft silk cravat matched fawn trousers that hugged his vigorous frame. His nearness melted sight and sense into a bewildering sensation that left me with a sudden quickening of fear.

"I'm sorry . . . I mistook you for someone else. . . ." he said apologetically, moving back. "Forgive me for startling you. I'm Ty Langston."

"Yes . . . I'm here with Budd Rafferty . . . he has an appointment with you at ten." My voice sounded thin and ineffectual. "I was looking around while I was waiting." I didn't realize until later that I had not given him my name.

"I see." He lifted a gold watch from a pocket of his embroidered waistcoat. "Yes, I believe I've kept him waiting."

Just then the small, dark-haired man I had seen before came in. "There are some people in your office, Ty."

"So I have just been reminded." His crescent-shaped eyebrows came together. "Cal, what are Maureen's things still doing here?"

"She left her stuff all over the place, but I think I've got it all gathered up now." He glanced at me as I dropped the cloak back into the wicker basket and then frowned as he asked Langston, "Has Maureen sent word where she wants them shipped?"

"No, she refused to tell me what her plans were, but she won't be back. When she left my office she slammed the door hard enough to break the pane. No use keeping the things she left . . . dispose of them." Once more his voice was subtly threaded with deep emotion.

Cal nodded.

Then, like someone coming out of a deep tunnel, Ty sighed and seemed to be aware of me again. His quick glance traveled over my dress, which seemed to me more shabby than ever. If he had offered me the clothes at that moment, I would have haughtily refused them, and the pattern for disaster might have been avoided before it even began . . . but he didn't. Something in my face must have warned him, for he made a polite bow and said, "Excuse me." He left the room with an easy stride and I could not believe the sudden emptiness that enveloped me at his going.

Struggling with the havoc my encounter with Ty Langston had made of my emotions, I stared after him. Then I felt Cal's dark eyes upon me and commanded some degree of composure as I turned and said politely, "It's a beautiful theater . . . are you an actor?" My voice was amazingly even, considering the peculiar fluttering in my stomach.

The small man's smile was slightly cynical. "Everything but, I'm afraid. Calabrese is the name, Cal for short. I play the piano accompaniment for the melodramas and variety skits. The rest of the time I'm the proverbial man Friday."

"Tara Townsend, the Rafferty Players. We hope to sign on here for next season."

He nodded. "Yes, I know. I hope it works out for you." Then he spread out his artistic hands in a rather helpless gesture. "I don't know what to do with all this stuff of Maureen's."

"Who is Maureen?" For some reason I found myself holding my breath, as if the answer was terribly important.

"Last season's leading lady, Maureen Cole."

"And she . . . left?"

"Yes. She walked after her last performance, a couple of weeks ago. She and Ty had a whale of a fight—don't know what it was about exactly—but she said she wasn't coming back for this season. I don't know what to do with all these things. Guess I could give them a good burning."

I must have given a horrified gasp. His dark eyes narrowed, and I felt him weighing some kind of decision. "It does seem like a shame. I don't suppose you . . . you could help me out and take them off my hands?"

Afterward I wondered if it was pure greed that made me finger the lovely cloak and feast upon the gowns. Or was it the need to somehow become the woman who had brought such emotion into that deep, resonant voice? I had felt Ty's touch upon my shoulders, looked into the translucent depths of those brown-black eyes, and trembled from the impact. His warm breath had bathed my face. A physical need like a deep ache had already permeated the deepest recesses of my emotions. Although I sought to deny it, I wanted to subjugate my own identity. I wanted Ty Langston to touch and speak to me in that tender fashion, as he had in the brief moment he thought me to be someone else. In short, I wanted to be Maureen Cole.

A tremble of excitement that I had never felt before engulfed me. I wiped sweaty palms on my faded dress and eagerly picked up the velvet cloak!

A warning was there, but my emotions had already spun out of control.

2

I'll always remember the festive air that permeated our boarding-house table at dinner that night. Jessie had allowed Budd to buy a bottle of cheap, robust wine in honor of the celebration—a contract had been offered to the Rafferty Players! As I had expected, it was Budd who had been signed, at a respectable salary of sixty dollars a week. Jessie had driven a hard bargain for the rest of us; Nell was to receive twenty dollars for minor roles in melodramas and farces; Farley Naylor, fifteen dollars for character parts; while I was hired as a supernumerary, or extra, at the bottom wage of eight dollars for walk-ons and background scenes.

I don't remember being the least bit disconcerted about my low position in the hierarchy of actors. Even at the height of my career as a child star I had never been puffed up by my popularity. The clapping and shouting was just a fun part of dancing and singing and playing the clown with Budd. Because of the protective distance Jessie and Budd had always kept between me and the audience, my only motive for pleasing the people who watched was the amount of coins thrown upon the stage at the end of my performance. Farley had more than once assured me that I had done my bit for the Rafferty Players and it was up to someone else to take over now. Since Jessie seemed satisfied with the amount of money I would be adding to her strong box this next season, I was content and felt as much a part of the Rafferty Players as I ever had. As we laughed and joked about performing in a legitimate theater, I was not aware that in accepting the wicker basket of clothes I already harbored an insidious viper that would soon thrust this complacency from me.

Of course, Jessie was delighted with my haul. Her clutching fingers pawed the rich garments of pluche, velvet, and soie de Londres, undergarments of purest lawn, tiny ribboned bonnets, hand-stitched gloves, and a dainty, beaded reticule. I could almost see her salivate as she held up each item and eyed it with the avaricious gleam of a miser. I knew that if she had her way, she would parcel out the clothes for the next five years, one at a time, to be worn until threadbare, or her nimble sewing fingers would turn them into curtains or spreads as the need arose.

Nell's good-natured laugh held only delight at my good fortune. Her plump shoulders shook as she exclaimed, "Heavenly days! Would you look at that!" She held up an oriental wrapper of blue satin. Her greenish eyes twinkled. "And who's this Maureen Cole? Someone's sweet darling, I suspect," she said with a bold wink.

"She . . . was Langston's leading lady," I managed.

"And that's not all, I wager." Nell's lewd grin

26

brought a flush of heat to my face. I was used to Nell's earthy, robust manner, but in this instance I resented it. For some bewildering reason, which I was not ready to pursue at that moment, I didn't want her talking like that. I was not naive. I knew exactly what she meant. I could feel the muscles in my jaw tightening.

"Well, come on, tell me a little about our new director, Tarry . . . is he really the legendary rogue that everyone says?" She laughed and prodded. "What does he look like?"

How could I describe the bold contours of that vigorous face, which could change from a crazed King Lear to the soft, adoring gaze of a loving Romeo? He was handsome to be sure, but his outward appearance could have been matched by many gentlemen of pleasing visage. It was something more. Ty Langston projected a masculine aura and virility, dangerous and bold, that made his presence on and off the stage dynamic and impelling. Looking into his eyes, he had snared my mind, my reeling senses, and sent my pulse beating wildly. Even now his features suddenly swam before me, and I quickly lowered my eyes, fearful that my dear Nell could look into them and see his face reflected there.

Jessie said primly, "Don't be thinking he's one of your good-time Charlies, Nell. You better stick with your button salesman." Nell's romantic exploits had been at odds with Jessie's puritanical upbringing, and although she loved Nell dearly, like the rest of us, she couldn't forgo the opportunity to show her disapproval.

Nell tossed a red mass of curls; her greenish eyes snapped mischievously, "Well now, I guess it don't hurt none to look over the merchandise. Right, Tarry?"

I must have flushed, for her reddish eyebrows rose questioningly. I didn't want to tell her about the incident in the greenroom, and the mistake Ty Langston had made as I stood in the cloak with my back to him. Just thinking about that moment when he spoke to me in those deep, compelling tones still set off a tremulous fluttering in the pit of my stomach. I remembered his nearness, that face bent close to mine, and the caring that had been there for that brief moment when he thought I was someone else. Those lips could be warmly passionate, for I had seen their softness and been drawn into their spell. I lowered my eyes without answering and pretended great interest in a pair of ladies' colored silk hose, delicately emroidered in fawn colors.

"He wasn't bold with you, was he?" she demanded, always the protective guardian, alerted to my inner confusion. "What happened, child?"

She knew me too well.

I shoved away the memory of those strong hands on my shoulders and those brown-black eyes briefly searching my face before disappointment set in. "I'm not a child," I snapped, "and nothing happened."

"Tyrone Langston gave you these things . . . why?" Nell prodded.

"He didn't give them to me. A fellow named Calabrese did! Mr. Langston told him to get rid of them," I explained. "Apparently, Maureen Cole ran off and left a lot of her things. Cal said he was going to burn them."

Jessie gasped. Such wanton waste was beyond her comprehension. "Oh, no!"

"Anyway, he asked me to take them off his hands . . . so I did."

"And you did right, Tara," Jessie assured me. She nodded, and the tight, graying black knot on the top of her small head bobbed vigorously. "We'll decide which outfit would be the most suitable and put the rest away in the trunk—"

"No." I pulled the wicker basket away from her. It was a childish gesture but I was exploding inside. It was as if a spirit outside myself had taken possession. My eyes were blazing and my muscles tautened. White-knuckled hands gripped the handles of the basket. The air was suddenly charged like before a summer storm. The two women looked at me as if I were a stranger. "They're mine!" My voice was almost a growl.

"And did I say they weren't?" Jessie snapped, her thin lips held in a disapproving line.

"Let her alone, Jessie . . . maybe it's time . . . seventeen is the right age to let the sap start running." Nell's green eyes narrowed in speculation. "It seems our Tara has grown up—all in the space of one afternoon." Then she tried to lighten the words with her ready laugh, but there was an uncomfortable tension between us and, though it was my fault, I didn't know how to smooth it over.

The balance between Jessie's rigid code of ethics and Nell's casual life-style had given me an outlook that was a blend of conformity and wanton willfullness. Jessie had assumed responsibility for my education and any rebellion on my part was quickly suppressed. She had been brought up in a proper home and our gypsy way of life did not interfere with instructions in proper speech, needlework, and ladylike graces—even if they had to be practiced in crude lodging houses or on the move to the next mining camp. No child or young girl had been forced to read more "good literature" or learn more passages from a well-worn Bible.

Nell, on the other hand, only laughed tolerantly at

someone else's puritanical morality. Her spontaneous, affectionate, hedonistic attitude toward pleasure had not passed me by without influence, causing me to dally backstage with a young fellow named Chad and invite some furtive, fumbling kisses and pledges of undying love. Farley put an end to the budding romance and set Chad on his way with a threat of bodily harm if he showed up again. Even Nell approved of the action in a surprising, hypocritical way, and I found her immune to my tears and threats to run away and find him. Since then, Jessie and Nell had increased their vigilance, making sure the affair was not repeated. I soon forgot about my broken heart and was content for the most part to accept their authority. Perhaps Nell sensed that those days of tight control were gone forever.

So that was how those fashionable, new clothes came to be mine . . . and I could wear them whenever I wished! I was satisfied with my little victory.

Before supper that night I freshened up in the community bathroom down the hall, and when I returned to our sleeping room I was glad to see that Nell had already gone downstairs to sit in the stuffy parlor with her drummer. I discarded the weary green tartan dress. With nervous fingers, I dug in the wicker basket, finding a pair of soft, lace-trimmed drawers, a soft camisole, and a lightly boned corset of muslin and Valenciennes lace. I had always avoided such uncomfortable lacings. As Nell's full figure increased, her struggles to keep her waist small had been rather ludicrous. I had decided that corsets and affectations of bustles and swelling bosoms were rather ridiculous, but I had been viewing them from a different perspective than the one I now held. Even though my waist was already a narrow span, the tight lacing gave me the illusion of a larger bust and more rounded hips, and as I practiced breathing in this new confinement, I decided that these womanly curves compensated for the uncomfortable, viselike squeeze around my middle.

A beautifully hem-stitched petticoat was cut fuller in the back than the front to accommodate a padded bolster over my buttocks. It swished enticingly as I slipped it over my head and let it fall in soft folds to the floor. Out of the basket I chose a pale blue lavantine dress with matching bodice and skirt. I discovered that the fit was remarkably good, and a little adjustment at the waist made the front panels lie smoothly across my hips and then gather in a saucy flounce at the back in a daring bustle. A rounded neckline was fashioned with an inset of lace curving the lines of my breasts so that their fullness was suggested more than revealed. In spite of its modest cut, the decolletage was more daring than any I had ever worn. This was no adolescent gown but one fashioned for a provocative, sensual figure.

A thinly silvered mirror above the washstand gave back a rather disjointed reflection as I turned and preened in front of it. I kept wondering if I looked anything like the woman to whom the dress belonged. She must be blonde, I thought, for my hair had fallen free of the cloak's hood when Langston turned me around. I could tell that our stature and figure must have been much the same now that the corset had elevated my bustline.

A flickering oil lamp sent an elongated shadow of my figure upon the faded wallpaper. I peered at my face, wanting it to be different. The blue-gray of my eyes had deepened with the reflected color of my gown, but I was dissatisfied with the slender nose and firm bone structure that thrust up piquantly in an oval face. My mouth was full and not cupid shaped, matching the rather bold jut of my chin. Crescent eyebrows engendered a wide-eyed, alert expression rather than a coy, demure one. For a moment I played with the muscles in my face. My talent at mimicry allowed me to assume an expression that was older, slightly suggestive of a haughty, regal demeanor. I curved my lips seductively and lowered my eyelids to a sultry angle. Then my natural, mischievous humor got the better of me and I began to laugh at my own reflection.

I brushed my hair and caught it modestly in its usual loop at the nape of my neck, despairing of the strong natural curl that eased wispy ringlets around my face and made a fringe on my forehead. I sneaked some of Nell's rice powder and violet eau de toilette and bit my lips to increase their natural light pink color. Satisfied that I had made enough of a metamorphosis for one evening, I wondered if I dared go downstairs and let the boarders have a look at the new Tara.

Now that I was ready I dallied. I knelt down at an open window and let cool evening breezes bathe my face. A valiant sun had burned off the fog and misty clouds during the day and left a luminous, freshly washed, exciting mecca that was San Francisco at night. I pulled back cheap curtains that obscured my view of the street below. The boardwalks were crowded with people, talking, gesturing, smoking, spitting, and hurrying into saloons and shops or just promenading and taking the night air. A cacophony of noises greeted my ears in the delightful medley that was the city; mounted riders sent a steady clop of horses on the cobbled street, rumbling carriage wheels struck iron upon the stones as the fashionably elite rode to a variety of engagements on California, Montgomery, and Kearny streets; the blare of a long trumpet from a coach and six heralded its passage; cries of vendors and peddlers mingled with piano music and laughter pouring out of saloons and gambling halls, where fortunes rose and fell. There was no scene to captivate the senses like this boistrous city as the population swelled with a flow of immigrants, all with stars in their eyes, all clinging to the promise that a fickle fate would grant them their most cherished dreams. My deepest longings cried out for such a dream. My breath and heartbeat mingled with the pulse of the city as if it were my own. As I daydreamed, I allowed my imagination full rein until the dinner bell broke my reverie and put an end to my romantic musings.

I was excited but relaxed as I went downstairs. If the world is a stage, so was Mrs. MacPherson's dining room, and I swept into it with all the exaggerated posture of a femme fatale. I couldn't keep amusement from playing at the corners of my lips as I touched my hair in a coquettish fashion.

My audience was ready to receive me and they laughed and clapped as I took my place at the long oval table. "Bravo! An entrance worthy of Lola Montez. Who is this lady of fashion? Surely not our own Tara Townsend."

I grinned and bowed and exchanged light banter with my affectionate theatrical family. Budd had a paternal grin on his craggy face and Nell's eyes shone with laughing appreciation as her bright gaze swept over my corseted figure, noting the fashionable bustle on my derriere. Her new conquest, Mr. Strosky, a middle-aged man with thatches of black hair spouting all over his head and upper lip leaped to his feet and gave me a polite bow at the introduction, as if I were truly a fashionable lady. Nell watched him, amused, as if secretly delighted that he had been fooled by my impersonation. Jessie's sharp eyes traveled over me, still assessing the quality of material in my gown and seeming pleased with the wear left in it.

I took my usual seat by Farley, our import from Australia, who had been with the Rafferty Players since he was about fifteen years old and I was six. He had an odd expression on his face that startled me. For a moment he seemed like a stranger instead of good old Farley.

With bewildering, sudden insight I realized that he wasn't much older than Ty Langston. I suppose he had a kind of unpolished handsomeness; thin face, nice eyes, and gangly frame. As a boy he had been enamored by the budding Shakespearean actor, Edwin Booth, then an unknown touring down under. The flamboyant Booth, in his usual garb of a black serape over a red shirt, fitted dark pants, and Hessian boots, captivated the fourteen-year-old Farley and the lad attached himself to Booth's company when it returned to California. Farley often told the story of dragging Booth, dead drunk, out of the Sacramento River and pouring brandy down his throat until the actor growled, "Who wo' me up?"

For as long as I could remember he had laughed and teased me the way Budd did so I wasn't prepared for the expression on his lean, angular face as I sat down and laughingly turned toward him. Dark-flecked hazel eyes were fixed upon me with sober questioning. I saw the muscles in his ruddy face tighten and I thought he was terribly angry with me.

"What's the matter?" I asked, startled. I touched his arm in my usual, casual way. I couldn't remember Farley ever being coldly displeased with me. He was the brother I never had. I could depend upon him to interfere when Jessie was in one of her cantankerous moods, and more than once he had gotten me out of trouble of my own making. "What is it?" I murmured, bewildered and anxious.

"Nothing . . . I . . . just startled, I guess." Peering through the shock of sandy hair covering his forehead, his eyes suddenly had a wintry glint. "I mean . . . that's quite a get-up."

"It's not a get-up," I insisted stubbornly. "It's time I started dressing my age."

"It seems to me you're adding a few years to it in that outfit." His eyes fell to my swelling decolletage.

"You better get used to it," I answered pugnaciously.

He didn't respond, but his expression eased.

"Don't you like the new me?" I prodded.

"I can't say that I do," he answered frankly.

I swallowed a caustsic remark just as Mrs. MacPherson bustled in with a Chinese servant holding white crockery dishes, steaming with mounds of mashed potatoes and pieces of mutton swimming in gravy and carrots. Identical bowls were placed at both ends of the table, with thick slices of homemade bread on a wooden board placed in the middle. As if a whistle had been sounded, the food was attacked from all directions. Boarding-house fare went to the aggressive and the quick. For a few minutes all attention was centered on filling up one's plate before the food disappeared and the empty bowls were taken back to the kitchen.

Budd passed around the jug of wine and soon conversation began to compete with the sounds of the meal. Story-telling was always a part of dinnertime, and soon a one-upmanship brought one tale after another about early San Francisco days . . . when Little Egypt danced the hootchy-kootchy at the Midway Plaisance . . . the time Charlie Fairfax, the Beau Brummell of the day, was stabbed, his blood spreading on a Sacramento street . . . and, of course, Sam Brannan, whose cry of "Gold, gold!" initiated the greatest pilgrimage of fortune-seekers in history. I had heard most of the stories before, but I delighted in the raucous history of this city that refused to conform to any established, decorous behavior. Already the town had been nearly burned down three times, new and better buildings simply rising again.

"I hear the new Crystal Hotel is being heralded as the finest hotel in the country," said Mr. Strosky. "A palace of opulence, catering to San Francisco's elite clientele." He said it as if he might be assessing how many people might reside there who would be customers for his bone, pewter, and glass buttons. Although mansions were beginning to grace Nob Hill, many of the wealthy preferred to live in hotels catering to their every wish.

"And who might the 'elite' be?" Budd laughed. "You've heard the ditty, 'The miners came in '49, the whores in '51 . . . and what came after are called the native sons . . .' "

We all laughed, knowing that San Franciscans had tried to mimic New York's society and identify their elite "four hundred," without much success. Wealth was held by too many upstarts who often could only trace their genealogy back to a wandering father.

I was only mildly interested in this talk of a new hotel until one name jerked me up like a taut wire. "I heard Langston is one of the major investors," remarked Nell's button salesman. "He's got one whole floor for himself and part of his company."

"Well now, I wonder if he's got room for the Rafferty Players?" Nell laughed facetiously and without rancor. We all knew that Mrs. MacPherson's boarding house was as grand as we were going to get.

Jessie didn't like this kind of talk. If she had her

way, we would move into cheaper accommodations even though we had landed jobs that would pay for our board and room and a little left over for her strapped box.

"A toast to Ty Langston . . . and the greatest season the Imperial has ever had!"

My hand trembled as I raised my glass, and in the swimming liquid I saw a pair of brown eyes shining like stone under water, and for a second my vision blurred. "To Ty Langston," I murmured, and let the raw, robust wine burn down my throat.

After supper Nell settled herself on a settee with Mr. Strosky in the small, crowded parlor. In a cozy, intimate manner, punctuated by giggles and soft murmurings, they began looking at some European scenery through Mrs. MacPherson's stereoscope. Nearby, in her usual corner, Jessie thrust a tatting shuttle in a growing band of trimming as she sat in a straight-backed rocker that took her tiny feet off the floor with every rock.

Sensing my restlessness, Farley asked if I'd like to take a walk. The day's excitement had left me keyed up and tense so I readily agreed. Portsmouth Square was nearby and since our coming to San Francisco we had enjoyed taking several turns around it before bedtime.

"I believe I'll be stretching me own legs," Budd said casually, joining us at the door as I slipped my new, warm cape over my shoulders and pulled the satin-lined hood around my face.

Farley and I exchanged amused looks, for we knew it wasn't exercise Budd was seeking but a mug of beer at some nearby saloon. We hadn't gone a half block down the street before the Irishman verified it by asking Farley for the price of a couple of drinks. Jessie never turned loose any coins for such indulgence, but

Farley kept enough from his wages to buy tobacco for his pipe—and beer for himself and Budd.

"Sure and it's a dry throat I have." Budd grinned, giving us a jaunty salute. As we watched his easy amble into the Bella Union, we felt like conspirators successful at outwitting dear Jessie.

Portsmouth Square had been laid out early in the city's history and had been the site of hangings and vigilante activities. Even now, it was the favorite site for Washington's Birthday celebrations, fire-fighter drills, and community gatherings. Even though the financial and commercial center of the city had spread to the south and east, property flanking the square was still deemed to be the most desirable. On all sides a variety of buildings rose tier by tier, some delightfully adorned with balconies and bay windows, others flaunting intricate gingerbread eaves, stained-glass windows, and wide doorways that gave enticing glimpses of flamboyant interiors.

I stilled an audible sigh as we walked past them. If only my escort was the elegant Ty Langston. In a foolish moment of tantalizing fantasy, I imagined that firm, muscular form moving in rhythm at my side, our thighs slightly touching as we brushed against one another. We would laugh and talk and touch. Who knows . . . perhaps the gown I wore had been on such an outing. He had recognized the cloak, so I knew that at some time Maureen Cole had worn it in his presence. Where had they gone? Had he slipped his arms around—

"What are you thinking, Tarry? You have a peculiar, glazed look in your eyes." Farley's voice shattered my reverie.

"Nothing . . ." I stammered. "Just enjoying the walk."

We had entered the square. A variety of stimuli

assaulted our senses. The night air was scented with heliotrope, lavender, lemon verbena, and deep green foliage. As we walked along its criss-crossing paths, music from the nearby amusement houses sent the strains of violins and flutes to mingle with the offerings of a lone harmonica player sitting at the base of a crude statue donated to the city by some artist. Couples strolled under the canopies of arching, forest green branches and lingered behind flowering shrubs. It was a night for lovers and the thought brought new emptiness to me.

"Shall we sit for a moment?" he asked as we approached a rustic bench just off the path.

I nodded. It was foolish to indulge myself in fanciful thoughts that charged the night with excitement, but I could not subdue a gnawing ache, a growing need that I did not quite understand.

On some level of attention I listened to Farley reminisce about the high Sierras, where we had ridden horses and mules from one camp to another. He had been our front man, riding ahead into a crude settlement, beating a drum, and alerting the inhabitants that an entertainment troop was coming. He was the one who arranged for space in some accommodating store, saloon or stable, and housing for us if we were to give more than one show. When we traveled he was usually by my side, making certain I got safely across a rampaging stream and didn't get too close to the edge of a treacherous mountain precipice.

When I outgrew my drawing power as a child performer, he was the one who made light of it. The gangly, ruddy-faced fellow was not a talented actor himself, but the Rafferty Players had become his life and the acceptance of his limitations was a help to me when I outgrew my childhood fame. He had been there like a big brother when I tried to make the transition from "Wee Tara Townsend" to mature roles—and had failed. The extent of his protective role had come to light during my brief romantic tryst with Chad, and that was the first time I had seen him truly angry.

As we sat together on the bench, I suddenly realized his posture was stiff. I forced my thoughts away from Ty Langston. A furtive look in his direction caught him accessing my face, framed by the ruffled satin edging of my hood, as if he found something strange there.

His manner made me self-conscious. Did he sense something different in me, a change that was more than the wearing of another woman's clothes? Was the sudden quickening of my body obvious—like the sudden opening of a bud to the sun?

"Why are you looking at me like that?" I demanded. "If you are trying to make me self-conscious, it's working," I added, tossing my head.

"I'm sorry . . . I guess you caught me off-balance, Tarry," he said softly, using the nickname he had given me.

"You're like everybody else. You want me to plait my hair in pigtails and wear little-girl dresses for the rest of my life."

"That's where you're wrong. When you came sweeping into the dining room tonight I felt as if someone had hit me in the middle of my stomach."

"But why?" I looked up at him, innocent of the emotional upheaval hinted at by the heated flush in his face. What was the matter with him? Why was he gazing at me in that peculiar way? When he leaned over and touched my forehead with a soft, caressing kiss I stiffened, stunned by its sensual overtones. I drew back. With a plunging certainty I knew that nothing would ever be the same between us again.

"Didn't you know, Tarry?" he said huskily. "I've been waiting a long time for you to grow up."

3

We gathered in the green room on the appointed day and waited for our director to make his appearance. As we wended our way backstage, the bustling activity there was in sharp contrast to my first visit to the Imperial Theater. Several grips, men who moved scenery about, were busily organizing the chaotic mess left by previous productions. I looked up and saw agile flymen working on an iron grid above the stage. Their job was to make certain lines and pulleys were free to move side wings, backdrops, and overhead flies. These men were strangers now, but I was confident that I would soon know them all. Some of my happiest moments had been spent sitting on a keg or trunk while stage roustabouts rolled cigarettes and exchanged humorous and disastrous stories backstage. I wasn't surprised when Budd greeted Billy O'Dell, a fellow Irishman who had worked backstage in the first Jenny Lind Theater before it burned down. Billy bragged that he had been in charge of the stage crew since the Imperial opened.

I felt perfectly at home as I coughed from the dust bellowing from sandbags that counterbalanced the drop curtains. I stopped and gawked as battens were raised and lowered efficiently by an assortment of ropes that ran up overhead blocks and pulleys. Billy had a good crew. Rope ladders were hung along the wall leading upward to a rigging loft, and more than once I had scurried up and down similar ladders with the same joy with which other children climbed trees. Often the ropes would get tangled, and a flyman would have to climb into the high rigging and walk on the iron girder to handle the snarled lines. Even cheap variety halls depended upon painted backdrops with various scenes to divide up the stage so that the next act could be readied while another was being performed. As a child I loved to dog the heels of some grip and was always underfoot; I had my fanny smacked more than once when I was slow in getting out of their way. Billy gave me a hug and nodded, " 'Tis a fine lass, you've grown into . . . and to think I used to box your ears."

These memories brought a smile to my lips. The familiar mixture of odors teased my nostrils. There was no smell like it; paint, canvas, dust, rope, oil, leather, powder and rouge, and lingering effluvium of persons who had graced the stage and dressing rooms. A vibrant energy was captured in these surroundings; the stage was empty now, but pent-up human emotions portrayed there would be released in catapulting words and action. The theater, with its painted backdrops, was no make-believe world for me. In these surroundings my whole being was encased in a capsule of laughter, tears, pain, and joy, waiting to be shared with a greedy beast called an audience. This world of studied emotions was the only reality I had ever known. It was little wonder that I had no yardstick for measuring the pretense that was to take over my life.

On this occasion I wore the same blue levantine dress I had chosen first from the basket. It seemed to lead me gently into the woman I wanted to be, while the other garments I had gleaned in the wicker basket mocked my girlish face and naivete. I wore a small feathered bonnet of Nell's over my naturally curly hair. My stubborn efforts to smooth my hair in a twist at the nape of my head had been in vain. Rebellious wheat-colored strands slipped forward into wayward tendrils that defied the womanly look I sought to achieve.

As we waited in the green room, moisture beaded on the palms of my hands. Despite a stern scolding, my romantic and foolish self could not quell the tremulous excitement that bubbled through my veins. I was going to see Tyrone Langston again! He had been in my thoughts like a whisper of a song that is always there, encroaching upon my waking moments and invading my dreams. I wondered how he had put such a spell on me. Perhaps I hoped to verify that my fascination had been fleeting, a momentary reaction that would instantly fade once I saw him again. Then I would have a good laugh at myself and accept the fact that for some bewildering reason I had allowed myself to be momentarily mesmerized by his voice and touch.

A murmur of excited voices filled the long, narrow room as the new company assembled for the first time. It was a large group and the five Rafferty Players were lost in the collection of actors, singers, dancers, acrobats, jugglers, and magicians that made up the Langston Theatrical Players. It was apparent that the Imperial was going to present a variety of attractions: Shakespearean drama, riotous farces, minstrel shows, melodramas, and several after-piece acts.

Farley renewed acquaintance with some actors who had been in San Francisco nearly as long as he. They stood about, sharing some stories about Edwin Booth's experience ''seeing the elephant,'' which was a euphemism for a luckless trek into the goldfields. As I had feared, Farley and I had failed to recover the friendly, easygoing companionship that had existed between us, and I had begun to avoid his company.

Across the room, Nell's infectious laughter rose merrily as her mischievous and inviting eyes collected several gentlemen around her. I could tell that Mr. Strosky's moment in the sun was already waning as Nell prepared to move on to newer pastures.

Nervously, I paused in front of a newly posted listing of rules and scanned them.

Green Room Rules

The Green Room is a place appropriated for the quiet and regular meeting of the company, who are to be called thence, *and thence only*, by the call-boy, to attend on the Stage. Every Performer is to be dressed for the performance ten minutes before the time of beginning as expressed in the bills or forfeit Five Dollars.

After due notice, all rehearsals must be attended. The Green Room clock, or the Prompter's watch, is to regulate time for the first call; Four Dollars fine for each ten minute tardiness. A Performer rehearsing from a book or part after proper time has been allowed for study shall forfeit Five Dollars.

A Performer introducing his own language, or improper jest not in the script, or singing songs not advertised in the bill shall forfeit Five Dollars.

Every Performer's costume is to be decided on by the Director, and a Performer who makes any alteration in dress without consent of said Director, or refuses to wear costume selected, shall forfeit Three Dollars.

A Performer absenting himself from the Theater on the evening when concerned in the business of the Stage will forfeit a week's salary, or be held liable to be discharged, at the option of the Director. A Performer's refusal of a part allotted by the Director forfeits a week's salary, and/or may be discharged.

There were more rules, twenty of them, in fact, but I stopped reading. It was apparent from the severity of fines that Ty Langston was a stern and formidable director. I couldn't help but worry about Budd. His easygoing manner and love of stout ale could easily wipe out a month's wages in the run of a play. Jessie was going to have her work cut out for her. I wondered if she had already read the posted rules.

Jessie had accompanied us to the theater in the hope of securing employment as a seamstress for the company; her fast needle had saved many of our costumes from the rag bag. She sat primly in a chair in an unobstrusive corner, her small feet together, her head erect and those sharp currant eyes evaluating every performer in the room. Budd, on the other hand, stood casually near her, one thumb caught in his belt, his weight resting on one foot. He bent his tawny head and said something to her. For a moment there was a flash of softness in Jessie's prim, little face, and I thought she might have been quite pretty when she was young.

More than once I had mused over the incongruity of this couple and their apparently happy marriage. Their backgrounds were as different as their personalities. Jessie was the daughter of a Protestant minister who had felt "called" to leave his comfortable church life in Boston and become a circuit preacher in the expanding western frontier. Unfortunately, his Bible was no protection, and he was shot in a skirmish between two claim-jumpers. His death left Jessie with the responsibility of taking in sewing and washing to feed a consumptive mother and three young brothers. It was a temporary job sewing costumes in the first Jenny Lind Theater that brought her in contact with Budd, a friendly, out-going Irishman who could make an audience roar with his comic antics. The son of a railroad huskie, Budd had started his comic routines in ramshackle bars and gambling saloons. His delightful sense of timing and Irish humor had a broad appeal. No one knew the whole story of their romance, but Budd sometimes teased Jessie about sobering him up enough to get married and then signing him up for a six-week run at the popular American Theater.

It was very likely that Budd would have ended up singing in some saloon for his next beer if it hadn't been for marrying Jessie. He owed her a lot, as did the Rafferty Players for keeping us together for all these years and navigating a treacherous course from bawdy mining camps to this prestigious acting company. I felt guilty about my selfishness over the clothes I was hoarding, but something within me would not relent. There was no going back to girlish frocks that I had blissfully worn before that moment when a man's voice had called me by another's name.

A new overtone rippled over the laughter and talking in the room, and then there was a hush. I turned and saw that our director had entered with two other people. The waiting was over.

Suddenly my heart drummed loudly in my ears and I foolishly moved behind Budd, as if I expected Tyrone Langston's eyes would instantly seek me out. My thoughts had centered upon him so often day and night since I first saw him that I expected him to be aware of the domination he suddenly exercised over me. Cowering behind Budd, I shot furtive looks at the dark-haired young woman and the blond man who had accompanied him into the room.

Langston let his eyes rove over the gathering. An easy smile of welcome brought crease lines around his eyes. Even as I stole glances at him, I thought he might have caught a glimpse of me hovering behind Budd. If I had thought my memory of his appearance too perfect, seeing him once more proved that his handsomeness had matched my romantic musings. He wore a double-breasted dress coat that molded his shoulders and tapered to his waist, accenting the hard flatness of his abdomen. The dark wine color of the coat was repeated in fanciful embroidery on his vest and harmonized with tiny stripes in his gray trousers. His deep brown hair fell casually across his forehead, softening the lines of his high cheekbones with their deep shadows. I savoured every detail that my darting, surreptitious glances provided.

He introduced the actress at his side as Miss Lila Fontaine, who had been with the company last year and who would be moving up as leading lady. Dressed in a dove-gray gown of velvet and satin that was fashioned to lend regal lines to a rather sparse figure, the actress acknowledged the introduction with a slight lowering of her head. Her hair was drawn back severely in a smooth coil at the nape of her neck, and its ebony luster gave her large, round blue eyes dominance. Her petal-smooth face and arresting features would undoubtedly project commanding beauty on stage. There was a proud glint in her eyes that indicated she was satisfied that she had finally come into her own as the Imperial Theater's leading lady.

Next, Ty Langston quickly introduced Dana DelMar, a tall, blond man, who was in his twenties. A broad forehead, slender nose, and lean cheekbones combined in an aristocratic handsomeness that matched his rather imposing stature of six feet. If he was aware of every pair of feminine eyes feasting upon his admirable figure, he gave no sign of it and apparently was not embarrassed by any adoration that might come his way.

"Dana was with us last year," Langston said in that full, resonant voice that made each word clear, full, and comanding, "and we are delighted to have him back as the male lead in many of our productions. Miss Lila Fontaine will replace Maureen Cole, who will not be with us this season."

Was there a tightening of his lips? Suddenly the dress I wore was rough and chafing against my flesh. I felt like an imposter, an intruder. Would he recognize the gown I wore as hers? Would he point an accusing finger at me and demand an explanation for my presumptuous behavior? I cowered behind Budd, daring only to sneak furtive glances as the three stood before the company.

"Miss Fontaine will play Rosalind in our first

production, *As You Like It*, and will, I'm sure, give us a memorable portrayal of the beautiful, charming daughter of the banished duke.''

The actress's lips curved in a responding smile. There was little doubt that Miss Fontaine had set her sights on something more than leading roles. She touched Ty's arm possessively. All around me there were knowing glances and smirking whispers among some of the women. If Ty Langston was aware of the coquetry in her manner, he did not openly respond to it.

He made a few prefunctory remarks, calling attention to the posted green-room rules, which I had already read. ''We will have two productions in rehearsal at one time—a Shakespearean offering and a farce or melodrama—we also will be offering a variety of after-pieces to round out the bill. I am looking forward to a prosperous season for all of us. Now Cal will pass out roles and scripts for our first performance. We will begin blocking out *As You Like It* tomorrow at ten o'clock.'' He gave a business-like smile that did not invite questions. None were offered.

Before I could move back, he made a purposeful stride across the room in my direction. I thought for a moment he was going to speak to Budd, but his glance went beyond him to me. My knees threatened to buckle with weakness as he stopped in front of me. Once more that clean, spicy scent washed over me. I knew then that he had caught glimpses of me as I peered around Budd.

My wide-eyed stare and lurching breath brought an amused twitching to his mouth. ''I really do not bite, Miss . . . ?''

''Townsend.''

"Oh, yes, Tara Townsend. I must say your popping in and out behind Mr. Rafferty's back has intrigued me. I want to assure you that it is perfectly safe for you to approach me without fear. Rest assured that I'm not an ogre who devours pretty young ladies—except, of course, on the nights of a full moon." His eyes betrayed a teasing glint. "Then, perhaps you'd better beware."

It did not matter that everyone in the room was observing this foolish repartee. Joy was spilling through me like water over a spillway. Boldly, I matched his grin with one of my own. "Thank you for the warning, sir," I replied with mock seriousness. "I shall take care."

The twinkle in his eyes deepened. "It was a bit unnerving to watch you dart in and out from behind your cover, as if you were preparing to send a missile of some kind in my direction." He chuckled. "I didn't know whether to duck or stand my ground."

"You were in no danger. I haven't launched a pebble from a slingshot since I was eight."

He threw back his head and laughed. "Perhaps I will have to challenge you to a contest then. It's been about that long since I had a pea-shooter in my hands."

At that moment Lila succeeded in making her way through the crowd, and she plucked at Ty's arm. "Ty, I do think we'd better see to those contracts." Her scowl dismissed me as an insignificant annoyance. "I believe the lawyers are waiting."

"Ah, yes, back to business." He gave me a reluctant smile. "I fear our contest will have to wait, Miss Townsend."

I wanted to say something terribly witty, but my tongue seemed stuck and I only managed a nod as he

52

turned and left.

"Hello, again." I turned in surprise as Calabrese handed me a script. His dark Italian eyes registered on the dress and he smiled at me in a knowing manner. "You look very nice."

"Thank you." Then I stammered, "I've been wondering . . . what if Miss Cole comes back for her things?" I was embarrassed to voice what had been worrying me.

"I don't think that's likely, but I'll just tell her Ty told me to get rid of them. We won't have to tell anyone what happened to them."

"Did you tell Ty that you had given them to me?" It was suddenly important to know if he had recognized the gown I wore.

"Nope. Ty has more important things on his mind . . . and to tell the truth, he doesn't have much of a memory for details. Ty automatically expects someone else to take care of that kind of thing. His background, I suspect."

"And what is his background?" I pried boldly, still reeling from the knowledge that he had talked and laughed with me.

"He comes from a wealthy southern family that has roots in England's aristocracy. I think his uncle is Lord somebody or other."

I should have been embarrassed to encourage this gossipy conversation, but any sense of propriety was drowned out by my great need to learn everything I could about the man who was wreaking havoc with my emotions. "Why did he come to San Francisco?"

"I think Ty was something of an embarrassment to his family when he took up with show people, so he came to the West Coast and made a fortune of his own." Cal shrugged his thin shoulders. "Some people say he's as ruthless and mercenary as a tight-fisted robber baron. He takes what he wants, that's for sure, and he demands a deep commitment from everybody around him. You'll work hard for your eight dollars a week.''

Then he gave me a script of *As You Like It*. As I expected, I was assigned three nonspeaking roles in the production; a shepardess, a court lady, and one of the duke's merry men, who lived in the woods with him like Robin Hood. ''I hope you don't object to wearing a young man's costume,'' said Cal.

''Not at all.'' I laughed and told him how I had performed Irish jigs and songs in green britches and a buttoned jacket. More than once I had played a youth in boy's clothes when the Rafferty Players were short of actors.

''Good.'' He smiled and moved on to hand out a bound script to the next person. Budd was delighted with his role of Touchstone, a ''motley minded, roynish'' court jester who ''sometimes speaks wiser than he is aware of.'' Nell's face fell when her part was marked, Audrey, the Goat Girl. Although she played opposite Budd as Touchstone's own love, she was obviously disappointed in the sluttish, unromantic character. She'd hoped for a gay, teasing, courtesan role that came easily to her.

''Maybe he's just trying to let us get our legs under us in this first production,'' Budd consoled.

''Just show 'em what you can do, Nell,'' advised Farley, ''and next time you'll get a better part.'' The advice might be an echo to what he was saying to himself, for his role as Jacques De Boys was slight, scarcely more than a messenger. It was apparent Tyrone Langston was not overly impressed with the Rafferty Players if this first casting was any indication.

With her usual down-to-earth attitude, Jessie quickly dismissed any wounded vanity among us as a luxury we could not afford. The strapped box was nearly empty. Our lodgings at Mrs. MacPherson's left little extra, and it was important that all of us contribute to the coffers as soon as possible. Jessie had been hired by the wardrobe mistress as a temporary seamstress, and she expected to work long, hard hours for piecework wages, and she expected the rest of us to do the same.

Rehearsals began, and we had little time to think about anything but the pace Ty Langston set for the company. As I had suspected, only a performance that bordered on perfection would satisfy our handsome director. More than once I was grateful that those critical eyes and demanding gestures were centered on other members of the cast. It was nearly a week before he began to block out the crowd scenes. He strode across the stage in fitted nankeen trousers, coatless, and a soft, full-sleeved cambric shirt. His boots made a clicking rhythm as he moved about the stage.

Suddenly his full gaze was on me.

It was the first time he had singled me out since that first day. "Miss Townsend . . . I assume you left your slingshot at home?" Grinning, he took my arm and moved me to a position that balanced a grouping of several persons involved in a court scene. Heat flared under his touch and consternation must have been visible on my face. His eyes searched mine, but it was difficult to read his thoughts. Was he aware of this leaping of response between us? There was a glint of puzzlement in the way his forehead furrowed. For a split second he seemed to relate to me with a disturbing intimacy that made our eyes cling like grappling hooks. Was it my imagination that what I was feeling had found an echo in a sudden rise of heat in his own face? His voice did not betray any hidden feelings as he gave me instructions. "I want you to move forward with me to stage left as the messenger enters. That will keep the stage in balance. As soon as my speech is completed, you will move off with the others. Understand?"

I nodded, cursing the heightened color that must be flushing my cheeks. "Good." He moved on to the next player, and I knew I was forgotten.

The days went by. It took all the willpower I had not to approach him on some pretext. Like a greedy miser, I collected moments when I was on the fringe of his attention. There were times when something peeped out of his eyes as he looked at me and then vanished so quickly that I wondered if my imagination had tricked me. I hoped, waited, longed for his eyes and smiles to light upon me.

As I wore Maureen's clothes, I grew more daring in my choices. Surely he would find me attractive enough to look at me in that intimate way which had sent my senses reeling as he peered into my face. I tried to use all the information that came my way about his last season's leading lady. Every time Maureen Cole's name was mentioned, I was like a scavenger, collecting this tidbit and that, trying to piece together information about the woman I wanted to be like. I changed my hair so that long curls hung beside my cheeks because someone had said that's the way Maureen wore her hair.

None of this fascination escaped Nell. "I think you're possessed by that girl. I wish you'd never taken her clothes . . . it's eerie," she said, more out of irritation than anything, not realizing how ominous the statement would prove to be.

Two days before opening night Maureen Cole's body was dragged out of the San Francisco Bay with a cord tied in a strangle knot around her throat.

4

Many of the Langston Players had worked with Maureen the previous season. They collected in little groups and talked in low tones about her ugly death or looked at each other, maintaining tight, raspy silences. *Who had done it?* Everyone knew Maureen had left the company after some explosive confrontations with Langston and other members of the cast. It was obvious that the leading lady was unhappy, resentful, and ready to vent her anger in all directions. The last production had been hard on everyone, and Dana DelMar, who had played opposite her, had come in for a great deal of verbal abuse. No one knew if Ty had ended her contract with the last performance or whether she had just walked out on him. Whatever he told the authorities seemed to satisfy them, for they declared her death to be at the hands of some unknown person or persons. The cord around her throat made it murder.

Law enforcement agencies had been less than effective in controlling lawlessness in the burgeoning city. They made routine inquiries, but, saddled with more than a hundred homicide cases a month, there was no real enthusiasm for pursuing this particular one. After all, she was an actress, wasn't she, and what more could one expect? After a small story appeared in the *Examiner,* The tragedy was ignored by the press.

"They says she'd been in the water some time." Cal and Dana talked in low tones as I hovered close by.

"Good God, it must have happened right after our closing performance. No one seems to have seen her after she steamed out of here that night." Dana ran agitated fingers through his tawny hair. "I can't believe it . . . I just can't believe it. I knew she and Langston had a knock-down battle just before curtain time."

"Ty wasn't the only one who was at cross purposes with Maureen," Cal countered loyally. "I heard plenty of shouting going on between the two of you. Don't lay this at Ty's doorstep. Who knows what company Maureen was keeping?"

"She wasn't like that and you know it, Cal. She must have really been hurting inside to throw such tantrums and disrupt the company. Why . . . why would someone want to kill her?"

Cal shook his curly head. "Damned if I know! We thought she'd just taken off. I kept thinking she'd come back for her things, then Ty told me to get rid of them."

"Yeah, our director seemed agitated about that, didn't he?" said Dana pointedly. "I mean, maybe the sight of her belongings disturbed him. . . ."

I turned away. The memory of Ty's emotional voice calling her name as he spun me around fell into a different perspective. Had I misinterpreted the reason for the intensity of his reaction, the emotion in his voice? Had he been surprised to see Maureen—alive? Even as the thought surfaced, bringing a pricking of goose flesh to my neck, I shoved the disturbing possibility away. No, Tyrone Langston had nothing to do with her death! His expression had not been that of a murderer startled by the appearance of his victim. I clung to the belief that he had looked at me with lover's eyes, and the memory of that impelling, passionate gaze dispelled any qualms about my continuing to wear the dead girl's clothes.

At times an inner voice taunted that he was a selfish, demanding, heartless man who cared for no one. He drove the company mercilessly with brutal, verbal lashings and an insatiable need for perfection. Every rehearsal he levied fines ruthlessly and without any sign of remorse. Even though he must have known that our salaries barely covered expenses, he continued to exact fines for unlearned parts and tardiness and other infractions laid out in the green-room rules. Budd lost twenty dollars of his sixty-dollar salary to his first month's fines. Despite my efforts and those of Farley and Jessie, Budd would wander off when he wasn't in the scene being rehearsed and talk blarney with an old codger, Billy O'Dell, whose Irish brogue and infectious laughter was more pleasant than learning lines. Or he'd wander next door into the Golden Nugget and forget to report for the next scene until Cal was sent after him . . . and another fine posted.

Every night at the boarding house we would cue Budd on his speaking part, since it was the longest in the group. Nell helped him on stage as much as she could, but Langston soon caught on to her tricks of covering up for Budd by keeping Ty talking while the rest of us scurried to get the Irishman back on stage.

Our director was seemingly immune to Nell's broad smiles, inviting looks, and lascivious winks as she pleaded, "Come on, now, Budd just got a wee bit mixed up. He knows the line."

"Then he'd better say it—he's changing the tempo of the whole scene! It has to move or the comedy is lost. Now, run it again . . . and I want you to run with that scene, keep it in focus!" The only consolation was that Langston had to work as hard as the rest of us, for he played scenes as well as directing them. He had a cane that he pounded on the floor like a metronome to set the pace of a scene. All of us came to hate the sound of that demanding cane tip.

Most of the hours I spent during rehearsals were backstage waiting, and I might have been consumed with boredom if my driving love for everything involved in theatrical productions had not been all-consuming. I made friends with all the crew handling scenery and lights, and gave them a hand whenever I could. Billy O'Dell was a flyman as well as the stage manager, and I saw his gnarled hands handle coils of ropes as if they were ribbons. The old codger answered all my questions about the workings of the battens, and I watched him climb the wall ladder and walk on narrow bars high above my head to loosen a snagged rope. Ty drove the stagehands at the same demanding pace as he did the rest of the company. Backsets and curtains had to be changed with silent ease, and if the wrong one was lowered or one was not put in place fast enough, the director vented his displeasure on Billy with the same ruthlessness he used on the actors.

At first all parts of the production were like a disjointed beast that one man, the director, was physically and mentally struggling to unite into a smooth, graceful entity. No natural harmony existed between the myriad facets of a successful production, and it was only by relentless force that a rhythm was established so that every aspect of *As You Like It* became a smooth-flowing, exciting mass of energy, ready to explode across the footlights on opening night. Watching all of it happen, I could not fault the man who gave as much of himself as he expected from others, and all the defenses I built against him instantly crumbled when he breathed a satisfied "Good . . . good . . . you've got it, people . . . you've got it!" Although his attention was always riveted elsewhere or on the whole group, there were times when I was sure he was aware of my presence. A quick smile or nodding glance was like the whiff of an addictive drug.

I had three costume changes for the production, and Jessie easily fashioned them to my figure. For my first scene in the forest as one of the duke's men, I wore a vest, doublet, and tight fawn trousers with my long hair tucked under a saucy, pointed cap with a green feather. Dress rehearsal was an exciting affair, and as we left the green room to take our positions in the wings, the atmosphere was charged.

When I reached the top step wearing my "merry men" outfit, I froze as Ty appeared in his costume. My whole body lost its normal rigidity. The day I had stared at his photographs in the lobby came back . . . and the same grappling emotions overtook me. I was not prepared for the onslaught to my senses when he strode into view in the velvet, jeweled robes of the arrogant and ruthless Frederick. His deep brown hair with shining auburn highlights had been swept back from his forehead and he wore a false mustache with an arrogant twist to it. All things rapacious and evil seemed to elude from his visage and carriage as he stood there.

My breathing quickened as it had when a similar surge of emotion had reached out to me from the photographs in the lobby. That first day his interpretations of King Lear, Macbeth, and Romeo had caught me up in the intensity of his portrayals. Now he projected Frederick's evil nature without saying a word! All the base meanness of man was there in this character Shakespeare had described as "of rough and envious disposition"—a man who could have tied a strangle cord around a lovely neck and committed murder!

He strode over to confer with Billy about some prop that apparently was not in its proper position. I felt sorry for the gnarled little stage manager, who was trying to make certain nothing would go amiss during this first dress rehearsal. I could see beads of sweat on Billy's brow as the two men conferred.

I turned away with a peculiar lurching in my throat to make sure that Budd was ready for his entrance; then I made my way to a corner backstage where I was out of the way but ready for my own appearance with the duke's merry men. A moment later Billy's groan broke into my heavy thoughts. His graying head was tipped backward and he was staring high above. I followed his gaze and saw that one of the battens wasn't working smoothly. A twisted rope on the open mesh of the iron grid above the stage was jamming the lowering of a backdrop.

Without thinking, I jumped down and whispered in a rush, "I'll get it!"

"No, lass . . . no!"

I ignored his shocked gasp. It wouldn't take a minute to straighten out the lines. He had his hands full and I could see where the trouble was. In my boy's clothes, I went up the wall ladder with the ease of my childhood days. The dizzy height above the stage did not bother me. I reached the top rung, swung out on the iron grid, and moved across the open mesh of beamed ribs until I could grasp the place where the ropes had twisted. Balancing on one beam, I stooped and had the knot in my hands when a furious, commanding voice assaulted me.

From below, fury and utter disbelief were like pointed daggers as Langston shouted up to me, "Tara! Get down from there! Now!"

Some stubborn, determined streak made me blank out his voice until I finished laying the ropes smoothly in their proper position. Then I looked down between the open spaces of the grid. Billy stood there with a sickly pallor making his freckles stand out like red blotches. I saw Ty at the bottom of the ladder, waiting, glaring up at me.

"I . . . fixed it," I called down, smiling, as if these feeble words might dissolve the negative vibrations floating up to me with the force of a brewing storm.

I came down the rigging with as much poise as I could manage and had almost reached the bottom when he jerked me off of it. Those firm, muscular arms encased me, and I felt imprisoned against him. "Of all the stupid, idiotic behavior!" he lashed out. His villainous makeup and costume harmonized with the fright or anger that flared his nostrils. "Would you be so kind as to tell me what in the hell you were doing up there?"

If he had taken his arms away, my weak knees would have betrayed me. The length of his body radiated heat against mine and, despite his harsh tone, his hands splayed gently on my waist and back, slightly kneading my flesh. I could feel the pressure of his encircling arms through the thin cloth of my costume. There was concern in his eyes that was at odds with his glower. His eyebrows matted as his gaze swept my face, as if seeking assurance that I was truly all in one piece. He must have gotten the shock of his life, I thought, looking upward and seeing me crossing the open iron grid. His mobile mouth still betrayed some of his anxiety.

"I was just . . . helping with the ropes . . ."

"And that's your job?"

"No, but . . . the ropes caught and I . . . I thought—"

"That you would just climb up there and break your neck in the process?"

"I didn't break my neck," I countered, peering at him from under the brim of my pointed hat. "I fixed the ropes!"

"And disrupted the entire rehearsal."

"No, you did that," I responded boldly, refusing to be intimidated. Even though his nearness was playing havoc with my emotions, I summoned enough indignation to defend myself. "I would have been up and down that ladder without anyone knowing it if you hadn't raised such a hue and cry!"

"Yes, of course. I should have ignored your little games until you fell and made a dramatic entrance midstage." His hands slipped away from me—reluctantly, perhaps? He took a deep breath, like someone who had just been through a trying moment.

"I wouldn't have fallen!"

His lips tightened under the narrow mustache. "I believe I hired you as a supe, isn't that correct?" His tone was even as his penetrating eyes devoured mine. He had not moved back but still stood with only inches between us. "Climbing stage rigging and waltzing on stage rafters is not a part of your contract, Miss Townsend."

"I won't charge you for it!" I said facetiously before I thought.

"Dear God in heaven," Nell breathed, standing just beyond us, her ample fist held against her mouth and her eyes rounded wide with horror. The crowd that had collected held their breaths and I heard some suppressed titters.

Langston's sideburns and mustache quivered. Anger? Amusement? Exasperation? I couldn't tell from his voice. "I'm afraid it is I who must charge you," he said bluntly, but I thought I caught a glint of softness in those dark eyes that belied his gruff tone. "Two dollars. And now, with your permission, Miss Townsend, we will return to our rehearsal." He called for the first scene to begin again.

I suppressed a flicker of satisfaction.

At least he had noticed me!

That night, at dinner, everyone talked about the incident. Jessie's pinched nostrils flared at the loss of two dollars because of my foolhardy behavior. Nell's scolding was mixed with suppressed laughter. "Imagine, Tara telling high-and-mighty Langston that she wouldn't charge him for the deed! It was enough to make me faint dead away."

"Sure and I thought she was going to get the sack, right then and there," Budd said, but his eyes betrayed a secret amusement and admiration.

Farley had obviously been frightened by the incident. "She could have broken her neck!" he said. "I thought we were finished with all that—no more fishing her out of the mill pond or jerking her off a rank mule before he pitched her. Somehow I got the idea Tara was trying to be a 'lady' these days."

I refused to meet his eyes. I was surprised when he asked me if I wanted to take a walk after dinner. Apparently the incident had reassured him that I was still "Wee Tara," needing some help getting out of scrapes.

"Shouldn't we help Budd with his lines?"

"We're either ready for opening night tomorrow or we're not," said Nell, giving Mr. Strosky one of her flirtatious smiles. "Time to relax a little, I'd say."

"I agree," said Budd. "Me legs are needing a little stretching."

"Humph!" Jessie snorted, not the least bit fooled by the charade.

I did not want to take a walk in the square and invite the kind of intimacy that had arisen between Farley and me the last time so I suggested to my escorts that we wander down Kearny Street. It was a fascinating stroll, bordered by steeples, storehouses, towers, hotels, gambling halls, theaters, and merchant establishments. Tiny windows flaunted exotic wares. Oriental colors blended the palest pinks with brilliant reds and fiery oranges, all making a riotous assault from flower baskets, silken fabrics, and delicate porcelain. Every block resounded with a cacophony of noises and filled the senses with a myriad of sights and smells.

A carnival of people surged along the walks. Bearded miners fresh from the silver diggings in the Comstock mines brushed by us, heading for the best-known taverns and other gathering places. We dodged elegant coaches with liveried coachmen depositing the wealthy at establishments like the Bella Union and Langston's Golden Nugget. Financial magnates exuded a successful air as they strode down the street wearing tall silk hats, their evening capes flipping haughtily in the breeze, often with women in silks and satins mincing along at their sides. It was easy to identify professional gamblers in their black coats with white linen and diamond stickpins in their cravats as they shoved their way into brightly lit establishments, hopeful that Lady Luck would bring them a profitable evening at the gaming tables.

We had only walked a couple of blocks before Budd stopped in front of Barnacle Bill's and asked Farley to lend him the price of a couple of beers. "Sure and me throat is as dry as a weathered plank lying in the sun," he said with a sheepish grin.

Farley dug in his pocket and handed him a couple of coins. "Don't be drinking more than a couple or Jessie will have my skin," he warned Budd. "You have to be fit for opening night, remember."

" 'Tis a fine friend ye are, dear Farley . . . and I'll be remembering your kindness when I become a great star and begin spreading my wealth around." He closed one eye in an exaggerated wink, his mouth parted in a broad grin, and then he turned and ambled into the smoky recesses of the saloon. I knew there would be the piper to pay when Budd got home and Jessie smelled rank ale on his breath.

"I hope to heaven he doesn't start telling jokes or singing for drinks," I said anxiously, for Budd could always make instant friendships and, more than once, he'd come home staggering drunk after only buying one drink, but gratefully accepting all the free ones that came his way. "Maybe you should have told him no, and not given him any money."

"You know I couldn't do that," said Farley, lighting his pipe and puffing as we strolled. Its heavy, aromatic fragrance mingled with the spicy foodstuffs piled outside food stores in open stands. Chinese merchants in black pants, blue shirts, and bobbing black queues bowed and smiled and invited our inspection. A growing Chinatown had attracted coolies originally brought to the area to work on the railroad or as laborers along the waterfront. Despite the growing animosity against them, they had settled in to make San Francisco their home.

Farley started talking about the first time he had

seen San Francisco from the decks of a schooner when he had accompanied Edwin Booth on his return trip from Australia. "Looked like a ragamuffin town," he said, "rows of tindery frame buildings and many colored tents pitched above the town, flapping and snapping. How the wind did blow!" He laughed. "Up on Telegraph Hill the black wooden 'arm' was raised to signal the arrival of our boat. Tom Maguire, the gambler who kept rebuilding the Jenny Theatre each time it burned down, was expecting Booth, so he even had a brass band down at the wharf playing 'Oh Susanna' to greet us!

I loved to listen to Farley's stories. When I was just a little girl he sat me in front of his saddle and held me tight as the horse picked its way along a dark trail from one mining camp to another. We often had to leave right after one night's performance in order to be at the next camp on the following night. I was never afraid on those nightly treks, and later, when I had my own horse or mule, I could even sleep as slack reins let my mount follow in the steps of the others.

When we reached the financial and commercial center between California and Washington streets, we continued one more block to the Palace Hotel, built between Bush and Sutter streets. Glittering lights, smart carriages, and elegantly attired men and women were coming and going through its vaulted doors. Involuntarily, my eyes were drawn upward to the rising stories with rows of ubiquitous bay windows that had become San Francisco's hallmark. I wondered on which floor Ty Langston had his suite of rooms. I could visualize him there, bathing and dressing for an evening out. His attire immaculate, clean-shaven, and projecting an elegant handsomeness. This last night before an opening was probably a time for an elaborate dinner and celebration. I knew that Lila Fontaine had rooms at the Palace, and it was a good guess that she probably would be dining with him, as undoubtedly other leading ladies had done before her. Had Maureen Cole stayed at the Crystal during the last season? Perhaps; the last anyone had ever seen of her was when she walked out through those doors.

Her velvet cloak was suddenly a weight on my shoulders. Where had she gone? What had happened to her after she left this glittering, crowded hotel? She had been found in the chilled, windswept waters of the bay. Someone had tied that viscious cord around her white throat and hoped her bloated body would not be found.

I shivered.

"What's the matter? Are you cold?" Farley asked.

"Yes." It was true. I felt a chill bone-deep, and some sixth sense picked up danger even as I stood there staring at San Francisco's newst and finest hotel. "Let's go home," I said, suddenly needing the warmth and security of Mrs. MacPherson's boarding house.

5

As You Like It had a good run and was followed by a
farce, *A Sailor's Sky,* in which I was cast as one of the
ship's crew, yelling and jeering in the background. I
also appeared in the final act as one of the ladies
welcoming the whaler back to port. Despite my
efforts to catch our director's eye again, he seemed as
oblivious of my presence in the theater as he ever
had. That emotionally charged scene at dress
rehearsal had not shortened the distance he kept
beween us. Memories of those firm arms around me
and his expressive hands molding the contours of my
waist and back continued to suffuse my body with a
tingling warmth as I savored them. He, on the other
hand, seemed to have forgotten the whole incident.

Miss Lila Fontaine demanded most of his attention,
off and on stage. I watched the way she held that
imperious head of hers and I practiced her graceful,
smooth carriage, hoping that whatever our director

found attractive in his leading ladies he would find in me.

I toyed with the idea of trying for one of the song and dance numbers that were added to the bill of each dramatic performance. Cal let me watch rehearsals of these after-pieces. His dexterous fingers flew across the keys, rendering a bouncing melody or thumping a chord accompaniment to jugglers and comics as he sat on a dais at an upright piano stage left. The musician always had a cigarette dangling out of the corner of his mouth and one eye squinted against the trail of smoke. You could tell he was in a world of his own as he belted out the piano tunes because his whole body bounced in rhythm with the vibrating notes and rollicking tunes.

I couldn't help but laugh and keep time by clapping as he caught me up in delightful old favorites and new compositions that he wrote for specific dance numbers. Sometimes he gave me a private recital after the stage was cleared and rehearsal was over for the day. I enjoyed these impromptu musical sessions and even coaxed a couple of backstage roustabouts into harmonizing on some old favorites with me.

"I could arrange for an audition with Ty," Cal teased, puffing on his cigarette.

"Thanks for the compliment, but I'd just make a fool out of myself." My singing voice was not a professional one and had only been adequate for a child belting out ballads on crude stages. "As for dancing," I shook my head, "I know a couple of Irish jigs that Budd taught me, but that's about all. I could never manage a professional routine. I'm strictly a has-been."

My face must have looked pained and my smile forced because he said quickly, "Don't sell yourself short . . . maybe if you practiced?"

74

"Thanks, Cal, but it would just be a waste of your time. I'm afraid the best tutor in the world couldn't improve this voice of mine. No use day dreaming . . ." My voice trailed off. I smoothed the deep burgundy dress I was wearing for the first time. A lace chemisette gave a teasing peek of my full, swelling breasts and draped my figure in a seductive long bodice and flounced skirt, but so far the man I wore it for had not even looked in my direction.

"You look mighty attractive in Maureen's clothes, Tara," he said, giving me an encouraging smile as he watched my preening. "With the right training, I bet you could get a new career going. You don't lack for looks—or guts either," he added, grinning, obviously remembering the "flyman" incident.

"Thank you, sir." I gave him a mock curtsy. "And thanks for letting me hang around your piano." Then I sobered. "You're the talented one, Cal." My compliment brought a peculiar shine to his eyes. I realized then how much thankless work Cal did around the theater and a spurt of resentment flared against Langston for taking advantage of him. "I mean it, Cal. That piano talks to you . . . and you could make almost anybody look good with your accompaniments."

"I wish I could help you in some way."

"You already have, by listening. Now, I'd better get into my sailor's garb before our dear director levels another fine at me."

In truth, that talk with Cal proved to be the push that set me into a new pattern of thinking. Without intending to do so, he had planted a seed that must have lingered in my subconscious.

With the right kind of training . . .

I mulled this phrase over and over until my willful nature latched on to it and looked at it from every direction. Imperceptibly, murky waters began to clear. A different perspective about myself slowly came into focus and brought with it some basic questions. Had I been selling myself short? Had I accepted limitations about my ability that might not be valid? Since I hadn't grown into a consummate, mature performer with the ease with which I had become a child star, everyone, including myself, assumed that I lacked the ability to become a good actress. *Maybe I just needed to work at it!*

Everyone in the Rafferty Players had accepted as inevitable my theatrical demise when I outgrew my boyish britches and small-girl appeal. The few times I had tried a dramatic role as an adolescent I had failed miserably, but no one had pointed out what I had done wrong or what I should do to improve my acting. They just said I was terrible . . . and the audience had obviously agreed. It was true that Budd had a natural talent for comedy and character portrayals, but he probably was at a loss when it came to coaching anyone on the fine points of acting. Farley had not been able to make his own professional stature grow and was pretty much at the same level as he had been when he trailed after Edwin Booth in worshipful ardor. Looking back, I realized he had been the one to assure me over and over that I needn't distress myself about not being a good actress. As always, Nell had been sympathetic about my failures, but she really only played variations of her own personality, the out-going, crude, lascivious, naughty female of low class. Any instruction she might attempt to give me was bound to be slanted and doomed to failure. In retrospect, it seemed to me that everyone had assumed, including myself, that my theatrical career was behind me when I became too old to be "Wee Tara Townsend, Entertainer Extraordinarie."

For the next two weeks I worried with these questions and finally all my mental gyrations brought me to one conclusion: I needed to study acting, and I needed someone to instruct me! As excitement suddenly flowed through my veins, my usual lassitude was subtly edged with the prodding, jagged points of ambitious drive.

The real reason I wanted to grow as a performer was lost in a rationalization that I wanted to be of more value to my surrogate family. If there was some mocking voice within that chided my new dedication, I was able to smother it. By the time I had determined my first step was to talk with Ty Langston about a suitable coach, I was convinced in my own mind that my motives were purely professional.

I waited until our director had scheduled two days between productions before I summoned my courage and sought him out one afternoon in his office above the foyer of the theater. As I moved up the same red plush staircase Budd and Jessie had taken that first day, my heart was hammering wildly. The palms of my hands were moist under my silk gloves as I clutched the chain of a crocheted reticule Jessie had made for me. I had chosen a teal-blue gown, fashioned with ecru lace accenting a dipping neckline and darker French blue sleeves and flounces. The sarsenet material with its taffeta sheen was flattering to my fair hair and ivory complexion, I thought, and I had chosen the gown after many moments of deliberation. A borrowed bonnet that Nell had worn several times in a skit was settled over one eye and its nest of flowers and ribbons gave me a look of feminine coquetry that I did not feel.

Up to this time none of the offerings of Maureen Cole's wardrobe had seemed to make the slightest

dent upon Langston's interest or attention. The only
time he had really noticed me, I was dressed in boy's
clothes with my hair hidden under a woodman's hat.
During rehearsals, I had been a human prop to place
correctly on the stage so the balance of actors would
not be disturbed. Other actresses, like Nell, who
smiled saucily at him or demanded his personal attention only received swift professionalism in return.
Even his treatment of Lila Fontaine during rehearsals
gave no indication as to what the personal relationship between them might be. It was little wonder I
almost turned back a dozen times before I glided
down the hall in my long skirts and reached the door
with gold-leaf lettering that identified his office.

The oak door was partially open and through the
crack I could see a heavy oriental carpet spread across
the floor and the carved legs of some heavy, black
walnut furniture. Brass fixtures held round, etched
glass bowls and flickering light sent an irridescent
glow upon polished, paneled rosewood walls. The
director's office seemed as impeccably elegant as the
man himself. As bravely as my trembling hand could
manage, I gave a sharp rap on the door panel.

Almost immediately his vibrant voice responded.
"Come on in . . . I'll be with you in a minute."

The invitation seemed genuine. Such open friendliness was reassuring and I did as he bade, moving
forward into the room with a rustle of skirts.

"Well, what do you think of that?" he asked.

I saw then that his back was to me. His arms were
raised and his head uplifted as he hung up a painting
on the wall behind his desk. The long, masculine lines
of his figure were defined by a tight-fitting afternoon
coat with broad tails and trousers that were narrow at
the top, wide at the knee, and tight again below the
knee. Both garments, in shades of russet brown, were

flattering to the reddish glints in his dark brown hair, curling longish upon his neck. He continued to talk to me without turning around. "It was painted from Telegraph Hill and I think it really catches the liquid shades of a sunset on the bay, don't you?" He stepped back and peered at it. "Don't be bashful. What do you think, Lila? Was it worth the hundred dollars I paid for it?" He continued to gaze at the painting with his handsome head slightly cocked as he waited for my answer.

Lila! He had left the door open for his leading lady! His welcoming tone was not for me. He was expecting Lila Fontaine! My silence must have finally alerted him. He swung around with eager expectancy, only to have that expression fade when he saw who it was. Sudden furrows creased his forehead. "I'm sorry . . . I thought you were someone else." The words and his tone had a *deja vu* ring to them.

"I think the painting is very nice," I said boldly, stubbornly refusing to allow him to dismiss my opinion as unimportant. I fastened my eyes on the painting, mainly because I could not bring myself to watch a disinterested glaze settle in his eyes. I dug in my memory of conversations I'd had with some painters who had lived at the same boarding house with us and came up with a term. "Impressionistic, isn't it?"

"Yes." He seemed surprised. "I like its romantic touch, don't you? You can almost smell the summer sun and hear the languid ripple of the water." His eyes traveled over me as he spoke, and he moved back so that he was standing beside me as we gazed at the picture. I felt mystically drawn into the painting, a warm wave engulfing us in a shared experience. The artist had captured an indolent summer evening with two figures settled in the grass watching the sun go down; a woman with her hair loosened and a large summer hat abandoned nearby on the grass, a light summer dress hugging the contours of her feminine shape. A young man was looking at the water, but the placement of his lounging body near hers bespoke an intimacy that was captured in line and posture. It was not a picture of a sunset but of two lovers, their senses satiated with color, movement, and each other. I felt my own senses reeling from the picture . . . and the nearness of his body. I was aware of every movement in is breathing and reeled from a spell he seemed to cast upon me by virtue of his physical presence.

I took a deep breath, as if to pull free from some invisible snare, and abruptly moved away from him. Pretending to look around the room, I noticed other pictures he had hanging. Copying the languid, slow carriage of Lila, I moved across the room to a wall where several lithographs of sloops, schooners, and frigates were arranged in a grouping. I allowed one of my gloved hands to lightly touch the lace ruffle at my throat in a studied gesture as I viewed them.

With him still standing in front of the desk, I deliberately held my head at a regal angle, as if judging the pictures. Then I turned and surveyed the rest of the room before I let my eyes come back to his face. For a moment I was pleased to see a quizzical smile putting small fan lines around his eyes. Then his mobile mouth quirked as if amused. "Are you an artist, Miss Townsend?" he asked politely, but I knew laughter was rumbling in his chest.

The questions put an end to my pretense. My worldly air disintegrated and I gave an honest chuckle. "No. I guess I know what I like . . . and that's about all." I had always been able to laugh at myself and it was a relief to put the grande dame pretense aside. I was not going to impress Ty Langston with any pseudosophistication and I knew it.

"And do you like my ships?"

"Not as much as the painting, but then I'm no judge of art."

"Someone defined art as anything that finds pleasure in someone's eyes. It can be almost anything . . . even a woman." His warm eyes were bold.

"And you are a collector?" I parried, returning his roving glance.

He laughed. "Like you . . . I know what I like." Then he cleared his throat, as if determined that the conversation should not continue in this vein. "Is there something . . . I'm sorry, I have an appointment momentarily. . . ." He let the sentence hang politely.

"May I sit down?" I requested. His presence had already put water in my knees, and I knew I could never state my business standing up.

"Yes, of course. Make yourself comfortable, Tara."

I was disconcerted by his use of my first name, although he had used it angrily once before when he ordered me down from the rafters.

"Now what can I do for you?" He sat on the edge of his desk with one of his legs lightly swinging. Under the tight stretch of his trousers I could see muscles rippling and quickly stopped myself from staring at this provocative section of his body. When I raised my eyes I knew he had noticed their quick jerk away from that intimate part of his anatomy. He was rude enough to grin.

"I . . . I want to talk to you," I said with as much poise as I could muster with him grinning at me. "I think I am capable of doing something besides my present assignments." I faltered and searched for the right words.

"You mean, you want to hire on as a flyman or grip?" My expression must have been laughable because a deep rumbling came from his chest. "I suppose I could talk to Billy about it," he said, his eyes holding a teasing glint.

"I'd rather do that than what I'm doing now," I flung at him.

"I see." His grin was still there even though he was trying to match my seriousness. "And what did you have in mind, Miss Townsend? Lady Macbeth, perhaps?"

"Don't patronize me!" I snapped, infuriated that he refused to understand what I was struggling to communicate to him. "I know that I have nothing to offer now, but I know I could learn if I just had a chance . . ."

"I'm afraid the Imperial productions are not learning exercises, Miss Townsend," he said gently. "I struggle with each performance to make it as professional as possible." He had reverted to the use of my formal name and I knew he had set all social amenities aside.

I nodded. "I know that . . . and that's precisely why I've come to you. I want to study, to learn my craft." As quickly as I could I told him a little bit about my background. "Somehow I fell into being a child star without any effort . . . it just happened. I wandered out on stage and people loved me. I wore white dresses or green britches and sang songs about home. Lonely miners flung gold nuggets at me."

He was listening intently. I could not tell how much of this he knew already, but suddenly I was myself again, not pretending to be a seductive woman in a taffeta gown. I talked to him as I would have to anyone about those early days, riding a mule from one mining camp to another, setting up stage at the end of a barn or above a feed store. "I never thought about acting, the 'theater,' or about doing anything else but being a part of my family, the Rafferty Players. When my career ended as child entertainer I helped out wherever I could, and that meant that when Budd, Nell, and Farley signed on with you, I came, too, in whatever capacity I could. But now . . . now I want to . . .''

"Become an actress?"

I nodded.

"And you think that all those past glories and adoration will come tumbling your way again?"

I stiffened. "That's not what's important! I mean, I really never thought about all the clapping and applause as something special. It was just part of the business. I was never starstruck," I said firmly, and my level gaze dared him to deny it.

"Then why aren't you satisfied enjoying show business from an easy berth?"

He waited, those intense dark eyes fixed on my face, but I couldn't give an honest answer to that. I had deluded myself too well. "I have to be an actress," I said firmly.

"Is it money?"

"No, not really, not for myself. . . ."

"I find that hard to believe," he said with a lift of an eyebrow. "Everyone is always talking to me about more money."

"I'll work for the same salary—and do extra work—here or backstage—to pay you."

"Pay me?" He was startled. "For what, pray?"

"For tutoring me."

His expression was almost laughable. His mouth fell open and those deep-set eyes the color of polished wood rounded in amazement. "And what makes you think, young lady, that you would be worth my time? Me, tutor you?" he repeated, aghast.

"Are you afraid?" I challenged with my usual

obstinance.

"Afraid? Of what . . . ?" He seemed intrigued in spite of himself.

"That you might fail . . . that you couldn't make me into a decent actress!" The retort was born of some acuity that seemed to be acting on its own. I had not planned to say such a thing.

"How deftly you put the challenge in my corner, Miss Townsend." His response was crisp, but a begrudging admiration flicked briefly in his steady glance. "I must confess that I've never been challenged to prove myself as a drama coach before." His eyes crinkled, as if the idea were somehow amusing. He rose and walked around his desk until his hands rested on the back of his chair as he studied me from some distant point. I watched him, and it seemed to me that his thoughts might be on different levels, perhaps analyzing, discarding, and evaluating the challenge I had flung at him. He gazed across the desk at me until I felt compelled to speak.

"I'm sure you could take someone with even less background than I and make her into a leading lady," I pressed.

"If your talent is anything like your audacity, I'm certain of it," he responded thoughtfully with a flicker of a smile.

"Then you'll do it?"

"No." He shook his head and straightened up, letting his hands drop away from the chair. Once more the pull between us was so charged that my mouth went dry. He had not taken a step closer to me and yet I could feel his gaze touching my face with caressing warmth. "I'm afraid I must turn away from the challenge."

"Why?"

"Many reasons . . . some of which you would not

understand." The timbre of his voice changed and he became briskly professional, but there was still a hint of amusement in his tone as he said, "At the moment I have too many obligations to even evaluate your offer to let me make you a famous actress, Miss Townsend."

The blunt rejection hurt, but I refused to plead with him. Pride stiffened my neck as I kept my gaze rudely fixed on his face.

He took a gold pocket watch from his vest as if my scrutiny was uncomfortable for him. "Well, it seems that Miss Fontaine has chosen to ignore our engagement. She is already forty minutes late. I suppose that's the penalty men must pay for the privilege of her company."

A leaden coldness brought a prickling of skin over my body. "Well, thank you for your time." At least I could leave graciously with my head held high, as if my failure was of little importance. I rose and started toward the door without looking at him again.

"I don't suppose you would like to accompany me?" he said in a rush, as if he didn't want to give himself time to reconsider the invitation.

"What?" I stammered, turning around.

With the purposeful gait I knew so well, he came around the desk to my side and smiled down at my startled expression. "I have ordered a carriage for a drive out to the battery. I have some holdings in one of the navigation companies and some business requires my attention. Would you care to keep me company and view the waters from the deck of a ship, Miss Townsend?"

Pure joy must have instantly flooded my eyes because he didn't wait for my answer but took his tall hat from a coatrack and guided me out of the office. I forgot all about pretending to be one of his sophisticated leading ladies. With effervescent delight coursing and bubbling through my body, I floated along beside him. The guiding hand he held on my elbow was sure and possessive.

A driver tipped his hat to us as we emerged from the building. Langston helped me into the elevated seat of the waiting carriage and then took his place beside me. A humorous sparkle in his eyes set me at ease. In a moment a trim pair of horses set a nice pace along California Street, taking the hills in easy rhythm as our driver jostled for position between horse-drawn trolleys laboring up and down hills to most parts of the city.

It was a dream . . . a wonderful, glorious dream! There was no way I could feign disinterest as we moved with the flow of the traffic. Bells hanging from the harnesses made a lovely accompaniment to the horses' clopping hoofs. Chinese street vendors darted quickly along boardwalks, flexible poles slung over their shoulders with baskets filled with vegetables and fruits swinging merrily with their bobbing gait. Langston pointed out some new construction proudly and I suspected that he was adding to his real estate holdings by buying stock in these new companies. The road rose and dipped over sand hills reaching to the bay.

The carriage swayed and tilted as it moved, and there was no way to avoid physical contact with the man sitting beside me. Several times I was thrown against him in an inviting fashion and reddened as he put a steadying hand on me until I had righted myself. I felt my pulse racing in the hollow of my neck and I wondered if he was aware of the havoc his nearness was creating. It couldn't be happening! I shot him a quick look and caught an expression of puzzlement before his eyes shuttered. What was he thinking? Was he sorry he brought me? Was he wishing Lila were sitting here beside him? I had no doubt that she would know how to tease and entertain him. She wouldn't be gawking out the window with the eagerness of an urchin. A surge of despair dulled my excitement. I struggled for something scintillating to say, but before I had gleaned something suitable, we went over the last sandy rise and the bay stretched before us, beautiful, serene, gently rippling waters in reflecting tones of blues and green, touched with a shimmer of silvery white. I struggled to keep a gasp of delight from issuing from my lips.

At the foot of Market Street the Ferry Building, a long, wooden structure, served as the "front door" to San Francisco. Everything was movement as we approached Long Wharf. Horses, hackney carriages, wagons, landaus, and elegant broughams maneuvered at full tilt in a chaotic surge of traffic in front of the building. Seamen just off schooners, barges, and riverboats joined travelers, merchants, drunkards, and gamblers in a flowing mass of humanity.

As we alighted from the carriage, a soft breeze teased my nose with scents of unloaded cargoes of tea, canvas, ropes, silks, spices, and incense. Nearby shops with narrow doors and crowded interiors displayed the practical with the esthetic in crowded stacks and heaps; mining tools, gold dust, velvet paintings, perfumes, and raw fish. Merchants chattered, gestered, and offered their wares in a variety of tongues. All of San Francisco and the world seemed to come together at the Bay.

Snubbed up to various wharfs, I could see masts of ocean-going vessels, sloops, and schooners; sailors and dock workers clambered up and down boat stairs and gangplanks on riverboats transporting cargoes and passengers from as far north as Canada. My heart quickened from the sounds and sights—and the presence of the man at my side.

He deftly guided me through crowds of people clustered in front of ticket offices. Prices and schedules for ferries, riverboats, and steamers were posted on large, colorful billboards. Outside, shrill whistles and shouts accompanied the anchoring and departing of crafts upon the water. Workers, travelers, and knots of people of every lineage gave the crowded building an international air; Italian, Greek, Slav, European and Asian . . . all bringing their dreams to a city that was like a brand-new coin, offering prosperity and happiness with the flick of a wrist.

Several fashionable ladies let their eyes travel discreetly over Ty as we passed, and I pretended to myself that I had every right to be there with this handsome, debonair man who kept a guiding hand on my elbow. I wondered where we were going.

An officer in a maritime uniform greeted him as we emerged at the lower level of the dock. "Good afternoon, Mr. Langston."

"The *Athena?*" Langston inquired.

"Her regular berth, sir. She docked on schedule last evening." He seemed about to say something more, but he must have changed his mind. Sending Ty an anxious look, he clapped his mouth shut as if he had decided not to invite trouble.

As we threaded our way around boxes, barrels, and stacks of unloaded cargo, Langston pointed ahead. "There's the *Athena*," he said in a voice tinged with parental pride. "She's a trim princess that holds the fastest time from San Francisco to Sacramento City. The newest addition to our California Navigation Line . . . and the best! A single-cylinder, vertical-beam engine and paddle wheels thirty-six feet in diameter, and her accommodations . . . '' He caught himself and chuckled as he gave me a sheepish grin. ''Why don't I let her speak for herself?''

There was a boyish enthusiasm about him that I had never seen in the theater. He looked younger and almost carefree as he gazed ahead at the *Athena*, and his nostrils seemed to sniff the air as if it held a rare perfume instead of the sharp, dank smell of wood, fish, hemp, and salt. With a quickening step, we reached the gangplank of the riverboat with *Athena* painted in royal-blue letters on her side. She was white with forest-green trim, brass trimmings glistening, and three decks with smooth and graceful railings. Everything seemed in perfect order until we reached the deck.

''What in the hell—'' Ty stopped short and stared in angry disbelief.

Part of the deck had been torn loose, and an ugly, gaping hole several feet wide yawned around charred planking. Blackened and sooty red plush furniture and singed timber bore evidence of a fire.

''A little trouble, sir,'' offered a ship's officer, hovering nearby. ''Captain Whitney would like to speak to you, sir.''

''As well he should! What happened here?''

''Some foolhardiness on the part of some militiamen, sir. They set up a small cannon, sir, to signal a salute to those waiting on the wharf. Unfortunately, sir, they neglected to remove the power keg to a safe distance.

Langston's jaw was clenched in a rigid line. His muscles tensed, and rage was evident in every line and plane of his body.

''One of the culprits has been detained, sir . . . by the captain.''

"Please wait for me in the Ladies' Salon, Tara."

"I'm sorry, sir," the officer said quickly. "The salon sustained some damage."

"I'll look around the decks . . . if that's all right?" I suggested.

Langston nodded curtly and was gone.

"Would you like me to accompany you, miss?"

"No, thank you, I'll just stroll about. I'm sure you have duties elsewhere." I gave him a reassuring smile and walked away.

I mounted a wide stairway to the passenger deck and looked over the railing. Then I strolled along the deck, peering in doorways. It was obvious why Ty was proud of the *Athena*. Her dining room was elegantly paneled in rosewood, beautifully lighted with crystal chandeliers, and plush, armless chairs surrounded tables spread with white linen, silver, and crystal. A slight contrast to Mrs. MacPherson's boarding house, I thought ruefully. Undoubtedly delectable feasts were served in this opulent room.

Next to the dining room was a large salon that I concluded must be used for relaxation and perhaps entertainment. I could not believe that people traveled in such comfort as this. My feeling was doubled when I reached the cabins and noted that they were also paneled in rosewood, with brass and crystal lighting.

With a light step I made my way around the stern, past a huge paddlewheel with eight-foot buckets. Suddenly, raised voices and the sounds of a physical struggle vibrated from the deck below me. The noise brought me to the railing and I peered over it to the deck below just as a man was flung against a supporting column, Ty's hand at his throat. I saw Ty's rigid profile as he growled, "I'll tear every limb from your body and throw you to the sharks if you make another threat like that!"

A husky man wearing a captain's uniform was trying to separate them. "He's just a loud mouth, Mr. Langston. We'll see that he cools down in the brig before we set him ashore."

Despite the captain's efforts, Ty retained his grip on the man's throat. "You deliberately sabotage one more plank in any of my ships—just one—and you'll hang from the yardarm until you're meat for the buzzards! Mark my word!"

I gripped the railing and fought back the impulse to scream at Ty to let the man go. His eyes were bulging and glazed, and he was losing consciousness. I closed my eyes in a wave of dizziness. When I opened them a moment later the three men had disappeared from view.

Trembling as if suddenly chilled, I stared into the water, shaken by the violent scene I had witnessed. Ty Langston's displeasure had been evident before, at the theater when things weren't going well, but I had never seen that black, raging temper. The force of it had invaded the marrow of my bones and put a deep chill there. Deep waters sloshed against the hull of the boat; the haunting sound was cold, sinister, chilling. *Had Maureen's body come from this area of the bay?*

Someone touched my shoulder and I turned with a gasp. Terror must have widened my eyes for Ty said quickly, "What's the matter?" He stood there utterly composed, a smooth veneer of good humor on his face, his stance casual, as if he had been having tea with the captain instead of threatening some man with his very life—but then, he *was* an actor. I had to keep reminding myself that chameleon changes were a part of his talent. "Has something frightened you?"

I could have lied, but too many warring emotions were rushing through me. "I . . . I heard you . . .

below.''

He frowned. ''I'm sorry; an unpleasant scene. The competition for river trade has spawned some villainous acts. There are some men who will do anything for the smell of gold dust. But let's not talk about that. Come, let's have some refreshment and put the matter behind us.'' He smiled. ''After all, I didn't bring you here just to be upset by some regrettable business. You must give me a chance to redeem myself.''

I searched his face. Eyes soft, rippling with a glint of tenderness, delved into mine.

''This is our chance to get better acquainted.'' A hint of a cleft deepened in his chin as he raised one hand and let his fingers lightly trace a cheek before they cupped my chin. ''Don't look so worried. You are much too lovely to wear such concern upon your face. Where is that delightful sparkle and the glints of stardust in those liquid eyes? Do you know that your whole face smiles, not just your sensuous lips?''

My lips quivered. His changes of mood bewildered me. Even as I summoned my defenses, I hadn't the strength to jerk away or to break the lock his eyes kept on mine. I forgot about everything but the nearness of his face. He could have kissed me then and there on the deck of the riverboat, like some cheap woman brought aboard for his pleasure. The invitation must have been in my eyes, for a bewildering need made me lean slightly toward him.

With a sigh, he let his hand trail away from my face. ''You sorely test the limits of my chivalry.'' He stepped back and gave me a smile of devastating potency.

I managed to murmur, ''I might say that you, in turn, are guilty of undermining any decorous behavior on my part.''

He laughed softly. "I take full responsibility," he said, "for both our behaviors." I wondered if he was aware of his thigh brushing against mine as we made our way around the deck to the dining room.

I do not remember much about the refreshments that were served. A small bouquet of fresh violets had been placed on the pristine white cloth and their delicate scent teased my nostrils. His nearness bombarded my senses. With graceful ease he handled a silver tea service placed by our table on a small cart. There were no other patrons being served, and I realized that the dining room was not open to anyone but Tyrone Langston.

"You own the *Athena*?" I pried, sipping my tea, unable to keep my eyes from surveying the sumptuous surroundings.

"Yes. I have always had a secret longing to be a sailor . . . an occupation that would probably have pleased my family more than acting, I might add."

"But you are such a successful actor and director."

He shrugged. "I am fortunate to have other interests that allow me to indulge in the theater. I was lucky when I first came to these golden shores with the legions of grasping, greedy men who thought a fortune was theirs for the asking. I decided to let them take the gambles, and I would share their success by providing them with the things money could buy. It has worked out very well for me." He eased back in his red plush chair and looked about with a sense of satisfaction.

"Why were you so angry with that man?"

"Ladies don't need to concern themselves with such matters."

He knew he had cleverly checkmated me. My endeavor to pattern my behavior after his leading lady had not escaped him. Did he recognize the gown

I was wearing as one belonging to Maureen? Would he have invited me here today if I had been wearing my own tartan plaid dress with the let-down hem? I thought not.

I did not have to feign interest as he talked about his arrival in San Francisco and the first time he had sailed a schooner up the Sacramento River. When we left the *Athena* I had forgotten all about the unpleasant scene I had witnessed. I knew that the rivalry among the navigation companies to control the prosperous water trade was lawless at times, and undoubtedly Ty was within his rights to be furious that someone had tried to sabotage his beloved boat.

As soon as we were settled once more in the carriage, he pointed out Telegraph Hill, where a wooden arm signal was given when a ship was sighted. He told me an amusing story about an actor on stage throwing out his arms in a familiar fashion in a dramatic scene and pleading, "Tell me, what is it?" The whole audience answered without prompting, "A side-wheeler!"

We laughed easily together. I confessed that once I had loosened the seams in a magician's top hat so that at a dramatic point in his act the bottom fell out and the hidden white mice ran in every direction.

"I bet you were a mischievous, little devil! I couldn't believe my eyes when I looked up and saw you waltzing across those iron beams like someone going for a Sunday stroll!"

"There was no reason for you to get so angry," I countered.

"I was concerned about your safety."

"I wasn't going to fall!"

"So you told me!" He chuckled, and reached over and took my hand. "Well, now that I've been warned,

I suppose I can expect you to be playing some tricks on me."

"Oh, I would never do that," I gasped, horrified.

"Why not? Am I that formidable?"

"I don't think anyone would dare play a joke on you."

"Not even Tara Townsend?"

"Especially Tara Townsend!"

"I can't believe that you're the least bit frightened of me."

His hand tightened on mine, and the warmth of his touch spiraled through me. Suddenly his face was poised close to mine. I felt the power of those dark eyes searching my profile, and I tried to keep looking out the window, but my determination failed me. I turned my head and lifted my eyes to his. "No, I'm not afraid," I murmured in a husky voice that betrayed the emotion underlying my words.

He sighed heavily and then pulled me toward him, lowering his lips to mine in a purposeful, possessive gesture that I knew I had invited. My whole being reached a zenith of awareness that sealed out all thoughts and feelings beyond the exquisite pleasure of his mouth on mine. A bewildering response flowed through my veins like a sudden ascent to the summit of a mountain top, and it was as if I had only come truly alive at that moment. The longing for his kiss had been there from the first moment his sensuous lips had taunted me as Romeo in the foyer photograph.

His hands moved gently around my waist, and then exploring fingers eased along my back, pressing, caressing, maintaining a soft stroking until a tingling explosion shot down my spine. As he held me close, his mouth left my trembling lips to trail kisses down the softness of my neck.

"Tara . . . Tara," he murmured in a voice strained with the sensual stirrings between us. I could hear his quickened breath and feel the heat of his body pressed close to mine. He moved his lips into the soft swell of my peaking breasts. In the midst of a passionate kiss he suddenly lifted his mouth and made a studied, half-lidded survey of my face . . . and then moved back.

At first I thought that we had reached the theater and he wanted to give me time to compose myself, but a glance out the window told me we were still far from the populous city streets. He had not withdrawn from our embrace for that reason. Why, then?

Startled, bewildered, I turned my face away as hot shame burned like a brand in my cheeks. I could not even bear to look at him. An inner voice mocked me for my presumption that I could replace Lila Fontaine in an afternoon tete-a-tete. He had been angry that she had kept him waiting and asked me along in a moment of whimsy.

At least he didn't insult me with a lot of glib talk as we finished our ride back to the theater district. The carriage continued to jostle us together, but he was strangely tense and silent beside me. A quick glance told me his jaw was set, and those bold cheeks were more pronounced than ever. He seemed to find the situation as untenable as I did. When we arrived at the Imperial he sat for a moment without speaking, and I couldn't even summon up the superficial niceties of thanking him for the excursion. My heart was lurching around in erratic rhythms, and I still couldn't bring myself to look directly at him.

He finally cleared his throat. "I'm sorry, Tara. I didn't mean for that to happen."

"It's all right," I said with a toss of my chin. "No matter."

"I'll have the driver take you to your lodgings."

"I'm perfectly capable of walking."

"Don't argue." He got out, turned, and through the open door said in that commanding voice of his, "And if you're serious about becoming an actress, I should have some time on Saturday mornings. That is, if you haven't changed your mind?"

I looked at him then. His gaze was steady and unreadable. For a moment I felt suspended, breathless, uneasy, as if wavering on some precipice. I was amazed to hear my voice quite steady and firm. "No, I haven't changed my mind."

"Good." He nodded, shut the door, and left me staring at his retreating back in a whirlwind of emotions that made me want to cry and laugh with abandonment.

6

When I arrived at his office the first Saturday morning for my coaching Ty was busy with his accountant, a wizened little man behind huge spectacles who seemed to look at the world through watery eyes. The huge ledgers he carried about were almost as big as he was. When I arrived the men were in a deep discussion, looking at papers spread out on Ty's desk. Ty asked me to wait in a small sitting room adjoining his office.

Airy and spacious, it was a pleasant, masculine room with walnut wainscoting and wallpaper depicting a variety of hunting scenes. Sunshine like warm honey poured in from a large window and spread talons of golden shafts across a homespun rug. A huge wardrobe dominated one side of the room. Its carved doors were slightly ajar, and I glimpsed a crowded rack of clothes, some familiar costumes and what appeared to be items from his personal wardrobe. Along one wall a long leather couch seemed to retain an imprint of those long, firm legs and that masculine torso, as if he had been lying there a short time ago. Everything had a personal touch, a slightly askew stack of scripts on a pier table near an upholstered chair, a silver pen and scribbled notes on the floor near the couch, and some gold-edged books piled nearby. I glanced at crowded bookcases fashioned with thin curtains to keep the sun from fading the leather-bound volumes. An identifying spicy tonic lingered, like a taunting specter, mocking and chiding, forcing me to remember his embrace and the warm ecstasy of his kisses. I wished he had chosen a different place for my lessons.

I sat down in a spoon-back chair, with my feet together and my back straight, a posture Jessie had instilled in me as correct. I was wearing a simple white bodice with leg-o-mutton sleeves and a navy skirt from my own wardrobe. My hair had been plaited into tight rosettes, a coiffure that kept willful curls from escaping into natural ringlets. I was determined to show him that I had put our little tete-a-tete behind us and that I was serious about the instruction he had promised to give me.

When he came in he apologized for keeping me waiting. I hoped the folded hands in my lap did not betray my inner tension. I felt like getting up and fleeing the room before I made an utter fool of myself. I thought he sent an approving glance over my attire, and his tone matched the crispness of my posture. The smile he gave me was perfunctory, and I knew he was as determined as I to keep our relationship professional.

"All right, then, suppose I have you read something for me. Do you have any preference?"

I shook my head. Although I had become used to

the tight lacing, at the moment every bit of air seemed choked out of my lungs and I wondered if my voice would be more than a pitiful croak.

He picked up a script, flipped to a page, and handed it to me.

It was a familiar scene from *As You Like It*. Lila's part.

I began with a rush.

"Too fast. Don't run your words together."

I started again.

"No, stand up. Take a deep breath, and don't read with your chin down. Hold the script out in front of you.

"The quality of your voice is promising." He peered at me, and a flicker of a smile softened his next words, "but that's about the worst reading I've ever heard. We have no place to go but up."

Since the worst had already happened I began to relax. For the next few minutes I tried to do everything he told me, hoping that I was improving.

"Breathe from your diaphragm. Lift your head and pull the air up from here." He had just placed his hand on my abdomen when a movement in the doorway stopped his next instruction.

Lila swept into the room. "Oh . . . am I disturbing something? I didn't know you were engaged." Her smile deprecated my presence as important as she smirked, "How quaint you look, Miss Townsend."

Her attire was elegant as always, and she was tall enough to show her clothes off to an enviable perfection. Her chiseled features were softened by a bonnet fashioned with a high crown and decorated with satin trimmings and white ostrich feathers. She wore a pelisse of indigo merino styled with gigot sleeves and broad wristbands confining the edges of her white kid gloves. Her bust was suspiciously full, as if hidden padding was lifting up her breasts. A protruding, gathered bustle was quite pronounced, indicating a large padded bolster underneath to fill out a bone structure that hinted of a natural angularity rather than the rounded curves her attire presented. The chain of a fringed, brocaded reticule hung over one arm and I saw a script in the other hand.

Ty glanced at his watch. Then he gave me a quick smile. "I guess our time is gone. I want to give you some things to practice. Excuse me a moment."

He went into his office, leaving Lila and me in an uncomfortable silence. I was determined that I would not give in to any nervous babbling. As casually as I could I seated myself once more in the spoon-backed chair and tried to borrow an air of complete confidence.

"I didn't know Ty was working with you," she said, looming over me. "How long has this been going on?"

I could have parried her questions or indicated it was none of her business, but I saw no point in it. "Today was my first lesson."

She gave a haughty sniff. "Poor Ty, he just doesn't have much judgment about the best way to use his time."

"Yes, it does appear he allows himself to be exploited at times. I should think an accomplished actress like yourself would be above needing tutoring sessions." I sent a pointed glance at the script in her hand.

She drew up. "My role as Portia in *Merchant of Venice* is worthy of his time and attention. There is a difference between working with an accomplished actress and an ambitious little twit appealing to his generous nature." Her nostrils flared and her eyes shone with the glint of a sharpened knife.

Her obvious jealousy only made me smile. I wondered how she would react if she knew Ty had taken me with him to the waterfront in her place. It was a hollow victory for me, and one that would not be repeated, but there was a touch of smugness in my reply. "I have every confidence in Ty as a director, don't you?"

It was an open-ended question that she could not answer without being in the wrong. Her expression was almost pinched, and an angry color rose up from that imperial neck, flushing her cheeks and narrowing her eyes. Before she could summon any kind of vitriolic reply, Ty returned and handed me a folder. If he was aware of the negative vibrations in the room, he ignored them. "Practice reading these aloud and remember to control your breathing. Give each word its full due. Next week we'll work on interpretation."

I rose and, without looking at Lila, smiled my thanks. If we had been alone he might have said something intimate. For a split moment a kind of pleading for understanding crossed his face. Then it was gone. We murmured polite good-byes. Both of us had stepped back behind barriers. We had successfully contained the sexual tension that exploded between us in the carriage—at least for the moment.

I had to tell Nell about the lessons. Her green eyes snapped as she gave me one of her knowing looks. "So that's how it is, is it?"

"I don't know what you mean. I'm just trying to improve myself. . . ."

"Improve yourself! Getting tangled up with Langston is no improvement. It's inviting trouble . . . like playing with a loaded revolver. You know his reputation with women."

"I'm not getting 'tangled-up.' "

She shook her head. The emotional rise in my voice

was evidence enough that her words had hit a
sensitive spot.

"I don't want to see you hurt, Tarry. You're a babe
in arms."

I refused to listen to warnings.

Farley was furious. "The arrogant bastard's got you
chasing rainbows. An acting coach! You've had
plenty of opportunity to develop your talents."

"If I had any? Is that what you're saying?" I flared.

"You damn well know what I'm saying."

"Yes, I do," I said coldly. "You have made it quite
plain, but I intend to continue the lessons as long as
Ty will give them to me."

He sent Nell an exasperated can't-you-do-anything-
with-her look. Nell shrugged her plump shoulders.
"You know Tarry. She's got to learn everything the
hard way."

Even Cal seemed disturbed. "I can't believe he
agreed to it. Better be careful," he warned. "Ty never
does anything unless there's a chance of increasing
his investment . . . and he never neglects to demand
payment."

These words disturbed me, but I soon rationalized
them away. Of course Ty expected me to become a
good actress and be an asset to the company, making
the time he spent with me a profitable investment.
Several times I offered to help in the office to pay for
the coaching, but he curtly refused. "Spend your time
watching Lila and Dana. See how they draw their
portrayals from the inside."

I tried my best to improve with each lesson, and
sometimes despaired that I wasn't making any
progress at all.

"No . . . no . . ." When he shook his head I automatically started the reading again . . . and again . . .
and again.

''Pain, joy, love, despair, and anguish you project on the stage starts within; it's not just tacked on the outside like a patch on some clothing. Acting is more than outward mimicry, Tara.''

I knew I wasn't progressing as he wanted. All the hours I struggled with assigned scripts accumulated in a deepening frustration. Then one Saturday morning the assignments changed. Instead of giving me Shakespearean material to practice, he gave me a melodrama—and in the next production I was given a small speaking part.

Jessie was almost as delighted as I was. In spite of my offer to take any part for the pay of a ''supe,'' my wages were increased from eight to ten dollars with this new role in *The Face of the French Coquette*. Dana DelMar played the hero in this production, and I wondered if Ty had asked him to help me, for, unlike Lila, he offered constructive criticism that improved my performance a great deal.

I found Dana to be a very intense, serious young man who labored at his art with the ardor of a religious zealot. He took a rollicking farce or melodrama as seriously as his lead in *The Merchant of Venice* or *Richlieu*. As Langston had instructed, I watched and learned and was receptive to any suggestion Dana made about my performance.

In the next farcical play I was cast as Lila's younger sister and played two scenes with her. Never once did she do more than haughtily acknowledge my presence. She was an artist and as such she remained upon her pedestal, granting only slight acknowledgment to the rest of us, her subjects.

Cal told me that last season she had been trailing in Maureen Cole's glittering dust. I couldn't help but mimic her in private, imitating her regal head with its long neck stretched upward at an imperial angle and her hands lightly wafting a hankie to her aristocratic nose. She wasn't like Dana, who viewed any production as a theatrical challenge. It was obvious she felt the farcical plays and melodramas beneath her and was quite vocal about it. I was ecstatic about having a few lines of dialogue.

"Maybe Ty is schooling you like he did Maureen," said Cal. "He brought her up from the ranks to play opposite the hero and villain in all the melodramas. She was very good, too, just like you're going to be."

"Thanks, Cal, but I don't think he thinks much of my acting."

"You're doing great. Keep it up and you'll steal every scene away from Lila."

I knew he was exaggerating, but it helped. At least I felt I was making some progress if Ty had made Maureen into a leading lady in the same fashion he was working with me. The first time I saw a photograph of Maureen a peculiar twitch went up my spine, like the brush of something furry. I stared at her face with unblinking eyes. Her fair hair was smoother than mine and her curls more orderly. She had a fuller face and a pretty sweetness. Her lips were curved softly and her eyes held a knowing, flirtatious sparkle. She wore a gown I immediately recognized but had never dared to wear, an off-the-shoulder emerald satin with a lovely lavaliere hanging on a gold chain in the cleft of her breasts. The picture lodged itself in my mind and I could not forget it. I wondered if the lovely necklace had been a gift, and from whom.

That night I lay awake and remembered the first time I had heard Ty's voice, calling her name. A deep ache was even more poignant now that I had felt his lips and allowed myself to be plunged into a maelstrom of desire. I wanted him to look at me like that, to hear my name on his lips, vibrant and caring. In every way that I could I was trying to become the kind of woman that would attract and keep his attention. What had Maureen been like? I had unabashedly asked questions to satisfy my insatiable curiosity. I knew that Dana had played opposite her all last season, but her untimely death had made him cautious about talking about her. Theatrical people were a superstitious lot, and bad luck was always a specter hovering nearby. I could not tell what Dana's relationship had been with Maureen. If it was anything like the one that existed between him and Lila, it was a controlled and impersonal respect.

Cal had said he had found Maureen to be rather taken with herself as an actress, and he thought that Ty's interest in her fostered it. That was as close as he had come to saying that they were lovers. How serious had their relationship been? Had the last quarrel been between lovers? When Ty had mistaken me for her he had spun me around as if eager to talk with her and perhaps put everything right between them. But Maureen was already dead. I could not believe that Ty already knew that when he called out her name.

The police had apparently filed her death away as an unsolved crime. It was little wonder that I was startled at making a discovery that suddenly drew me back into her past. One afternoon I decided to use a small beaded reticule of Maureen's that had been in the belongings that Cal was going to throw away. The only reason I had not used it was because I didn't want to hurt Jessie's feelngs by putting away the bag she had crocheted for me. I started to shift my ivory comb and small, silvered mirror into it and discovered that the small bag contained a scented hankie, a tiny vial of perfume, and a scribbled note.

"G-Church, Father Inghram, Tuesday, 2 p.m. Don't forget."

The *don't forget* was underlined, signaling the importance of the reminder. I was intrigued. Why had Maureen made an appointment to meet with an Episcopal minister, for the G-Church must be Grace Cathedral, I reasoned. Could the appointment have had anything to do with her death? Should I tell someone? But who? Had she kept the appointment? No date was on the note. Maybe the appointment was a trivial thing that would make me look utterly ridiculous if I made a fuss about it. The sensible thing to do was forget it.

But I couldn't.

I held my counsel for nearly a week, thinking about it, and then gave vent to my curiosity. I decided the best thing to do was to follow it up myself. If it was a dead end or I determined that nothing was amiss about the appointment or the reason for it, then no one need know about my prying.

I reassured myself that it was not my own fixation on the dead woman that made me lie to Farley and Nell the following Sunday afternoon about taking a walk in the Square to study my lines. It was all I could do to keep Farley from accompanying me, and I picked a quarrel so I could flounce out of the house without him.

As quickly as I could I hurried away and headed up the steep incline of California Street. A boisterous wind was sweeping up and down the hills, lifting sand and lowering dark clouds. The knitted, multi-colored shawl I wore over my teal gown was not heavy enough to keep out the chilly air, and I realized that in my haste to leave the boarding house I had forgotten my umbrella. I dared not go back. In fact, I kept looking back over my shoulder in a stealthy fashion. It would be just like Farley to keep a protective eye on me. Why I felt so furtive about my errand I could not really tell . . . it was just a feeling that I didn't want anyone to know what I was up to.

I passed St. Mary's Church on the corner of Dupont Street and continued up the hill until I reached the Grace Episcopal Cathedral, an imposing stone structure with vaulting belfry and stained glass windows. Since my religious training had consisted of private instruction by Jessie in the fundamental beliefs that had been given to her by her evangelistic father, I felt intimidated by this massive structure, built specifically to guide mankind's souls heavenward. Had Maureen Cole been a member of this congregation? Could she have driven up in front of its portals every Sunday morning and alighted from a carriage for services? Maybe she had worn this very same dress as she knelt for blessings and forgiveness, I thought, feeling my skin prickling in a peculiar way.

My resolve was growing weaker by the minute and only my well-honed stubbornness kept me moving on the path at the side of the church that led to the church offices. As I stepped inside the hushed, somber building a white-haired gentlemen greeted me through an open door as he moved about his study, busily collecting books and papers. A sign on his desk identified him as Father Inghram. "Yes, may I help you?"

With an apology, I introduced myself, stammering that I had a question that he might be able to answer . . . that I really didn't want to intrude upon him . . . that I was rather embarrassed . . . and perhaps I shouldn't pursue the matter further . . .

"What is it, child?" he asked, stopping my flow of

nervous chatter by asking me to sit down. He folded aging, purple-veined hands placidly on the desk and tipped his gray head attentively in my direction. "Now, Miss Townsend, I have a few moments before my Bible class. Please tell me how I may be of help."

His unhurried manner and gentle smile did much to quiet my mind and let me proceed in some reasonable fashion. "I am an actress at the Imperial Theatre. . . ." I hesitated, tempted to qualify that remark. It certainly sounded more impressive than my position warranted. "I came into possession of some things belonging to Maureen Cole." I waited to see if the name brought any outward signs of recognition. The man's round face remained serene and there was nothing to indicate that the name meant anything to him.

I dug in the beaded recticule and brought out the crumpled slip of paper. "I found this in her bag." I handed it to him and watched him read it. That smooth, broad forehead furrowed slightly.

"I don't seem to remember such a person, but let me think. What did you say the lady's name was?"

"Maureen Cole. . . . She was also an actress."

His face cleared. "Oh, yes, now I remember. I received a written message from her . . . the stationery was perfumed." He looked a little abashed that it had been this frivolous detail that had made him remember. "I set up an appointment for her."

"I was wondering if there was something that might shed some light on her death."

"Her death?" He looked startled.

I nodded and then told him as evenly as I could the circumstances of her death, as far as they were known. "You can see why I was wondering if you might know something . . . if she might have confided in you."

"I'm sorry, but Miss Cole was not a member of my congregation."

"I thought—because of the note—that you had met her."

"Miss Cole never kept the appointment. Let's see, that must have been sometime late last summer. She asked me to meet with her concerning plans for a wedding in my church."

"Wedding," my voice croaked out the word. "She was planning to be married?"

"I assume so, since that's what her note said. I was surprised that she was coming alone. Most arrangements are made by the couple."

"Did she say whom she was going to marry?"

"No."

An unwilling bridegroom? Someone who would rather kill than be led to the altar? My mouth went dry.

"I set up the appointment," Father Inghram said, "but, as I've told you, she did not keep it. I was not aware of her death. I'm truly sorry."

"She didn't say anything else in her note to you?" *Don't forget.* The underlined words burned into my brain. Why had it been so important for her to come alone to make arrangements for a church wedding?

"No, I'm afraid I can't tell you anything more. It's sad . . . I shall remember her in my prayers." He stood up then and collected his books. I knew Father Inghram was not going to indulge in any more meaningless speculation. "I hope I have been of help." He smiled benignly.

I managed to thank him and then fled the church. During the few minutes I had been inside the sky and wind had changed to match my mood. A lowering haze was already bringing a spattering of small drops of rain, making dark spots upon my dress and bonnet. A freshening wind tugged at the streamers of my bonnet and sent loosened strands of hair flying across my face. All around me people rushed along the wooden sidewalks, frantically opening umbrellas or hurriedly mounting the trolleys. A downpour was imminent, but a thunderstorm could have been rumbling overhead and I would not have noticed it.

Wedding. Maureen was making plans—she was going to be a bride. Things had gotten far enough for her to talk about engaging a minister and a church.

No, no! I did not want to handle the thoughts that were spilling over me with the force of a floodgate. She had not kept her appointment because she had already been murdered. Instead of a bride she had become a bloated corpse. I covered my mouth with my hands as a sickening bile lurched up into my throat.

Imperceptibly, the descending mist gave way to distinct drops, chasing each other downward in thickening, silver streaks. In a matter of minutes the flowers and ribbons on my hat drooped, my hair became plastered against my face, and the hems of my gown and petticoat were weighted with water as they swished through collecting rain puddles.

I didn't notice any of it.

The memory of the dark fury upon Ty's face and his vicious hands tightening at a man's throat came back to haunt me. The same unanswered questions rose up in my mind. What had that last quarrel between him and Maureen been about? Had he told her that he would never marry her, that their affair was over? The need to know was like a drug flowing through my system. I turned toward the Crystal Hotel without consciously making the decision that I would demand that he tell me. Even though my feelings about him were irrational, I told myself I would know if he were lying. I would know if that powerful, masculine strength had exploded into unleashed fury because Maureen was going to hold him to a marriage he didn't want.

In my confused and tortured thinking I never once considered that such wrath might be turned against me. As I stumbled through the lashing wind and rain, I had only one driving thought . . . I must talk to Ty and find some peace within myself.

Like a listing vessel bracing against the downpour, I reached the Crystal Hotel, with its ornate facade of decorative stone and cast iron. Seven stories of looming bay windows and balconies rose above an inner court where carriages, broughams, and landaus were disgorging passengers.

Gratefully, I darted into this luxurious hotel that combined European grandeur with a golden gaudiness that was San Francisco. I was short of breath as I crossed the expansive lobby. My sodden clothes dripped water upon a deep plush carpet and I peered through water-laced eyelashes, trying to get my bearings. Gas-lit crystal chandeliers dispelled the darkened shadows and gloom that pressed up against the outside windows. The almost blinding glitter of shimmering prisms transformed the lobby into a glistening, luminous world set apart from the elements. Polished, inlaid tables and chairs and settees in deep green and gold brocade were scattered gracefully about in private and secluded groupings near potted plants. Fresh floral bouquets, dominated by deep crimson roses, had been artfully arranged in silver, pewter, and cut-glass containers. Rose perfume scented the air as if continually dispensed from the soft spray of an atomizer. Massive Ionic columns, vaulting ceilings, and paneled walls captured a hushed elegance that was almost overpowering. There were no disturbing sounds or loud voices. Everything was serene and melodious.

I was completely out of place. Only the force of my inner anguish drove me to the polished reception desk to ask for the number of Mr. Langston's suite.

An austere gentleman behind the desk let his bespectacled eyes register disapproval of my disheveled state before his thin lips moved almost imperceptibly to give me the information.

Tugging at my loosened hair and smoothing my clinging skirts, I walked over to one of the five hydraulic elevators stretched along one wall. Such was the discipline of the hotel's staff that I received no more than a quick, cursory glance from the uniformed operator as I stepped into the elevator and gave him the floor number. I was conscious of what an impropriety it was for me to be here, alone, intent on calling upon an unmarried man in his hotel suite. Even though my theatrical family, including Nell, had protected me and formed a rigid barrier between me and the public, I knew very well I was putting my reputation in jeopardy by this rash action. At the moment social proprieties seemed of little importance. I was not thinking clearly about anything except the deep need to hear that commanding voice and know that all my wild suspicions were unfounded.

I left the elevator on the fifth floor. My high shoes made a squishing noise as I moved down the carpeted hall past elegantly carved white doors with brass numbers and door knockers. My teeth were threatening to chatter. I knew the drenching I had received had gone bone deep. I reached the number that I had been given and knocked.

The door was opened almost immediately by a small Oriental man who nodded politely and waited for me to speak.

"Is . . . is Mr. Langston in?" I managed, my lips touched with blue from the chilling rain.

"And who, please, is calling?" His eyes narrowed beyond their normal slant and I knew that he was ready to politely turn me away.

"Tara . . . Tara Townsend."

My voice was almost a gutteral croak but it must have floated into the apartment. Even before the servant had turned away to deliver my name, Ty was at the door. He took one look at me and swore. "Good Lord, Tara! What are you trying to do, catch pneumonia? Come in. Sit down over there by the fire. Let me have that shawl and that miserable-looking bonnet." He issued orders as if we were at the theater and his word was law. "Ching, get something warm for Miss Townsend, coffee laced with a bit of brandy. What on earth are you doing taking a stroll in a downpour like this?"

Now that I was face to face with him, the urgency to speak with him was shriveling. Words seemed to fail me and I let him guide me to the fireplace and ease me down into a comfortable parlor chair with curved arms and a deep seat. I sat on the edge of it and hugged myself, as if somehow that would hold me together until I regained my composure. I didn't even protest when he deftly knelt down and spread the folds of my water-logged skirts toward the fire. Before I could protest he had slipped off my soaked shoes and placed a pillow under my feet.

"You really should get out of those things . . . you're drenched to the skin."

"No . . . I . . . I'm fine," I stammered, and realized

that my teeth were chattering.

"Sure you are—half drowned, chilled and shivering, looking like someone in shock—but you're just fine. Here, drink this." He took a cup and saucer from Ching, as he quickly padded into the room, and handed it to me.

I tried to keep the china from rattling as I took a sip of the steaming liquid. Fiery warmth plunged down my throat and sped to the extremities of my body, easing away the wintry flow in my veins and soothing the ragged edges of my emotions.

He waited until I had finished the drink before he disappeared for a moment, then returned with a soft towel. He sat down on the arm of my chair and began taking out the pins from what remained of my coiled twists.

"No," I protested, my hands flying upward to stay him from my falling hair.

"All right, you do it." He tossed me the towel.

Even as I rubbed the dripping, heavy strands, I knew what my hair did when it got wet: It tightened into unmanageable ringlets in a blowsy mass of curls. My struggles to try and keep it smoothed back were a mockery now as I took the towel away and it fell around my shoulders in a cascade of wheat-colored ringlets and waves. I knew he was staring at it in a bemused fashion and I felt a warmth that had nothing to do with the brandy I had drunk, easing into my cheeks.

His Chinese servant had discreetly disappeared. Undoubtedly, lady visitors were not a rarity in these premises. This knowledge reminded me of the urgency that had brought me here. Despite the unconventionality of my appearance at the moment I managed to put a little starch in my manner as I said, "I have to talk with you."

"All right." He sat down next to me and crossed his legs casually in front of him. I noticed then that his collar was loose and he was wearing a smoking jacket with deep velvet pockets and a tie belt. Apparently, he had not been expecting visitors this Sunday afternoon and was lounging about in this casual dress. I felt even more embarrassed about his lack of proper dress than I did my own.

He watched my traveling gaze and apparently read my thoughts, for the cleft in his chin deepened with amusement. "Would you be more comfortable if I retired and put on my vest and jacket, Miss Townsend?"

His mockery and the use of my formal name helped me collect my thoughts. The suspicions that had grown like a malignancy since I had learned Maureen's secret made me fix my eyes on him with vulturelike intensity. I wanted to be aware of every flicker of those thick crescent eyebrows; I wanted to measure every movement of his curved eyelashes; I wanted to weigh every response and body movement for truth or falsehood. In short, I wanted nothing of his manner to get by me.

"Is there some problem at the theater?" he prodded at my silence.

"No, this has nothing to do with that," I said quickly. He must think I was there for some extra tutoring or with some complaint about my part. "This is . . . personal."

"I see." He nodded gravely, and I was certain there was a momentary flicker of amusement in his eyes.

It gave me some sense of satisfaction to deal a direct blow to that smug, patronizing manner. "I have just learned that Maureen Cole was making arrangements to be married at Grace Cathedral."

His face closed against me. "Is that so?"

"Apparently, she never kept her appointment with Father Inghram . . . because she was murdered instead." I faltered and then said bluntly, "I want to know whom she planned to marry."

"So you've come to me, through wind and rain, to find out, is that it?" His expression was passive and his thoughts indiscernible.

"Exactly." My breathing quickened.

He had not moved a muscle that I could see. "Have you considered the fact that such knowledge may be none of your business, Tara? Not only that, but the girl was murdered. I caution you that, considering the circumstances, the particulars of the dead girl's affairs might best be left undisturbed."

"Not if they shed some light on who killed her," I countered boldly, a sick feeling developing in my stomach. *Please, say it wasn't you . . . please. . . .* "Were you planning to marry Maureen Cole?" I was shocked to hear the question in my own ears.

"No."

There was his answer. Short and prompt. Perhaps too prompt? Could I believe him?

"That's all?" he taunted. "Aren't you going to ask me if I murdered her?" I knew then that he was furious.

I leaned my head back in the chair and closed my eyes. "No." I believed him. I had to. Relief sluiced through my body.

In the next instant he was by my chair, his hands placed on the armrests as he bent over me. "You little fool," he said in a quiet, deadly tone. "Don't you have any brains in that stubborn, willful head of yours? Going around asking questions that might put a cord around your own fragile neck. It's dangerous. What on earth can I do to make you leave this thing alone?" His eyes raked my face.

118

"You could tell me what really happened."

Letting out an explosive breath, he pulled me to my feet and we stood there, looking into one another's face like figures frozen in a moment of time.

"Please, Tara, believe me," he whispered hoarsely, "what happened cannot be changed now. Let it go." His hard mouth descended angrily on mine, as if to force my acquiescence. There was no tenderness in the arms that held me in an iron embrace. Hard, muscular sinews pressed against me and the hands splayed across my back held me with viselike firmness.

I could not move away from the desire surging between us, engulfing my senses. I had longed for his embrace, turned restlessly in my bed dreaming of kisses and caresses that would carry me into the swells of passion, and there were no defenses I could summon now that fantasy had become reality.

All the professional distance he had maintained between us was shattered, and I was foolish enough to think it didn't matter. I returned his kisses with the pure, honest delight of my inexperienced ways. When he drew me down to the rug in front of the fire I remained in his embrace. He buried his face in soft, unruly hair tumbling upon my shoulders and let tight, teasing kisses trace the lines of my cheek until his lips once again claimed the pliable softness that burned under his probing mouth.

"Tara . . . Tara . . ." he murmured as one hand cupped the arching firmness of a heated breast. Through the wet cloth hardening nipples responded to his light stroking. I had never felt a man's arousing touch before. A warm fullness spilled from my lips and breasts and spread, radiating heat into my thighs. I was lost to a desire as consuming as the curling tongues of bright flame in the fireplace.

I did not protest when he lifted me up in his arms and carried me to the bedroom. I had been in love with him since the first time my eyes had feasted upon his photographs that day in the theater lobby. My life had changed from the moment he called me by another's name with a softness in his eyes that I longed to claim. There was no going back to the innocent young girl I had been before I met him. I wanted him as totally as a woman had ever wanted a man.

As he slipped off my clothes and abandoned them in a heap on the floor beside his four-poster bed, I was suddenly frightened. Not because he was about to make love to me, but because of my inexperience. Would he find me wanting? I knew nothing about the art of responding to a man's passion. Was there a role I should play? Responses that I should make? all these anxieties were obliterated as he slipped under the covers beside me and pressed his naked body against mine. No rehearsal was necessary. My body responded without hesitation to the soft, undulating caresses that his hands made upon my full breasts and the kisses he buried in the smooth line of my throat. His mouth sought to taste the sweetness of my heated flesh and his touch left trails of exquisite sensation under his rampant mouth.

He murmured endearments, filling my ears with that rich, resonant voice of his until responding moans escaped my lips. Firmly yet gently, he swept my legs apart, transporting me into an unbelievable height of pain and ecstasy. In a rising crescendo, the rapturous sensations increased until my fingers were pressed against the hard muscles of his back, every sense filled with a need that defied interpretation. This wild, wonderful physical love between a man and woman had been orchestrated beyond my belief. And then, like a crash of cymbals, my body seemed to break apart into a shower of fragmented sensations, leaving me breathless and suspended.

A bewildering contentment and lassitude engulfed me. I lay quietly in his arms. He held me close, gently, and his heavy breathing eased into a quiet, regular rhythm. He closed is eyes and I wondered if he slept. I was content to memorize the handsome face turned toward me on the pillow. I was not dreaming. It had happened. He was no longer beyond my reach.

Then his eyes opened and his half-lidded gaze stroked my face; his expression was introspective as he smiled. I knew he was trying to gage my reaction to what had happened. He knew that he was the first, and, as far as I was concerned, the only man who would ever possess my body.

He raised up on one arm and looked down at me. My hair was in curly disarray around my face and yet I had never felt more beautiful. With one finger he traced the smooth curve of my cheek and chin. Then he bent his head and kissed me several times, ever so lightly. I wondered if he was going to make love to me again. I was disappointed when he drew back, a frown creasing his forehead. "I want you to promise me, no more questions of me or anyone. What happened to Maureen is not your concern. Let it be."

I almost whispered that I would do whatever he wished. For some reason I allowed my natural willfulness to thwart that response and whispered, "I have to know. I can't let it rest . . ."

"Why?"

I couldn't answer him. For some reason I had merged my identity with the dead girl far beyond my longing to attract Ty Langston. Perhaps Nell was right: Maybe I had become possessed in some mysterious way. Was Maureen reaching out to me from the grave? I could not throw off the premonition that some purposeful fate had given me her clothes and allowed me to find the scribbled note.

"Were you in love with Maureen Cole?" I dared to ask, fearing his answer.

"No, I wasn't."

"But was your relationship . . . professional?"

He impatiently cupped my chin and looked directly into my eyes. "Until now I have not had any trouble keeping my personal involvements separated from the theater."

I knew the moment had come when I must maintain control of my leaping desires or forever be lost to them. His words could entrap me, make me his captive.

"Forget about Maureen Cole. Promise me . . ."

"I can't promise. I have to know." My pulse still hammering from his kisses, I shattered the intimacy that had been between us. "What are you hiding from me?"

I felt his instant withdrawal and was not surprised when he stood up and loomed over me like a specter glaring down from some great height. His hair was rumpled where I had laced it with my fingers and I ached with the sudden rejection I felt vibrating from his virile body.

"You have to know," he repeated in an acid tone.

"I'll be careful . . ."

He gave me a rueful smile. "My dear, you don't know the meaning of the word."

7

The boarding house was in an uproar when Ty's
carriage deposited me in front of it a few minutes
later. I knew my arrival had been announced when I
saw the lace curtains move in the parlor, where glass
lamps were smudges of light in the late afternoon
grayness. Earlier heavy rain had changed into a
capricious mist swirling like low clouds around me as
I made my way up the cobblestone walk.

Despite my efforts to fasten my willful hair back
into a respectable twist, damp ringlets trailed on my
forehead and sprang out from my head in a curly
mass. My wilted bonnet looked more disreputable
than ever perched on top of my disheveled coiffure.
The moist hem and flounces of my dress were
wrinkled and water-spotted. There was little I could
do to repair the damage my unconcerned flight in the
rain had wrought. It was no wonder that my
appearance brought a sudden silence that was as loud

as a pealing bell when I closed the front door behind me and the parlor archway filled with people.

They stared at me en masse, Jessie, Nell, Budd, and Farley. Even weary Mrs. MacPherson, who took little interest in her boarders' coming and going was there, wringing her hands.

I flushed as Nell's snapping green eyes took in my appearance, a knowing glint going from the departing carriage to my flushed face. Jessie's prim features were pulled down in scowling lines and her posture was so stiff it crackled. "Such disgraceful behavior . . ."

Budd's expression of relief turned to embarrassment, and he shifted uncomfortably, as if he should say something to me but didn't know quite what was appropriate.

Farley was just plain furious. "So you're back . . . and how did you enjoy your . . . walk!" His lean face jutted forward and his usually passive eyes raked my appearance. I saw then that his clothes were dripping wet. *Farley had been out looking for me!* He must have come after me, and he knew I hadn't taken my walk in the square as I had indicated when I left.

"Would you mind telling us where you've been?" His slender nose flared and I wondered if he could smell the brandy I had drunk.

I firmed my chin, which was always a sure sign I was on the defensive. "Not at all . . . I just took a longer walk than I planned . . . and darted into the Crystal Hotel to get out of the rain. Mr. Langston saw me . . . and politely offered his carriage to take me home." Most of it was tinged with the truth, and I was rather pleased at the way it hung together.

"You've ruined that bonnet!" snapped Jessie, her parsimonous eyes registering its collapse. "And your gown. Look at the hem of your pelisse, soiled with mud and water . . .''

"You've been gone nearly three hours," Farley said pointedly, not letting me off with my vague explanation.

"We were pretty worried, lass," Budd scolded in his easygoing way.

"I'm sorry. I didn't mean to alarm anyone."

"You didn't go to the square at all," Farley accused. "If you had, you would have come home when it started to rain."

"I told you . . . I went for a long walk. And I need to get out of these wet things." I gathered up my skirts and swept by them with as much poise as I could muster and quickly mounted the stairs. A murmur of voices floated up after me and I knew what the topic of conversation would be for the rest of the evening.

Farley decided to ignore me during dinner. Afterward, he smoked his pipe; his manner indicative of an artic chill. Jessie had carried off my wet things with the air of someone entrusted with recovering a great loss. Nell let things simmer down before she brought up the subject as we made ready for bed. "I'm not about to lecture you none, Tarry. God knows, I ain't set much of an example for you."

"Please, Nell," I protested, turning my back to her. I hoped she would take the hint that I didn't want to talk about it, but she ignored my posture.

"You ought to know that you're a lot like your mother, bless her soul. Dear Nola watched me cavorting around with this fellow and that and she never said one thing about it, but we both knew she was different. Never once did she waver in her affections nor wander away from the one man she loved, your father. That's the way she was . . . and that's the way you are too, honey." She gave her broad, rather coarse laugh. "Not like me. Fellows never get under my skin very deep. Never have understood why gals take them so seriously. But some women do, they give their heart away only once . . . and more often than not to some guy that ain't worth a broken shoe hook. Come here, gal, sit down and let old Nell set you straight. Your pa an' ma would want me to tell you some things needing to be said.''

Most of the information I had gleaned about my parents had come from Nell. Any talk about them was like a shiny object waved in front of my eyes, so I curled up on Nell's bed while she eased her ample self back against some soft feather pillows. Her red hair flamed against the pillow and I mused, as I always did, how pretty she was. Above her ruffled nightdress, her white skin was still peaches and cream, her breasts full, her arms nicely round and firm. Her breezy voice was tinged with affection as she talked. ''I guess you kinda grew up on all of us, honey, before we were ready . . .'' She held up a plump hand. ''I know, you'll be eighteen in a few weeks. But we all think of you as our little girl, and I guess we all want to protect you a little. Farley was out of his mind, thinking someone had carried you off, but I was worried about something else.'' Her forthright manner got right to the point. ''You haven't fooled me none. I know you haven't been the same since you laid them dove eyes on Ty Langston.''

''It's . . . it's not what you think,'' I stammered.

''It's exactly what I think. You can't fool old Nell about some things.'' Her round, honest face was knowing. She gave me a sly wink. ''And you know exactly what I'm talking about, don't you?''

How could I lie to her? I let out my breath. ''Yes, I guess I do,'' I admitted, remembering how desire had run rampant through me when I was in his embrace.

''And I'm telling you that this kind of thing ain't for

you, honey. You'll get yourself all torn up inside over a guy whose mistresses read like a threatrical bill. For heaven's sake. Love, don't get yourself in a dither about a ladies' man like Langston. Better gals than you have tried to put a hackamore on him trying to get him to the altar.''

Like Maureen?

"What's the matter, honey? You're upset about something . . . you haven't been the same since we signed on at the Imperial.''

I could have told her then, and perhaps impending terror and tragedy would have been avoided. I loved her and I knew she loved me . . . and, in a way, I trusted her more than any other person on earth. She had always been there when I needed her, and yet I couldn't tell her about my errand that afternoon. It was some perverted sense of loyalty to Ty Langston that kept me silent about going to him to find out if he was the one Maureen was planning to marry. He had denied it and I couldn't chance having Nell proclaim it for the lie it might be. Maybe I knew that the reassurance I needed wouldn't be there. I opened my mouth and then closed it. She must have read the conflict in my eyes. "Why don't you tell me what happened this afternoon, Tarry?'' she said softly.

"Nothing happened.'' I set my chin again.

"You've got that willful look that means trouble.''

"That seems to be my middle name. I wouldn't be surprised if our director starts easing me out of the company altogether.'' I remembered his cold manner as he let me out of his suite.

"Don't be fooling yourself, honey. You don't seem to recognize the kind of effect you have on men, even on an experienced rogue like Langston. Take Farley, for instance. I've been meaning to talk to you about him .''

"Farley?" I knew in my heart what she was going to say. All my pretense that everything was the same between us was about to be shattered. "What about Farley?"

"The time for you hanging on his arm and cuddling up to him is over. He doesn't think of you as a child any longer. Any fool can see that he's in love with you."

"You're . . . you're out of your mind. Farley is like an older brother."

"Not old enough, I fear. He's probably only got a couple of years on your enchanting Mr. Langston. Sure, he treated you like a youngster during those years when you were growing up, but things change. He's been fighting a jealousy dragon every time he sees you hanging over Cal's piano, laughing and talking and spreading your smiles around. All that help Dana's been giving you, haven't you felt the smoldering heat coming from Farley's glare as you two work together? I don't think he's been aware of Langston as a possible rival, until today. When you rode up in his carriage . . . Lordy, I thought Farley was going to dash out and challenge somebody to a duel!"

I didn't want to hear this. Farley was one of the few solid, firm, comforting supports that had been there for me nearly as long as I could remember. I didn't want to think of him as a lover. What I felt for him was something apart from a romantic relationship. "No, it's not true," I protested. "You're imagining things." But I knew she was right.

"In spite of your newly found maturity, honey, you've got a lot to learn about men."

She began to enlighten me about some of her romantic pursuits. We talked until she was too weary to hold her eyes open.

I went to my own narrow bed and spent a restless night trying to come to terms with a bewildering rush of emotions that were threatening to spin out of control. It was a paradox—I wanted things around me to stay the same, and yet I wanted them to be different. I knew that my life was spinning wildly like a top thrown from a taut string—but I was not prepared for the changes that came quickly the very next morning.

When parts were handed out for *All That Glitters Is Not Gold*, a popular play that Langston had cleverly adapted to California's Gold Rush, I stared at my script as if the name beside the supporting female role could not be mine.

"Congratulations, Tara," Cal said, his black eyes shining with an odd expression. "I knew you could do it."

"So did I," said Dana, shaking my hand. I knew he was taking some of the credit for my advancement because of the help he had been giving me. "You'll be a leading lady yet."

Other members of the company collected around me in the green room. Budd and Nell gave me affectionate squeezes, but Farley stayed his distance. His mouth was clamped down tightly on his pipe, as if he was trying to control a response that had nothing congratulatory about it. He obviously thought my sudden rise in the ranks was due to something besides my budding theatrical talent.

I couldn't help but wonder the same thing. Ty's manner was certainly an about face! If I had despaired because our director ignored my presence before, all that had changed. He seemed to find all kinds of excuses to have me trailing around as he looked at costumes and made discussions about sets.

"Part of your tutoring," he said when I summoned

my courage to question him about it. "There's more to being a competent actress than reading lines."

The memory of his caresses and the passion that flared so easily between us was always there, but I followed his professional lead, knowing that he was trying to keep a tight rein on our emotions.

I knew everyone was talking about us. The change in his attitude was so obvious that I felt myself flushing when he directed a remark to me. Even so, how could I remove myself from this sudden attention when every pore in my body greedily drank up his presence? I assured myself that his behavior toward me was never suggestive or flirtatious. He continued to arrive and leave with Lila in tow, and he never asked me to come to his private office. He even put an end to the tutoring lessons. "Learning is best accomplished on stage. You have mastered the basics, now you must wrestle with refinements."

During rehearsals he flayed me with his driving whip the same as the others. "For Godsakes, Tara, tighten it up . . . tighten it up." Bang, bang, went his cane, and dust bellowed in clouds from the floorboards. "No, no, you've got to have more voice! Punch up that line. It's wrong, all wrong! Tara! Dammit it, run it again."

Often tears burned behind my eyes. My reaction to his professional criticism was warped by my personal feelings for him. Every sharp comment wrenched my insides into a painful knot. How desperately I wanted to please him. I could feel Lila's knowing eyes on me as he demanded perfection that I was not capable of giving.

She's enjoying this! The knowledge that she wanted me to fail helped me get through each demoralizing rehearsal.

At night, on the edge of exhausted sleep, Ty's voice

bit into my roaring ears "Bring it up . . . bring it up, Tara . . . you're letting the scene die!" In nightmare proportions, his voice grew. "You failed . . . you failed!" His threatening visage came closer and closer —until I awoke screaming.

Nell soothed me in her soft, full arms. "It's all right, honey, you're getting it. It's going to work out, you'll see."

"What if I fail?" I sobbed.

"You won't."

I wanted to believe her, but I was frightened, discouraged, exhausted, and I felt the whole company was embarrassed that I had been given a role beyond my abilities. I finally decided there was nothing to do but give up the part.

"I see," said Ty evenly when I told him what I had decided. "I didn't realize you were qualified to question my judgment."

"It isn't that," I said quickly.

"Then what is it? You say that I have made a mistake giving you this part, that you are embarrassing the company, that your decision to become an actress was a whim and not worthy of any hard work."

"It is not the hard work!" I flared.

"Then what is it?"

"I think you gave me the part . . . because . . . because of what happened between us."

He gave a short laugh. "Believe me, Miss Townsend, if I gave a role to every charming woman whose company I enjoyed, we'd have to put on three performances a day to accommodate them." His bluntness was cruel and to the point. "I assure you that you were given the part because I thought you were ready for it. Now, if you don't mind, I suggest you take your place before your tardiness costs you

131

another fine."

His callous behavior sent anger like molten fire surging through my veins. I hated him! His insufferable, conceited attitude was like a rasp. I writhed furiously under his unfeeling manner. When I returned to rehearsal I blotted out everything except dispelling steaming energy on that stage. Once I thought I saw him grinning, but I only heard his commanding voice. "Now that scene's beginning to play. I think you've finally got a handle on it."

We presented *All That Glitters* to an enthusiastic audience, and my debut as a supporting actress was made. I didn't even resist it when he laughingly chided me for ever doubting his ability as a drama coach. Backstage that night, he took my hand and brought it up to his lips, bestowing a lingering, light kiss that promised much more. The air suddenly held a mysterious sweetness as I savored the feel of those lips upon my flesh. His eyes burned into mine, and I waited for him to make the move that would break the stalemate of our relationship. It didn't come. He pulled back behind some invisible barrier. As he released my hand his smile was suddenly distant. Foolish tears swelled up in my eyes, and I turned away quickly so he wouldn't see them.

I don't know when I crossed over the line of becoming competent. Probably not in that play, or even the next one, but some time during the winter season I began to show some arresting presence on stage. I could tell when the pace of a scene was slowing and I didn't need to hear Ty's cane pounding on the floor to pick it up. I learned that a good scene played like the steady rhythm of a musical composition. When everyone on the stage was performing on one level, there was harmony, and the energy generated flowed out into the audience.

Ty maintained his professional attitude toward me, and although heat rushed to my face when he brushed against me or took my hand to lead me to my correct position on stage I managed to subdue my outward reactions, hoping that he didn't discern the effect his nearness had on me. Several times I caught a softening at the corner of his lips, which suggested that I had not fooled him with my distant manner.

Dana continued to work with me, making certain the cues he gave me were on target, and he seemed to find gratification that I was progressing with each offering. He was foremost an actor, and I never felt he was interested in me in any way but as a struggling artist. He and Lila seemed to have reached a new plateau in their relationship, but none of us could quite figure out if it had eased into the amorous. His tawny blondness was a contrast to her regal dark hair and eyes, and although they began to arrive at the theater together, they both gave the impression that the theater was their first and only love. I wondered if Ty had said something to the handsome, blond actor that made him receptive to the extra effort he made in my behalf.

During each performance, from his position on the dais, Cal grinned at me as his chords and trills accented the melodramatic action or put a sinister frame around the actions of the villain. Every melodrama demanded tight blocking, visual pictures, body language, extreme posturing, and was highly structured. A perfect vehicle for the schooling I needed.

My first leading role was as the heroine in *The Drunkard's Daughter*. It seemed less demanding than some supporting parts I had done because I was ready for it. The play was a classic one, and a sure winner with any audience. Ty had chosen well for me, and

133

my triumph was sweet.

I loved every minute on stage, feeling the same joy that I had experienced as a child. It was a miracle that I had discovered that my latent talent had to be developed by hard work and dedication. I might have gone through life lamenting the fact that the mantle of a mature actress had not fallen on my shoulders. The night of my first starring performance the audience filled my ears with applause. As I took my bows with Dana, who had played opposite me as the hero, his aristocratic face was as flushed as mine, and he seemed genuinely happy for my success.

Backstage was delirium. Nell cried and wiped at sloppy tears flowing down her face. I forgot about being reserved with Farley and threw myself into his arms for a bear hug. Once again I was an integral part of the Rafferty Players, and no one was more pleased than Jessie at my increased salary. Her black eyes actually beamed with parental pride as my debut as a leading lady was heralded by everyone—but the one who mattered most. Our director was strangely absent. At this moment of triumph I wanted to be with him without reserve, expressing pure happiness and allowing erotic feelings to spring free.

I couldn't keep my eyes from flowing across the crowd backstage as we made our way downstairs to the dressing rooms. Where was he? The voice I longed to hear praising my triumph was so silent that it made all the others have a hollow sound in my ears.

The women's dressing room emptied out quickly, and Nell and I were the last ones to put our costumes into Jessie's clutching hands. With a martinet step, she carried them off to tall wooden wardrobes in a sewing room where they would be kept until the next performance.

''Who's the lucky man tonight?'' I asked Nell as she

preened in the narrow mirror in front of her stool. Careful attention to her hair and the exact placement of a jeweled, feathered comb were sure signs of a romantic engagement. Tugging her off-the-shoulder neckline a little lower, she curved her reddened lips in a mischievous way. "Now don't be asking personal questions, love. You know I'm not the kind to kiss and tell." She flounced over to me and planted a hearty kiss on my cheek. "Budd and Farley have gone next door to the Golden Nugget for a couple of beers. They'll be back to escort you and Jessie home."

I nodded, somehow disappointed that no one had thought to prepare any kind of celebration at the boarding house or some inexpensive tavern. After all, it was my first real triumph! I knew Jessie did not hold with such foolishness, and no coins would be taken from the cash box for such frivolity.

Nell bustled out with a filmy shawl thrown over her shoulders, a taffeta petticoat leaving the echo of a whispered rustle in the room.

I stared at my reflection in the mirror, blinking back a sudden fullness in my eyes. After the cheering and clapping and accolades of a few moments before, the dressing room had a mocking emptiness to it. Why was I feeling sorry for myself? Sitting here, blubbering like some lovesick fool, when I ought to be giving my head a proud toss! I had been trying to prove that I could be as great a leading lady as Maureen Cole, that I was worthy of wearing her lovely clothes, and I had accomplished my goal!

As I sat there, I had a peculiar sense of her presence still lingering in the theater. How many times had she sat in front of this very mirror looking at her reflection? And what had she been thinking? Who waited for her upstairs? Had she sat here the night of her last performance while a murderer prepared to lure her to the waterfront and put a cord around her neck?

I shivered. Her scent rose from the lace handkerchief I had found in her beaded bag. I put the cloth to my nose and filled my nostrils with its cloying lilac fragrance. She could not be dead . . . she was alive . . . in some mystical way I had willingly merged my identity with hers. I felt it, and an instinct of danger was almost palpable in the darkened theater.

My neck prickled as if suddenly bathed by a chilled brush of air. I did not want to be alone in an empty theater. Some terrifying premonition was upon me. A sense of panic thrust me from my chair. Even before I reached the top of the narrow staircase I heard the cry! At the same instant I felt a cool rush of air from a nearby, half-opened door. Because the earth fell away sharply behind the building this back entrance to the theater was reached by a long, steep flight of steps. None of us used this entrance, and I couldn't remember ever seeing the door open before. The strangled cry had come from that direction!

Without thinking, I jerked the door open the rest of the way and rushed out onto a wooden landing. A small gas lamp sent a wash of feeble light down below. A cry lurched in my throat as I peered over the railing. A crumpled heap lay still at the bottom of the stairs with its head twisted at a grotesque angle.

"No!" I screamed and flew wildly down the plunging, treacherous steps. I sensed rather than saw a movement in the shadows at the dark corner of the building.

I was not thinking, just reacting in blind panic.

Sobbing, I lifted Jessie's tiny head into my lap. "No, no." Beyond the frontier of my grief I saw that she was clutching something bright in her hand. I recognized it with the plunge of a searing brand. I had seen it once before, in a photograph, lying in the soft cleft of Maureen's breasts!

A gold lavaliere!

8

My sobbing cries rose in a frantic crescendo. "Help
. . . somebody help!" All rational thought seemed to
have stopped as horror poured over me. Death had
never touched me before, and the icy stab of its talons
kept me hysterically cradling Jessie and calling for
help. An overpowering loyalty prevented me from
leaving her and seeing to my own safety.

Diffused moonlight shone wanly through clouds
scudding across the moon's face. As I looked upward
the gaslight at the top of the long stairs flickered
weakly, lost in a cavern of darkness. Deep shadows
hung the back of the theater, and the building
loomed darkly over me. Suddenly, a perception
intruded upon my anguish. Was that movement in the
shadows close to the building? My cries for help
caught in my throat. A wraithlike figure seemed to
waver, almost perceptible in the flickering blackness.
Was someone lurking there? The sense that I was not

alone was overpowering. I strained to look into the
shadows, my heart lurching wildly about in my con-
stricted chest—and then I heard pounding footsteps
on the stairs.

"What is it, lass? What's happened?" Billy's stocky
frame was suddenly crouched beside me, taking in
the crumpled body I held.

"It's Jessie . . . she's . . . she's . . ." I could not get
the words out.

"Mother in heaven!" he swore, and gently lifted
her head away from my lap. He put his ear against her
quiet chest and then shook his head. I covered my
face with my hands and gave in to a spasm of sobs.

"How did it happen?"

"I . . . I don't know . . . I heard her scream . . . and
found her . . . like this."

He swore again. "Sure and I'd better be getting
someone."

When I refused to leave he darted back into the
theater, leaving me alone once more. I don't know
how long he was gone, shock overtook me. I gave in
to sobbing anguish until voices were suddenly all
around me, and my hands were gently removed from
my face. Ty pulled me up into his arms and I sobbed
hysterically against his chest. "It's all right . . . it's all
right . . ." His hands stoked my hair and cheeks, and I
clung to the protective circle of his embrace.

There was nothing that could be done and no way to
know if Jessie had fallen or been pushed down the
treacherous staircase. Later, as I looked at the group
collected in the green room, a few figures dominated
my senses: Ty, Budd, Cal, Nell, Dana, Lila, Farley,
and Billy. Even in my state of shock I stiffened against
some insidious vibrations coming at me. I don't know
at what point I decided not to mention the impression
of a vague figure hovering for a moment in the

darkness of the building. Perhaps I did not trust my own perceptions at that horrifying moment, or I cowardly feared that voicing such a suspicion would unleash a new wave of madness. Everyone questioned by the rather indifferent law officer could account for his or her presence elsewhere. Although everyone declared they had not been anywhere near that open door, I knew it would have been easy for anyone to return to the theater and give Jessie a violent shove that precipitated her death.

The gold lavaliere was identified as Maureen Cole's, and Jessie's fingers had clutched it voraciously, as if determined not to give it up even in death. Where she had found it nobody knew. Her movements after she had left our dressing room with her arms loaded with costumes could not be verified. In my own mind I suspected that her scrounging ways had brought to light this piece of jewelry that might well have been removed from Maureen's neck the night she was strangled. If Jessie had been able to speak she might have identified the person who took it from the murdered girl's neck.

The entire company was stunned, but it was the Rafferty Players who had lost a mainstay who could not be replaced. Who would hold us together with Jessie's dogged determination, demanding that we share and give and sacrifice for the good of the whole? Who would keep a steady hand upon us when we were threatened? We had all railed against Jessie's frugality and rigid discipline, but her incorruptible strength had provided our security—and now it was gone.

We grieved and tried to console each other. Budd wandered around with dull eyes, listless, as if his wife's death had drained him and he was only an empty shell without her sustaining presence. All our efforts to support him couldn't begin to make up for his loss. Farley took over the finances, but there was no way that he could force Budd to give over his wages as Jessie had done, and the amount he kept back for beer money grew and grew. Langston was as lenient as he could be at first in levying fines on Budd for infractions of the rules, but he had to hold the line on discipline, and Budd's wages went down, as did the importance of the roles he was given.

Farley tried to assume an authoritarian role where I was concerned, but I would have none of it. Verbal outbursts became frequent between us, and I wished Nell had never talked to me about his feelings toward me. I could no longer relate to him innocently and I could not return any romantic feelings. It was ironic that my career began to hit zeniths at the same time the center core of the Rafferty Players was disintegrating. While Lila continued to star in Shakespearean dramas, playing opposite Ty, I was given major roles in *A Delightful Dailliance*, *The Factory Girl*, and *Beacons of the Rich*, all farces or melodramas. Dana played opposite me in these productions. Our similar blondness seemed to make a hit with the audiences.

Newspaper items about the Imperial Theatre Productions began to hint that there was a romantic attachment between us. I was furious. Ty laughingly assured me that there was only room for one love in Dana DelMar's life—the theater. "Let the gossipy tidbits alone," he advised. "They're good for business."

I could not understand him. He was willing to give all the time and effort needed to shape my career, but he never made any intimate advances toward me. My eighteenth birthday came and went, and I continued to feel that I was only an amusing protegee as far as he was concerned. I had long since ceased lying to myself. I was in love with Tyrone Langston, completely, idiotically, hopelessly. Nell's firm lectures did no good; Farley's knowing glares only made my growing frustration more acute. Fortunately, my pride kept me from blatantly throwing myself at him. I made every outward show of being happier in Farley's, Cal's, or Dana's company during rehearsals than I did in his.

Since Lila was no longer considered the only leading lady, the time came when Ty decided I was ready to be cast in my first Shakespearean role. It was a supporting role in *A Midsummer Night's Dream*, but rumor had it that Ty was schooling me to take Lila's place as Juliet, playing opposite him in the spring production. Most rumblings in a theatrical group must be discounted as mostly fantasy, and I had little faith in the truth of this one.

When it happened I could not believe it. The dream I had been chasing seemed within my grasp as I stared at my name posted for the Juliet role and Ty's as Romeo.

As soon as I could, I sought him out. "Are you sure I can do it?" I asked him in the corridor outside his office.

"When are you going to quit questioning my professional judgment?" Ty's tone was impatient, but there was a softness at the corner of his lips that almost tugged them into a smile.

"I think it's a mistake," I said as honestly as I could.

"You think the role is beyond you?"

"No, but I'd rather not do it. I'm . . ."

"Afraid? Don't tell me I have finally thrown out a challenge that Tara Townsend doesn't have the courage to accept? His taunting tone riled me as he probably knew it would.

"I don't think courage has anything to do with it!"

"Are you sure?"

He waited for my answer. His forehead was slightly furrowed, and there was a glint of uncertain light in the depths of his eyes. I knew then that he had agonized over this assignment. As if to echo my thoughts, his voice softened. "Trust me, Tara, to do what's best for you." Then he added rather ruefully, "On a professional level at least."

"I do trust you."

He gave me that warm, roguish grin. "Maybe you shouldn't, at least not where our personal feelings are concerned." His fingers tightened in an almost imperceptible squeeze as he slipped his hand in mine.

How could he do this to me? He must know that I experienced a sudden shallowness in breathing and a runaway quickening of the pulse every time he casually touched me. It wasn't fair that he could crumble away my protective mantle with a simple touch. "Maybe it's myself I don't trust," I stammered. *How could I play Juliet to his Romeo?*

"It wasn't an easy decision to make, believe me, but the part is right for you."

I suspected that the challenge of playing lovers on stage would be as much of one for him as for me; to be sure, for he had already mastered the part, but had he mastered his feelings about me? As certain as I could be of anything, I knew that he had deliberately erected a barrier between us all these months. That uncertain flicker in his eyes and questioning brow was not for me alone. *He had reservations about the whole thing!* This knowledge brought a sudden joy to my face and laughter to my voice.

"Why are you laughing?" he asked, startled. I knew my eyes must be shining, for the luminosity came from deep inside.

"Because I suddenly feel very much up to playing your Juliet."

I think he knew then that he had made a mistake. His confidence seemed to waver as we looked into each other's eyes. An honest longing leaped between us. Even though we were standing in a public corridor and there was a space of several inches between us, an exploding magnetism diminished all other reality, leaving us suspended in an intimacy that was laced with sexuality.

"It's going to be a lot of hard work," he said in a husky tone.

"Yes, sir."

"And I don't intend to present a second-rate performance just because it's your first major role."

"Of course not."

"The limitations of the role are only those you impose upon yourself, and I'm not going to be easy on you."

"I know."

"I expect you to become the definitive Juliet."

"Yes, sir."

"And quit agreeing with me like that."

"Yes, sir. I mean, no, sir."

We chuckled foolishly. The play was forgotten. Our wordless communication was so strong, it was unnerving.

Cal came out of the business office at that moment and caught the bemused glance that held us together. He cleared his throat. "I'm sorry. I've got the scripts ready to hand out."

"I'll help," I said quickly, turning away from Ty, knowing that my face was awash with a betraying pinkness.

"And I have a business meeting." Ty let go of my hand. "We'll talk about the new role later, Tarry."

I nodded, took a stack of booklets from Cal, and accompanied him back to the green room. "How is Lila going to react to my getting this role?" I asked him, already dreading her aristocratic fury and disdain.

"Don't worry about it. Ty knows how to handle things like this. He's promised Lila *Camille*, so she shouldn't make any trouble. He's had plenty of experience manipulating leading ladies."

Instead of being reassured, his words brought me down from my rosy summit. A few moments ago Ty had been smiling at me in that bemused way that recalled the capture of my lips under his. Now I wondered. Did he want me to remember those passionate kisses and the melting of heated flesh as I felt his sweet length pressed against mine? Had I been cleverly "manipulated" so that I would project a passionate, intense Juliet on stage? Had Ty allowed me to see what I wanted to see? I kept forgetting that he could project any image he wanted to, off and on stage. Shadows reached out for me again, and by the time the first rehearsal was called I was convinced that Ty was intent upon using my emotions to give him the kind of Juliet he wanted . . . inexperienced, passionate, devoted, and tragic. He knew me well, for the passages of declared love fell from my lips with an intensity that brought hushed silences even during rehearsals.

Fortunately, I had mastered a great deal of my craft, and this competence was a hidden structure that gave my performance alacrity. I no longer had to think about every detail; a natural stage presence began to flow through me, and Ty was right: I was ready for a more sophisticated role than I had done before. Perhaps if he had chosen a different vehicle for my debut as his leading lady, I might have disgraced us both, and the company as well. But he must have known how I would respond to his vibrant voice delivering passionate endearments. As he gazed into my face with lover's eyes that pierced my very soul, he *was* my beloved Romeo.

"Though his face be better than any man's, yet his leg excels all men's, and for a hand, and a foot, and a body, though they be not talked upon yet they are past compare" exults Juliet as she falls in love, and her words were mine . . . and her emotions as well.

Nell's attitude throughout rehearsals was the antithesis of her part of the nurse, the coarse confidant of Juliet, who made arrangements for the secret marriage of the lovers. "I don't like it at all. You're as innocent as a lamb being led to the slaughter . . . and he's turned you blind."

"Don't be dramatic, Nell. It's only a part."

"Is it now? You could have fooled me. All them passionate speeches and tender embraces are just pretend."

"Good acting!"

"Hogwash! I ain't been around this crazy business for longer than you have years without learning a few things, and one of them is the difference between acting and feeling. You ain't fooling me none. There ain't a mite's difference between you and that part you're playing. 'Oh, gentle Romeo, if thou dost love, pronounce it faithfully . . .' she quoted from the garden scene. "You're meaning every word of it, he's working your emotions for all they're worth."

"That's where a memorable performances comes from . . . the inside," I lectured. "You have to draw on your experiences."

"Well, you're setting yourself up for some good ones, young lady. Pain, heartache . . . disaster. Something deep inside tells me the only tragedy isn't going to be on stage."

Ty had cast Farley as the angry, bellicose Tybalt, who is Juliet's kinsman and who slays Mercutio, Romeo's best friend. Here, too, perhaps, Langston drew on emotions that were already surging within the actors. More than once Farley's protective attitude had brought Ty's crescent eyebrows arching when I was swept out of the theater on Farley's possessive arm. His attitude bespoke an adult relationship between us that wasn't there.

On the stage the two men brought tension up to a combustible level as impassioned speeches gave way to action. The two parried and thrust their rapiers with believable fury. My heart caught in my throat as I watched them. It was only good acting, I told myself. Why should there be any bitter rancor between these two men? I was being as foolish as Nell, I thought, trying to reassure myself that in different roles the two would be comrades.

Budd was drinking heavily. He always had a dour expression on his face, and his blurry eyes focused just beyond the thing he was looking at. His good-natured disposition had deteriorated, and he used his thick fists at the slightest provocation. He seemed bent on revenging Jessie's death on anyone who crossed his path. It would have been better if Ty had left him out of the production, but he was given the part of the apothecary who provides Romeo with the poison to kill himself: "Such mortal drug I have." Budd delivered the lines with such sadness, with a resignation that tore at my heart.

"Are thou so bare, and full of wretchedness, and fear'st to die?" flares Romeo when the old man holds back the drug he wants. "Famine is in they cheeks; Need and oppression stareth in thy eyes; Upon thy back hangs ragged misery . . ."

Upon thy back hangs ragged misery.

Tears filled my eyes. The lines had never been so apt . . . and Ty had dispensed them with such power that once more I felt a stab of uneasiness as I watched them exchange money for the lethal vial.

Budd's impassive glare made him a stranger to me. He had shut himself up in his own thoughts and I did not know what seeds of revenge lay there, nurtured by a bitter grief.

Surely we were just actors playing out roles upon a stage, but tragedy lay heavily in the air, and I began to wish that death and murder were not a part of our current production. I couldn't rid myself of the apprehension that at some time the tiny vial might indeed contain poison instead of a harmless liquid.

As usual, our director drove us with his fever. Almost too soon opening night was upon us. For the first time I felt faint from stage fright. I doubted that I could take one step out upon that stage. I rated a private dressing room now because of my status and two seamstresses hovered around me and helped me into my costume at each change.

Some strength beyond my own faltering courage brought me on stage right on cue, and the drama was launched. My ball gown for the opening scene was lovely; high-breasted, with blue folds of soft silk and intricate golden trimmings; full velvet sleeves that fell gracefully in sweeps to the floor. I wore a cap of seed pearls woven together in a mesh of gold; my hair was fashioned with dangling fair curls to frame my face and fall upon my shoulders. When Romeo first catches sight of Juliet in a shimmer of silver and deep blue I could believe his adoration, ''O, she doth teach the torches to burn bright! . . . Did my heart love till now? Forswear it, sight! For I have never loved till this night.''

I took the words as my own. There was no pretense as my eyes feasted upon his virile figure, encased in tight fawn breeches, high boots, white linen, and a russet cape clasped by a gold chain around his neck. His rich brown hair fell youthfully around his face, framing the bold uplift of his cheeks and giving added depth to the luminous intensity of his eyes. When he approached and took my hand it trembled without pretense.

"If I profane with my unworthy hand this holy shrine," he quoted, desire leaping in his eyes. "My lips, two blushing pilgrims, ready stand to smooth that rough touch with a tender kiss." He raised my hand and touched his mouth to my tingling skin. At that moment the love that flared between us was a living thing, and from those opening lines we drew the audience into the tale of "star-crossed lovers . . . who with their death, bury their parents' strife."

The words and caresses had no pretense for me. That haunting, spicy scent of his triggered instant desire as he bent his comely knee to gaze up at my face in adoration. He took my trembling hand and declared his love in deep, resonant tones. Every time his lips brushed my hair and his impassioned speeches filled my ears I lived the flights of passions and despairs of separation. I did not care if he was manipulating my emotions for the good of the play. Freely they spilled forth from the swirling depths of a love that reached beyond the boundaries of Shakespearean dialogue.

When, in the final act, he stood by my bier and drank the draft of poison, such sudden terror raced in my heart that only the sheer force of my will kept me lying still in drugged sleep. When he crumpled at my side on the bier my own breathing stopped completely.

He was so still! So dead!

An unspeakable terror engulfed me! At that moment an evil specter was on stage with us, laughing at our make-believe world.

Cries choked up in my throat from pure terror. It was all I could do to control my panic as the friar entered and gave me the cue for rising and discovering my beloved lying motionless at my side. My voice rose in anguish as I bent over him. "What's here? A cup closed in my true love's hand? Poison, I see, hath been his timeless end. . . . I will kiss thy lips; haply, some poison yet doeth hang on them. . . ." I pressed my mouth against his. Warm, vibrant flesh reassured me, and the kiss I gave him promised much more than the script called for.

I made my verbal farewell. "Oh, happy dagger . . . this is thy sheath," and thrust the fake weapon against my breast.

The curtain fell. Swells of applause sounded beyond its heavy folds.

My eyes sought his and he pulled me into his arms and kissed me as if he, too, had been swept up in the tragedy and had to assure himself that we were still vibrantly alive.

"I love you . . . " he whispered in a hoarse voice. "My own dear Juliet . . ."

My surprised and wondering gaze fixed upon his beloved face. The play was over, all the dialogue had been spoken, but he was still whispering endearments into my ear. Bewildered and floating in a heavenly euphoria, I let him guide me into a line forming in the wings for our curtain calls. All of the applause and cheering meant nothing to me at that moment. My ears were filled with his whispered *I love you*, and my gaze was captured by those compelling eyes delving into mine.

The curtain began to rise, and we took our turn as the final bows were made. I had never seen Ty so exuberant after a performance. As soon as the curtain came down for the last time, he invited everyone to join him at the Crystal Hotel for drinks and a late supper. This time there was to be a celebration—a party in my honor. Laughingly, the cast scurried to get out of costume and put on party attire. Ty kept his arm arounbd me as we lingered backstage, talking about the performance. I confessed that I had almost ruined the crypt scene with my sense of panic.

"I could tell you were taut and anxious. You silly goose, you didn't think there was really poison in that vial, did you?'

"I . . . I had a terrifying premonition that you were drinking something deadly."

"Well, your premonition was wrong. I'm very much alive." He lightly cupped my face as if it were something fragile. He kissed me again, this time with a languid delight. I did not care who saw us embracing. Still in my costume, I was his Juliet and reality was still only on the fringes of my awareness. Perhaps I knew that only a few minutes separated me from the shattering of this shimmering joy.

He let out his breath slowly and set me away. "You'd better go change. I have some things to attend to . . . and then I'll join you at the party."

In the cradle of his arm, I walked with him to the top of the stairs. "How do you like your new dressing room?"

"I don't. I'd much rather share with Nell and the others. My own dressing room makes me feel like . . ."

"A leading lady?" he teased.

"No . . . like I'm suddenly set apart from everyone."

"Sorry, but you'll just have to make some concessions for the change of status. You're a star now and must behave like one."

He gave me a light kiss on the forehead and then left me to change in his private sitting room.

As I went down the long hall to the end dressing room, I could hear laughter and chatter coming from the crowded one I used to share, and it made my small, private one even more solitary. Lila had a dressing room across the hall, but it was dark. I had not seen her backstage, and I wondered if she had even come to the theater to witness my triumph.

I closed the door and began removing my robes. Since Jessie's death there was no one to wait for the costumes or handle them with such efficiency. The new woman was an Oriental who didn't understand most of what was said to her. When she arrived I was already nearly out of my costume. Bobbing her head, she left with my gown and pearled cap.

Still flushed from Ty's adoration and whispered words of love, I changed into a party gown, my feelings exploding like fireworks. He had let the barriers down . . . he was no longer keeping me at a professional distance! With light laughter bubbling in my chest, I changed into an emerald-green gown that bared my shoulders in a provocative way. Soft silk folds fell away from my small waist to flounces caught in pale pink roses. I swept my hair up in a high twist and brushed soft, curly tendrils on my forehead and around my cheeks. I wore a pair of emerald glass earrings that Nell had discarded, and liked the way they dangled along my flushed cheeks. No need for even the most discreet makeup, for my lips shone with glossy redness and the glow of love had deepened the rose tints in my cheeks. A touch of rice powder on my nose and forehead hid the sheen of my nervousness. I preened until I was satisfied that the reflection in the mirror would meet with Ty's approval. Then I picked up my wrap and beaded bag —a strange thickness halted me.

I put the wrap back down. My fingers were suddenly trembling as I opened the bag. What had been stuffed into it? I drew out a wad of paper . . . no, a folded photograph. A fair-haired Juliet wearing a seed pearl cap and the same blue-silver gown met my rounded eyes.

I gasped, and a shiver like furry spider legs went up my spine.

Maureen! In the same Juliet costume I had worn that night! Ugly, jagged lines of writing ran across her face. Like grappling hooks, the words leaped up cruelly and tore at me.

"Alas, poor Juliet . . . her death awaits."

9

I heard the swish of a woman's skirts coming down
the hall and I furtively stuck the photograph with its
vicious note back in my bag just as Nell came in.

"Ready, honey? What's the matter? You look
peaked." She put a soft, plump hand against my forehead. "You feel hot."

"All the excitement . . ." I murmured. A mist of
nervous sweat had beaded on my forehead, and all
my natural coloring had drained away. "I'm fine . . ."
I brushed by her before she had a chance to argue.

We joined Farley and Budd, and the four of us left
the theater together.

"You're silent tonight," Farley commented as we
walked to the hotel.

I nodded. The photograph had brought its own kind
of shock. I tried to convince myself it was a vicious
joke . . . a harassment intended to spoil my success.

"I wish we could leave all of this behind and go

back to the camps," Farley said. "Life was much simpler then."

The glitter and glamour of the Crystal Hotel was in sharp contrast to my leaden spirits as we entered the elegant salon that Ty had engaged for the party. With a surge of apprehension, I saw immediately that this was no private cast party but a prestigious gathering of San Francisco society. We had arrived on foot, but affluent, fashionably dressed people were alighting from handsome carriages and making their way into the hotel.

An elegant courtyard with fountains and elaborate gardens was framed by the seven-story building. Orange, lemon, and lime trees, hanging flower baskets, Oriental shrubs, and marble statuary gave an illusion of a residential garden, and guests were greeted by violins from a gypsy orchestra. Balconies lined the courtyard on every floor and provided an ever-changing scene below as brightly uniformed employees hurried to greet the arriving vehicles. Tonight fashionably attired guests entered the hotel through high arched doors into a fantasy that was harmonious with a San Francisco built by gamblers and dreamers.

Nell and I moved across the deep carpet of a luxurious salon, making for a window seat set into a large bay window while Farley and Budd immediately deserted us for a bar set up at the end of the long, glittering, mirror-lined room. Jewels, silks and satins, vibrant colors, perfumed laces and fans, glittering gold cuffs and diamond breast pins blended together in a heady richness. Nell and I gawked at fashions that might have come from Paris or New York and smirked at others that were gaudy enough to have just come off a Mississippi riverboat. Apparently attempts to set standards by an elite four hundred had failed—there seemed little agreement about whom San Francisco's wealthy should ape.

Nell poked me and nodded to the doorway. With shining jet-black coils of hair piled high in an elaborate coiffure, Lila Fontaine moved majestically into the room. Her saffron gown of shimmering satin enriched with beaded embroidery was a stunning contrast to her dark hair and eyes. Instantly, she collected a bevy of admirers around her, as if she had been the star of the evening's production of *Romeo and Juliet*.

As I watched her my heavy thoughts made me wonder: If she had been the one who had played the Juliet role, would she have found the desecrated picture in her dressing room? Was it the role itself that threatened the actress? I wanted to think so. It was less ominous than believing that in some sinister, foreboding way the vicious words were meant for Tara Townsend. I was glad I had decided not to say anything to Nell about the photo. She would just lay the blame at Ty's doorstep, insisting that my foolish infatuation and obvious behavior during rehearsals had alerted everyone to my feelings. I did not want to hear these things, so I kept my own counsel. Ty's whisper that he loved me put a cocoon around me, and I would not allow anything or anybody to take it from me.

Glances came my way, and I gave a distant smile in return. Obviously the room was filled with theater patrons who had seen my performance, and a few approached me to murmur perfunctory congratulations. However, none lingered to pursue any conversation with me. I wondered if my inner turmoil was projected on the outside as haughty aloofness or dullness.

Nell's sparkling eyes and curving lips did not go

unnoticed for very long. A large gentleman with a florid face and rather large nose bowed in front of us. His currant eyes centered upon Nell as he introduced himself. "Willy Lambert, manager of the Golden Nugget." His flamboyant clothes, diamond stick pin, and manner verified his occupation as a professional gambler. Undoubtedly, Ty must have great confidence in him to put him in charge of his gambling house, I thought, curious to know how long he had been working for Ty.

Apparently, Nell found Willy Lambert a suitable recipient of her charm. She laughed, peered coquettishly at him, and soon engaged him in a vivacious conversation about himself.

Willy was obviously flattered by her attention. "I'm certain Ty would be unhappy to see you ladies without a glass of champagne in your hands," he said, and motioned imperiously to an Oriental man who was passing a silver tray of drinks through the milling guests.

"Now that's better." He smiled when he had placed a fragile-stemmed, crystal glass in each of our hands. "I saw the play tonight, and I must say you ladies were magnificent." Once more his gaze sidled to Nell, and I knew she was about to make another conquest. Her eyes took on that inviting, mischievous glint and her laughter rippled on a musical tone as she responded to his chatter.

I was relieved that I no longer had to make conversation. My thoughts were much too heavy for any idle chit-chat. What should I do? Ignore the picture as some malicious joke? If I made a big production out of it, Ty might take me out of the part. Could Lila have arranged this vicious prank as a way of getting back at me, using Maureen's death as a way to diminish my joy at playing Juliet or to scuttle the whole production? I caught her deliberate stare in my direction as she held court with her admirers. She probably was enjoying seeing me cowering in a corner with a long face. I couldn't help it. Holding my glass listlessly in my hands, I stared at my distorted reflection in the pale amber liquid. As my indistinct features wavered and elongated, my sense of disorientation increased. For an absurd, brief moment I wondered who I really was—for it was Maureen's face that swam in front of me!

There was a heightened ripple in the crowd. I raised my head and saw that Ty had entered. His handsome visage and figure commanded everyone's attention as if he had just made his entrance on stage. He smiled his greetings and, nodding, he moved among his guests. Lila pushed forward with a gasp of delight and took his arm possessively. Her yellow gown contrasted brilliantly with his black frock coat, dress trousers, and gold embroidered vest. As she pressed against him, she said something that made him laugh, and his mouth spread wide enough to show his even, white teeth.

The crowd framed Ty and Lila as a couple. He took a glass from a hovering waiter and then raised the goblet and clicked it against Lila's in some kind of toast. As I watched them my blood suddenly ran like arctic ice water. *Lila Fontaine was still his leading lady.* I was an upstart pretender. He had given me the Juliet role because he knew my infatuation would spill over on stage.

Dana joined them. His blond hair was brushed back in a high pompador, which accentuated the straight, smooth line of his patrician nose. As always, he maintained his stage presence in the midst of the most casual gathering. As the three of them stood together, an informal reception line began to form around them. It was obvious that the invited guests recognized the trio as the stars of the Langston Theater.

I lowered my gaze and sipped my drink.

"What are you doing in the corner?"

I looked up. Cal! My face broke into a relieved smile. "Hiding," I confessed.

He also was dressed for the occasion, and his slight figure took on added stature in an evening coat and striped gray trousers. Dark, heavy lashes blended with his black curly hair and Italian features. Without a cigarette hanging out of his mouth, he seemed quite debonair. I told him so, and the compliment seemed to embarrass him.

He quickly became quite businesslike. "Ty has arranged with the hotel for a banquet to be served shortly. He's gone all out with lobster croquettes, boned capon, truffle with glee and spring lamb with mint sauce. Doesn't that tempt you?"

I lied and said yes. I had never felt less like eating in my life.

"I thought the performance went well tonight . . . no question about the vibrations between you and Ty."

I was saved from responding by the arrival of Dana at Cal's side.

"I agree," Dana said as he joined us. He had played Benvolio, friend to Romeo, and had executed his lines with his usual professionalism. He began to talk about some of the near miscues that might have sent the dialogue in the wrong direction. I was glad that he was there to ease the situation. As always, his conversation centered upon his beloved acting and the theater. I soon found the tautness in my body easing and I laughed with Cal and Dana as they remembered another production where a rapier had fallen apart in the hero's hands at the beginning of a dramatic fight. I felt my spirits lifting and I accepted another glass of champagne.

When Farley and Budd joined us I could see that Budd was already well into his cups. His Irish brogue was thicker and his laugh too loud. Farley, on the other hand, seemed more withdrawn than usual. He had hardly spoken to me all the way to the hotel and he no longer treated me with any avuncular warmth. Obviously the surroundings were chaffing him, and he seemed to be a bundle of nettles, completely ill at ease.

When I heard Ty's voice nearby I stiffened. In a moment he appeared at Cal's elbow. "Cal, have you seen Tara? Oh, there you are! For heaven's sake, what on earth are you doing hiding in the corner?" He tried to put an amused edge on his words, but I could tell he was impatient. "Come on. This is a special night. You must enjoy it."

"I am enjoying it . . . with my friends," I said pointedly and in a rather childish manner. I couldn't help it. After all, he had ignored me to toast a clinging Lila, I thought, as a green serpent applauded my jealousy. I sent a smile around the circle: Cal, Dana, Budd, and Farley, Nell and her gentleman friend. When my gaze came back to Ty I was rewarded by a hard flicker that narrowed his eyes.

"I apologize for taking you away . . . from your friends," he said politely, "but dinner is about to be served. If you will do me the honor . . ." A question was there as he offered his arm. A short time earlier he had left me as a soft, passionate, loving Juliet. Was he wondering if I was more of a consummate actress than he had imagined? It pleased me to think he was unsure of my feelings, that he wondered whether my passion had dimmed now that the play was over.

As I settled my hand on his arm and moved beside

him toward the dining room, my resolve to be distant and mysterious dissipated as I felt his firm muscles rippling under my tingling fingers. He smiled down at me, and his fluid mouth taunted me with its softness and made mine curve in response. A swath of russet hair was easing down on his forehead, tempting me to raise my hand to tenderly ease it back. I forgot about Lila and about everyone else as we entered a sumptuous private dining room. The onslaught of crystal and silver was overwhelming. I was blinded by the snowy white linen and sprays of red roses. He must have felt the sudden trembling that engulfed me for he put his hand over mine. "Steady."

Other guests had fallen in behind us and were taking their places at a long banquet table. Two places at the center were obviously meant for the guests of honor, and Ty led me to them. I had never seen such an array of exquisite table service. Heavy silver utensils lay in a bewildering spread on both sides of delicate, hand-painted china. Damask cloths and napkins provided a background for huge silver tureens, pitchers, and an array of platters. Deep red roses were sprays of color, and their rich petals were reflected in the dangling prisms of a golden candelabra.

Ty was watching my expression as he seated me on a plush, armless chair of deep burgundy velvet. His hands rested lightly on my shoulders for a moment as he bent over and whispered in my ear, "You belong here, m'love, never doubt it."

I knew then that my eyes must have widened like those of an interloper in wonderland. I laughed as he sat down beside me. The play was over and still tender words were on his lips. There was no pretense in the responding emotion that flooded my body at his nearness. My heart raced in a foolish drumming.

Others drew out their chairs, Lila on Ty's left, Dana

at her side, and then Cal. On my right, Nell, and then her attentive Willy Lambert.

Soon an army of soft-footed, silent waiters began to lay the food upon the table. There was little chance to talk as the feast was brought and taken away. Ty pressed food upon me, entertained me with tidbits about other social functions given at the Crystal, and sent wordless messages with his eyes that obliterated everything else.

He paid polite attention to Lila, but it must have been obvious to everyone that for the evening I was his lady. It was a dream come true, a fantasy, and I had little rein on my thoughts or emotions. It wasn't until much later that I realized that Budd and Farley had not come in for dinner. They must have decided the free lunch at the Golden Nugget was more to their liking. Nell's laugh floated above the dinner noise, and I knew she was charming Mr. Lambert. No doubt, a new romance was in the offing.

I had just finished the last delicious morsel of strawberry tartelette swimming in fresh cream when Ty whispered in my ear. "Would you like to take a walk in the courtyard garden . . . ?"

"If I can move," I groaned quietly. I had never eaten such a sumptuous feast. Conditioned by Mrs. MacPherson's boarding fare, I'm afraid I took heaping helpings of everything, fearful that the food would disappear before it could be brought around again. I had tried to pace my eating with Ty's, but it was a real effort not to devour every dish with rather impolite alacrity.

As a signal that the meal was over, Ty stood up, eased back my chair, and then masterfully guided me away from the table before anyone could delay us with after-dinner conversation. I did not feel embarrassed that countless eyes followed our exit from the room through open French doors or care if I was committing any social improprieties. My impetuous nature was in charge and I gave it full rein.

The evening air was perfumed and warm. Stars above twinkled against an indigo background and wisps of clouds trailed like translucent ribbons across the moon's face. We strolled the circular paths of the courtyard under canopies of leafy branches. From a secluded bower came the strains of Gypsy music floating on the air, establishing a languid, romantic mood. Soft lanterns cast a green-gold patina upon the shrubbery, making every leaf seem polished and gleaming. Alabaster statuary caught a silver sheen from the moonlight, creating the essence of a temple in the depths of overhanging trees.

Ty pointed out favorite marble sculptures and the same boyish enthusiasm was there as it had been when he showed me the riverboat. All evidence of the taskmaster and actor were gone, and so were the memorized lines that we had spoken to each other on stage. Even though other couples strolling along the walks and the overhanging balconies gave us little privacy, the world did not seem to intrude upon us. He cupped my elbow gently and brushed against me as we walked in easy rhythm.

A small fountain gurgled musically in a miniature pool of liquid silver and indigo. We sat down on a carved bench in a secluded corner and watched glistening streams of water spout from a white dolphin's mouth.

''It's lovely,'' I murmured in a hushed tone, as if fearful that the moment was spun glass and would shatter.

''Yes . . . lovely.'' His eyes were not fastened on the fountain or the garden or the bejeweled sky. The tip of his forefinger and thumb touched my chin and brought my face around to his. A flame quickened in his eyes and his bold and vigorous expression made my breathing suddenly shallow and quick. All sophisticated pretense left me. I floundered under that look. He frowned. "Don't look so frightened . . . you're not, are you?"

What did he expect of me? How could I confess my naivety in this situation? "A little . . . I . . . don't know what to say or do."

"Do?" he echoed, amused.

"This is the first time I've been invited to a place like this. Of course, you already knew that. I wasn't exactly the worldly dinner companion, was I? I didn't know what to say . . . how to entertain you with scintillating conversation . . ."

"That's why I enjoy your company."

"Because I'm gauche?"

"Because your vibrant honesty is so refreshing . . . and appealing. I love you, Tara Townsend."

There, he had said it again . . . this time in the quiet, hushed seclusion of a garden.

"Don't look so surprised," he teased. "You can't have been oblivious to the way I feel about you. Heaven knows I've tried to keep from loving you, but you conquered me at every turn. I've been lost since that moment you climbed down from the rafters and saucily told me you wouldn't charge me for untangling the ropes." He laughed and put his arm around my shoulders. "You were the most attractive creature I'd ever seen. I wanted to shake you . . . paddle you . . . and kiss you . . . all at the same time."

"But you seemed to ignore me."

"I know." He sobered. "I exercised my willpower to stay my distance but finally had to give in. You assaulted every bulwark I raised against you. I gave in to the lessons because I wanted to be with you . . .

then you surprised me and met every acting challenge I threw at you. I admitted defeat when I cast you as Juliet. I knew it was the vehicle that would bring honest words of love to my lips and my heart would be yours for the taking. I hope you want it . . ." He looked almost shy. I felt him stiffen, as if waiting for a rejection.

I almost laughed. Ty Langston was afraid I was going to reject his declaration of love.

"Of course, I want it. What do you think I've been doing, wearing Maureen's clothes and . . ."

"Maureen's clothes?"

"You didn't know? Cal gave them to me that first day, after you mistook me for her in her cape."

"My God!" His eyes swept over my gown. "That's one of them? You mean, you're wearing her things?"

"Yes . . . I wanted you to notice me!"

"Me . . . and who else! You little idiot! Don't you know we're dealing with some kind of sadistic murderer? Nobody knows who killed Maureen . . . or why. Here you are prancing around in her clothes . . . now you're playing some of her roles . . . and . . ."

"And I'm in love with you." The declaration did not bring the softening of features that I expected. It should have been a moment of gentle intimacy, but the shadow on his face deepened. "Just like Maureen," I added in spite of myself.

"Is that what you think?"

"Isn't it true?"

"My romantic liaison with Maureen was brief and preceded our professional relationship. It was broken off with mutual consent when she joined my company. Contrary to what you obviously believe, I don't sleep with my leading ladies as *droit de signeur*. Romantic attachments are detrimental to good performances as a rule, and I try to avoid them. They lead to demands that can't be met.''

"Is that why you quarreled with Maureen just before she left?''

"That was strictly business. She was leaving me in a damn lurch, with only Lila to carry the female leads. I don't know who she was running off with." He ran his hand through his hair. "That's the frightening thing. Someone in the company knew what was going on . . . but who? I keep telling myself it was someone from the outside that killed her . . .''

"It was someone in the company," I said flatly.

"How do you know?''

I unclasped my small beaded bag and handed him the picture of Maureen with the ugly threat scrawled across her face.

"Alas, poor Juliet . . . her death awaits.'' He read the words in a hoarse whisper and then raised his head and stared past me at a fixed point beyond the shadows of the overhanging greenery.

"What do you think it means?'' I asked in a strangled tone.

For an eternity the gurgling fountain was my only answer. Strains of lamenting violins brought a haunting melody to my ears. The moment was suddenly framed by sinister overtones. I knew what he was going to say before the words passed his tense lips.

"It means that someone is planning to *kill* you.''

10

Like an ugly miasma his words hung in the air and settled around us. The shadows of the garden no longer seemed protective and romantic but sinister and waiting. A strolling musician was somewhere nearby playing a dolorous, lamenting melody on his violin, in harmony with my desolate spirits. Ty's hands captured mine and poured strength and reassurance into them from the contact of his fingers lightly stroking mine. I had never seen him visibly shaken before and, forgetting my own despair, I sought to ease his agitation.

"Maybe the note was just a . . . malicious joke," I said, voicing my early speculation with a conviction I didn't feel. "Someone wants to scare me . . . or harass me. It might not have anything to do with Maureen's death at all."

"That's what worries me, my darling. Don't you see, that would make the circle of suspects even larger than last year's company. Someone may be using the unfortunate affair of Maureen's murder for his own purposes. The threats on your life may not be connected with what happened to Maureen at all.'' He hesitated, as if not quite certain how to proceed. ''I don't want you to get angry, darling, but I have to warn you to trust neither Budd nor Farley.''

I drew back, instantly aghast and angry. He had attacked the heart of my surrogate family. I sprang to their defense. ''You don't know what you're saying! They would give their lives for me! When I was little . . .''

''Yes,'' he cut me off. ''I understand your devotion, but things change—and so do people! I've watched Farley's personality alter in just the few months he's been with the company. My dear, he broods and watches you with an unhealthy obsession. He is not pleased with the rising star of your career. You have to admit it! He would much rather have you at his level, an insignificant player of little talent.''

His words found a credence in my mind that couldn't be denied. Farley had always assured me that it didn't matter that I didn't have any talent—he had helped me accept my limitations. Had he perpetuated them? Aloud, I ardently protested that Ty was completely wrong about Farley.

''No, I'm not. He'd taken you out of the company if he had the chance. As for Budd, he's losing his grip on reality because of his drinking. I'm not going to trust either one of them to keep you safe.'' He loosened his hands from mine and gently cupped the sides of my face, holding it like something precious and fragile. ''You are no longer their concern, but mine.'' His lips brushed my hairline with the lightness of a fluttering butterfly, and his hands slipped down from my face to nestle at my waist. I wanted him to pull me to him in a fierce embrace, but strolling guests curtailed any passionate demonstrations. A furtive kiss was all we were allowed.

"I want you to move into the hotel, where I can be near you. I'll alert the hotel management to station someone outside your room; my carriage will take you to and from the theater; either Nell or myself will accompany you at all times. Don't argue. I'll even hire a dresser to be with you at the theater."

"You make it sound like I'm to be held prisoner . . ." My natural willfulness rose to challenge his dogmatic manner.

"No . . . you're a treasure that needs guarding . . ." He kissed the back of my hand slowly, lingeringly, sending quivers of delight up my spine.

"I'm not afraid," I continued to protest.

"I know. That's what worries me. I've seen that foolhardy courage of yours in action." He gave me a teasing smile. "I promise not to intrude on your privacy, but I must have you close by or I'll go crazy with worry."

"My family would be hurt if I moved out on them," I protested, trying to maintain some equilibrium as his warm breath bathed my face and his lips spoke endearments.

"Possibly, but I'm sure you can make some explanation that will not offend them. They surely don't expect you to stay in that boarding house now that you are making enough money to stay in a decent hotel. Both Dana and Lila have housing allowances and so will you, plus a raise, I might add."

"I won't move unless all the Rafferty Players can come too."

He was obviously irritated by my stubbornness, but I felt that there was also a begrudging admiration for my loyalty in his tone. He seemed to know it was useless to argue. "All right. I guess I'll have to settle for that, but I don't want you telling them about the note—not until we find out whom we can trust. Promise?"

I nodded. I didn't want to tell them about it either, but for other reasons.

"Good! Let's talk to the hotel management and see what can be arranged." Pulling me close, he stilled any further objections with a furtive kiss that might or might not have been viewed by guests looking down from the ring of balconies around us. "That's a promissory note . . . to be paid in full later," he said huskily, his eyes bathing mine with desire. "I love you, Tara Townsend, and I'll not let anyone hurt a fair hair on your head."

I believed him.

With his usual commanding, efficient manner, he arranged for adjoining rooms for Nell and me on one floor and the same for Budd and Farley on another. He would have sent for my things that night, but I insisted that I had to have time to talk to Nell, Budd, and Farley. I wished Jessie had been there to help make the decision.

That night I worried about trying to tell them what had been arranged. Nell came in late and I was still awake, agonizing over the best way to tell her what Ty had arranged. I finally just blurted it out.

"So he's moving you into his hotel, is he? Just a floor between you, eh?"

"It's not what you think." I saw her wise eyes assessing the situation.

"Isn't it, now? It would take a blind man to miss what's going on between you and Langston."

"He loves me, Nell . . . he told me so." I couldn't keep the tremulous wonder out of my voice.

"And you're believing every word that comes tripping out of that smooth tongue of his? Sure, he's the smart one, all right. He's got you so you don't know whether he's playing Romeo on or off stage!"

"Please, don't argue, Nell." I didn't want to listen to that kind of talk, perhaps because it had valid echoes in my own heart and mind. "Are you going with me or do I have to go alone?"

"You'd do that, move out on all of us?"

"No, I told Ty that I wouldn't come without you and the others."

She snorted. "What're Farley and Budd going to think, us putting on the dog like that, moving into the Crystal as if we belonged there!"

"Where's it written that we have to stay in a smelly old boarding house and eat lumpy potatoes all our lives?"

"Oh, it's Miss Snooty, you are now?"

I put my hands up to my face as my eyes suddenly filled with tears. The excitement of opening night and everything that had followed it had sapped my usual resiliency. Why did it have to be like this? I felt pulled in a dozen different directions.

At the sight of my face streaming with tears, Nell instantly flung herself down beside me, her soft arms cuddling me against her pillow breasts. "There, there, honey, I'm sorry. It's your own welfare I'm thinking of. Truly, it is. You've gone and given your heart away to someone who's had his choice of females from the time he buttoned up his first pair of long britches . . . and maybe even before that! I know what I'm talking about, honey. You ain't in the same league with his women, and none of them have ever held his attention for long."

"I'm not one of his women."

"Then why is he arranging this move?"

"To protect me," I sobbed. Ty had warned me about telling anyone about the scribbled threat, but . . .

Nell snorted. "Protect you! Now that's a new line—and, of course, you fell for it."

"It's not a line. It's the truth!" Cradled in her arms, my promise to Ty was forgotten. I told her what I had found in my beaded bag and showed the defaced picture to her. "Someone's threatening to kill me!"

"Lord love us!" she swore, staring at the photograph. "It's that Cole gal, isn't it? In the same Juliet costume!" Her eyes widened, and fear put ugly creases around her pretty mouth as it hung slack. Suddenly she looked all of her forty years.

"Maybe it's only a vile joke," I stammered, wanting to ease the horror from her face. "Someone wants to spoil my success and used this way to do it. It may have nothing to do with Maureen's murder," I said, remembering what Ty had said.

"It's him that's caused it!" she flared.

"Who?"

"Langston! Paying attention to you the way he has. If he'd left you alone none of this would have happened. Somebody's got it in for him and they're getting at him through you!"

"That doesn't make sense, Nell. He's not the one that's being threatened."

"He's causing it . . . that poor girl fished out of the bay," she wailed as if she hadn't heard me. "She was his leading lady too! And now it's you . . . dear God in heaven . . . we've got to get out of here . . . leave San Francisco. Your dear dead mother would never forgive me if we stayed. We'll pack up and get shut of this place."

"What . . . what are you talking about! We've got contracts."

"And what good will they do any of us with a murderer loose? We can find work someplace else . . . Sacramento . . . Nevada City . . . we'll start the circuit again."

"No, we can't," I protested, aghast. I hadn't expected this kind of reaction. "We can't just walk out."

"Budd and Farley are ready to leave. Nothing good's happened to us since we've been here . . . poor Jessie. . . caught in some evil mesh . . . and now you." She set her jaw. "We're leaving. Come on. Farley's drinking in Budd's room. I saw the light and heard them talking as we came up."

Nell seldom showed any dogmatic, authoritarian attitude but when she did, we all listened and obeyed. My growing up in her care had instilled this habit in me, and it could not be broken in one swift, momentary slash. Even though a hurricane of emotions warred within me, I was held by a bewildering inertia and couldn't think. She pulled me out of the room and I numbly and obediently followed her down to the second floor.

Farley and Budd sat in front of the small fireplace with a jug between them. I thought that they had been doing more talking than drinking, for both men were too somber to be in the high spirits of drunkenness.

While Nell talked to them, I sat on the edge of Budd's bed and stared at the worn carpet. The scene was familiar. I had been a part of hundreds of such conferences held during the years when the Rafferty Players were moving from one lodging to another, traveling to the next scheduled performance or hunting for work in any little camp that might add a few coins to Jessie's money box. Always they argued and discussed and swore at each other until agreement was reached about what the troupe should do

then that was the end of it. In the past whatever had
been decided by Budd, Jessie, Farley, and Nell met
with no opposition from me. Even now, I couldn't
shake the conditioning that kept me listening silently
as they made plans to wrench up the roots I had
planted in my career and destroy the love that had
flared so beautifully in my life.

I seemed trapped in that ugly room; stale air
harbored the lingering odor of cooked cabbage
mingled with an acidic tang of soot and smoke from
the fireplace. Even though it was well past midnight,
raucous sounds of lumbering wagons and screeching
trolleys laboring up Kearny Street vibrated against the
dirty panes of glass in the boarding house's tall,
narrow windows. My nails bit into my hands as I
clenched them tightly, but the pain did not dispel the
nightmare inertia that engulfed me.

"There's no help for it," Nell told the men, passing
around the picture I had shown her. "It's Tara we
have to be thinking of . . . we don't want to lose her
. . . the way we did Jessie."

Budd's craggy face betrayed the pain and heartache
eating at his insides. " 'Tis my fault. It was my
wanting to play the Imperial that brought all of this
upon us."

"Don't be a doddering old fool," Farley said
impatiently. "We all wanted to work for the great
Tyrone Langston!" He clenched his pipe in a tight
jaw. "If a mistake was made we all contributed to it!"
His hazel eyes were fastened on my face, and I stared
at him, trying to see beyond the familiar trappings.
Was Ty right . . . had he wanted me to remain inadequate and dependent? "We shouldn't have signed
on."

"That's neither here nor there," said Nell briskly.
"We're into something that has the stench of some-

thing putrid . . . we've got to take our losses and get out."

"I hate to leave before . . . before I'm knowing who killed my Jessie." Budd reached for the jug. "Somebody's going to pay."

"You want to get yourself strung to a tree, taking the law into your own hands?" snapped Nell.

"She's right, Budd," Farley agreed. "You're going to get yourself in trouble, going around threatening everyone. I think it's wise to get you away from here before you do something stupid. We were better off riding mules from one camp to another, missing a meal now and then."

"And not having to look over our shoulders and peer into shadows to see if someone's lurking there," added Nell.

Farley got up from his chair and came over and sat down on the bed beside me. He put his arm around my waist. "I'm sorry, Tarry . . ." His voice was soothing, laced with the brotherly assurance that I had relied upon so many times. "You've done us all proud, but we can't take any chances. Nell is right. There's danger here for you. We'll move on . . . take the bumps as they come . . . together."

"We won't let anything happen to you, honey," said Nell.

"I'll kill the bastard who tries anything," Budd swore, and wiped the liquor off his mouth with his arm.

I let my gaze travel from one to the other and tried to draw upon the comfort of their concern and affection. This was my family talking. They had closed in to protect me as best they could. From the time I was a toddler this family circle had provided for all my needs—and now it wasn't enough.

Bewildered, I withdrew from Farley's embrace and

walked over to the window. Nervously, I fingered the gray sheer curtain and stared out into the darkness. There was a murderer out there. Despite the reassurances I had given Nell, I knew that the warning was not an idle prank. Someone was watching my every move. Wherever I went, whatever I did, that evil presence was there, waiting, planning, anticipating the moment when I could not escape from his diabolical clutches.

I closed my eyes and leaned my head up against the window frame. Maureen had not escaped . . . she must have walked right into the vicious mesh that cost her her life. The prudent thing to do was to follow Nell's plan and leave the city and hope that the evil did not follow me. I could pursue my career elsewhere. I could make myself forget the explosive physical attraction that my first love had held for me. I could live a sensible and perhaps long life with these people who had cared for me so faithfully.

A heavy silence had settled on the room. I knew they were waiting for me to say something. I could sense the looks they were exchanging and heard the uneasy shifting of their bodies. There was a strangeness between us, as if they didn't know me anymore. As I stood there with my back to them, I wondered if I knew myself. I had moved forward in my career, in my desires, and little by little I had begun to cut them out of my life. I was grateful for the nurturing they had given me, but it had to come to an end. If I let them take me away now, I might never break free from a loving bondage that would try to keep me chained to the past. I wasn't Wee Tara Townsend anymore and they couldn't protect me forever.

I took a deep breath and turned around slowly, but with my chin firm. As I expected, their eyes were fastened on me. Even before my lips parted, I think

they knew what I was going to say. "I'm sorry . . .
please understand . . . I know you are thinking of me
. . . and I'm grateful for the sacrifices you are willing
to make . . . but I can't leave."

"Tarry . . ." began Farley.

"No, it's no use. My career is here and I won't turn
my back on it."

"He's put a spell on her," said Nell in hushed tones.

"I'll knock his goddamn head off," Farley swore,
clenching his lean, hard fists.

"Stop it! I'm not a child! Do you understand that!
I'm a woman and I have the right to control my own
life. You can't jerk me around from pillar to post
anymore . . . you can't make decisions for me. I love
every one of you, and I don't want to hurt you, but
this decision is mine. I'm staying here with or without
the rest of you!"

Sobbing, I fled out of the room and stumbled
blindly up the stairs to my own room. The old bed
gave a loud squeak as I threw myself across it. My
sobs came in great heaves.

A few minutes later I felt Nell's plump hand moving
gently across my back, massaging and soothing me. I
buried my face deeper in my pillow and let the tears
flow.

"It's all right . . . don't you be fretting so. Old Nell's
not going to let you face this thing alone. We'll move
into that fancy hotel, all right. Budd and Farley ain't
coming, and I think that's for the best, but Nell's
going to be there like always."

I turned and buried my face in her soft chest. I
wondered if I could have gone without her.

Nell gave a soft laugh and said brightly, "Lordy, I
can just feel them satin sheets right now." She patted
me and started talking about how surprised Willy
Lambert would be when he came courting and found

her living in such a place.

Listening to her easy chatter, anyone who didn't know her would have thought that her fun-loving nature had already won out over her reservations. But I knew better. She had given in to my willfulness, but there was no genuine joy in her light banter.

When I raised myself up and gave her a hug there was a suspicious moisture in her eyes.

We moved into the hotel the next morning at ten o'clock. Our travel-weary satchels and battered belonging were conspicuous as uniformed attendants took them from the elegant lobby up to the fourth floor rooms that Ty had engaged for us.

Nell apparently had put behind her the crisis meeting of the night before and was determined to make the best of what she considered to be an unwise decision. If my mind was made up, there seemed to be little question about whether or not she would accompany me. I knew that there was nothing petty or mean about Nell, and she always made the best of any situation. With her usual smiles and friendly overtures she accompanied the entourage up to the fourth floor and had our luggage deposited properly in our adjoining rooms. She winked at me as a chambermaid took charge and began to unpack our belongings.

We examined the private bathrooms with childlike glee. "Would you look at that," Nell exclaimed, pointing at a large, claw-footed tub gleaming with polished brass fixtures and so deep that it would bring delightful hot water up to our chins. "I do believe I could get used to this kind of pampering." We giggled foolishly as we hugged soft, thick towels with large *C* monograms.

There was no sitting room, but each bedroom was large enough for a small round table and two chairs to be set in a spacious window alcove. We fingered thick, damask drapes pulled back by golden ropes at the windows and peered through crisp lace curtains that hung in snowy white folds. A pair of French doors beckoned us out on a balcony, and we viewed the courtyard below. My eyes followed the flagged path to the fountain where Ty and I had sat, and a tingling flowed like effervescent bubbles through my veins. I could not see the bench where we had sat, but the memory of his caresses brought a betraying color into my cheeks.

I had been disappointed that Ty had not been at the hotel to greet us when we arrived, but I assumed he was already at the theater. We had a two o'clock call. It was his habit to take us through some of the rough spots that had occurred during the previous performance. Always bent on perfection, he continually tried for improvement up until the time of the last curtain call of each play. I knew that *Camille* was already in rehearsal and he was probably working with Lila this morning, I reasoned, but not without a slight twinge of irritation.

"I'm getting the hang of this already." Nell grinned, her eyes sparkling as she poured tea from a china pot and served a light lunch she had ordered for us. Like two conspirators, we sat in the alcove of our bay window and enjoyed looking out over San Francisco. Soft swaths of white clouds fluttered against a gentian blue sky stretching to the horizon above rolling hills dotted with colorful buildings flaunting red tile roofs, wrought-iron balconies, flower-laden window boxes, and the ubiquitous bay windows. We felt like interlopers in such wealthy surroundings and, laughing together, made remarks about the hustling, bustling crowds in the street below, where promenading ladies and gentlemen were taking daily strolls past the best-known restaurants and entering inviting shops. We sipped our fragrant tea, ate dainty sandwiches, and for the moment ignored the unpleasant circumstances that had brought us here.

"Now you take a nap and I'll wake you in time for rehearsal. Don't be arguing with me. I know you spent half the night staring at the ceiling. You're still as taut as a fiddle string." She shooed me into my room like a belligerent child.

This privacy was something I had never experienced before. I had always shared quarters with Nell, often the same bed. A quilted coverlet and puffed pillows on the brass bed was a heavenly sight . . . and it was all mine! With a playful bounce I landed in the middle of it and stretched out my arms and legs in delicious freedom. Nell laughed at me and then closed the door between our rooms.

I let my gown and confining undergarments drop to the floor. A delicious sense of freedom invaded my naked body as I slipped between silken sheets and stretched my legs. I raised my arms above my head and let my breasts arch upward, brushing lightly against the clinging cloth. A narcissistic delight brought an awareness of my body and I was glad that it was firm and smooth and inviting to the touch. He loves me . . . he loves me . . . the words rang like a tinkling sweet bell in my mind. For one sensuous moment I thought about his body pressed close to mine and blushed. I smiled upward at the pearl-white ceiling. A molded decorative design was a far cry from the spotted, cracked plaster that met my view from Mrs. MacPherson's sleeping room. My eyes feasted upon the intricate scrolls of vines that bordered the blue and green wallpaper. A picture similar to the one Ty had bought drew me into its depths and reminded me of the day he had taken me with him to the wharf. The view from Telegraph Hill must be a popular one with artists, I thought, as I languidly gazed at the lovely schooner with sails hoisted into the wind. There was movement there, and the impression of the smooth sailing craft across green-blue waters soothed my spirits. I felt that everything was going to be all right. I sighed again and closed my eyes. Ty had cosseted me in this wonderful place, and just thinking about him brought a euphoric feeling that mocked any lingering apprehension about my decision to follow his instructions. I remembered his kisses, and let myself float away on his imagined caress.

When I awoke I had a moment of disorientation. Where was I? I jerked up. Wine damask drapes greeted my eyes and muted light through crisp white curtains told me it was late afternoon. I had missed rehearsal! I leaped from the bed and jerked open the door into Nell's room.

It was empty. A glance in the connecting bathroom verified she was not there. Where had she gone? Why hadn't she wakened me? A sluice of panic sent me hurrying back into her room. Then I saw it! A note on the round table.

I grabbed at it and then eased out my breath. "Ty sent word . . . no rehearsal for us this afternoon . . . he's working on the fight scenes with Dana and Farley. Decided to take a trek around the nearby shops while you sleep. Nell."

I felt a little foolish. My panic was for nothing. Undoubtedly she would be back in a few minutes, her arms filled with purchases—a new length of ribbon, a fancy comb or fan, perhaps even a new parasol.

Annoyed with myself for overreacting, I freshened up in the elegant bathroom and brushed my hair

furiously before plaiting it again in a coronet braid on
the top of my head. I chose a simple white dimity
dress with a matching merino jacket, and the thought
that I would soon be with Ty again brought color into
my cheeks and a wanton sparkle in my eyes. I went
back into the bedroom to wait. Still Nell did not come.
The silence and emptiness of the unfamiliar rooms
began to eat at me. I decided to wait for her in the
lobby.

I stepped out of the room and was just locking the
door when I felt eyes watching me. I gave a furtive
glance both ways down the carpeted hall, but I
couldn't see anything. The sense that I was being
observed would not leave me. For a moment I
thought of unlocking my door and fleeing back inside.
As I hesitated, my heart plunged downard. A gasp
caught in my throat as a huge man suddenly filled the
corridor! His head and shoulders were the largest I
had ever seen, his features bronzed and weathered. A
full black beard and fringed leather jacket and pants
harmonized with the gun belt slung on one hip. He
had been waiting in an alcove where a potted plant
and small sofa were placed, and now he cut off my
advance as he came deliberately toward me. He
blocked my path, standing with his legs slightly apart
and his hands on his hips. "Sorry, ma'am, but I've got
my orders. You ain't suppose to go nowhere." His
tone was strangely polite and at odds with his
threatening appearance. "Mr. Langston's order's,
ma'am. Jim Perkins is the name, but they call me
Trapper."

"Ty . . . hired you . . . to keep me confined to my
room?"

"Yes, ma'am, unless you're with the other lady or
himself. You're not to go anywhere alone, and I'll see
you to and from the theater. I'm supposed to see you

there by six o'clock so I don't think you want to go anywhere now."

"You can't give me orders!" I flared. "I'm perfectly capable of taking care of myself."

"Maybe so, ma'am, but you'll have to take that up with Mr. Langston."

"You can believe that I will do exactly that!"

I flounced around and I thought a smile broke through that mass of black beard as he watched me retreat back into my room and slam the door.

I was in a fine dither by the time Nell got back and I told her what happened. She obviously thought the idea of a bodyguard was an excellent one and paid little attention to my tantrum about being kept a prisoner. She only laughed and said it might be fun to have a hunk of man like Trapper follow us around. I thought otherwise! When we arrived at the theater with my bodyguard shuffling behind I sailed into the building like a war frigate with all sails unfurled.

I had a few things to say to Mr. Tyrone Langston! But the rehearsed, indignant speech that I had formulated in my mind died the moment I entered the green room and saw him.

I screamed and lurched forward.

Blood ran like an open faucet from a wound as he stood there holding his arm. A deep gash had opened the skin across his wrist, and Cal was trying to staunch the flow of blood. Ty's face was bleached of color, making his polished black eyes saturnine with suppressed anger. I followed his furious gaze.

The floor wavered under me. Horror choked my throat.

Farley stood there, blood dripping from the tip of his rapier.

11

A flurry of people rushed to aid him, blocking off my view. As I tried to lunge forward, firm hands held me back.

Voices clanged abrasively in my ears, hollow, echoing, and spine-chilling.

"Tybolt and Romeo fight scene . . ."

"Farley must have stumbled . . ."

"No, he made a deliberate lunge . . . Ty tried to parry the thrust . . . luckily it caught his arm . . . and not his chest."

"Might have been fatal . . . fatal . . . fatal. . . ." The word went on echoing like a relentless, painful jab.

"Here's the doctor . . . give him room . . ."

"Tighten the tourniquet . . . he's lost a lot of blood . . ."

"Somebody get a chair . . . she's going to faint."

I fought to still an enveloping vertigo as the memory of Farley's fury last night came back with a rush. *I'll knock his goddamn head off.* The warning had been there, but I had turned a deaf ear to it and had moved out of the boarding house. I had broken up the Rafferty Players. If anyone had brought this confrontation to pass, it was I.

I ignored the chair and pushed forward into the crowd clustered around Ty and the doctor. As I passed Farley, he reached out a hand to me, but I brushed by him without looking into his face. I knew then that nothing else was important in my life . . . only Ty Langston.

When I reached his side he looked up at me over the doctor's shoulder and gave me a weak smile. It caught at my heart and hot tears swelled in my eyes. "No need to look so shaken, Tara. I'm not on my death bed," he assured me wryly. "Save that look for the crypt scene. The doc will patch me up, but I'm afraid it'll be up to you and Dana to carry the play tonight."

"No . . . I couldn't . . . not with you . . . like this," I protested, horrified.

His mouth tightened and some color eased back into his pasty cheeks. "Don't be ridiculous. I've lost a little blood, that's all, but my arm won't let me function tonight. Dana is a capable Romeo; he handled the part well last season." His voice softened. "You'll do fine."

"Not without you," I protested again. Didn't he know the role was only a reflection of words and feelings that were meant for him? How could I say those impassioned speeches to someone else? I was his Juliet, no one else's. "What if I can't remember my lines?"

"Well, then, I guess we'll find out the true mettle of your dedication and ability," he chided softly. Then he nodded to Cal. "Get her out of here, Cal. We've got a performance scheduled. Move things along."

Cal took my arm. "You heard what the boss said."

I bit my lip. I didn't want to leave; I wanted to ease back the swath of hair on Ty's forehead and kiss his pale lips. Cal pulled me away. I saw then that Farley had left the room.

"What happened, Cal, really? Was it an . . . accident?" There was pleading in my voice that he would say yes.

He lit a cigarette as we walked toward my dressing room. His eyes squinted up against the smoke and I thought he was going to say something, but he just shrugged his narrow shoulders. "I wasn't there." It was a lie—he had Ty's blood all over his coat and jacket.

"Budd Rafferty hasn't shown. Know where he is?" he asked me abruptly.

"No, I . . . moved out of the boarding house this morning, into the hotel."

"Well, he's had his last chance. We've already pulled in an understudy for him. If he shows up drunk tonight, he'll find himself in the alley."

I felt renewed responsibility for what was happening. Where was Budd? Would he do something as vicious as Farley had done? We were approaching the door of my dressing room, where a woman I had never seen before waited for me. "Who's that?" I asked Cal, lowering my voice.

"Mrs. Faraday, your private dresser. Ty's really setting you up in style, isn't he?" Cal said rather coldly. "Your first starring Shakespearean role and a personal attendant."

I wanted to tell him about the note so he would understand that I wasn't putting on airs. This time the promise made to Ty about not saying anything about the note restrained me. Giving me a curt nod, he turned his slender back on me and left. I could tell from his expression that he thought I was becoming a snob. He wouldn't be the only one, I thought. The whole company would soon be talking about my bodyguard, and the theatrical grapevine would be buzzing with wild speculation about the reason.

I wanted to cover my face and have a good cry. It was a good thing I had help getting into my costume. My fingers trembled nervously and I couldn't manage the simplest of fastenings. Mrs. Faraday had been one of the seamstresses who worked with Jessie, and her chatter about that ''poor Mrs. Rafferty'' did nothing to help settle my nerves.

Jessie was dead; Farley had nearly killed a man; Budd was going to be tossed into the gutter like worthless garbage . . . and someone waited in the wings for the chance to tie a chord around my neck. How could I go out on that stage and play Juliet to anyone other than Ty? I couldn't do it!

He must have realized the warring conflicts going on in my mind. He was waiting at the top of the stairs at my ten-minute call. He caught me to him with his one good arm and murmured against my ear, ''I'll be right here . . . go out there and let them see my very own vivacious, enchanting Juliet.''

''I can't go out there . . . I don't remember any of the lines . . .''

His unbandaged hand bit into my shoulders and I thought he was going to shake me, but he only gave a reassuring laugh. ''I've felt that way plenty of times myself. Just keep saying the first line of your speech over and over again until you step out on that stage and deliver it. The rest will take care of itself.'' His light kiss steadied me. ''Now, let's see what kind of actress you are, Miss Townsend.'' I wanted him to stay near me, but he briskly turned away and gave his attention to some last minute scenery preparations.

I took my place in the wings when I heard Nell say "Where's this girl? What, Juliet!" I managed to move forward like someone stepping off a precipice and it seemed to me my voice cracked as I picked up the cue and replied, "How, now; who calls?"

I couldn't tell how it was going. The magic of last night's performance was missing, but the scenes flowed and the audience seemed caught up in the drama of the play. Dana handled his role of Romeo with his usual professionalism and his smooth delivery kept me going. Speeches came out of my mouth of their own volition and Ty's relentless instruction gave my performance a polish that was almost automatic.

Ty was always in the wings as I made my entrances and exits, and I drew strength from his approving nod and shining eyes. The play seemed to go on forever, but finally it was over. Dana and I took our bows; he kissed me lightly for the audience and the applause was almost deafening. I came off the stage to reap Ty's praise—and found him gone.

Cal saw the disappointment that flooded my face as I looked for Ty backstage and told me that Ty had gone back to the hotel at the beginning of the last scene. "He was satisfied that you were going to carry the play off."

"Is he all right?"

"Just weak . . . and tired, I think. You did a nice job tonight," complimented Cal. "You and Dana make a good match."

"Thanks. Most of the credit goes to Dana. He carried me through."

"Don't sell yourself short, Tara," Dana responded when I told him the same thing. "You handled the role with extremely good style." His blond head nodded approval and his patrician features softened as he gave me a smile.

I stammered my thanks; coming from him, the compliment was almost jewel-studded. I couldn't believe I had performed that well.

Nell, Trapper, and I took Ty's carriage back to the hotel and Willy Lambert was there to greet Nell as we alighted in the courtyard. "My dear lady, I've been waiting for your arrival. May I have the pleasure of offering you a late supper this evening?"

Nell batted her gleaming eyes, her smile rather teasing and mischievous. "A late supper . . . ?"

Her suggestive tone made Willy grin broadly. "I've made preparations in a private dining room at the Golden Nugget . . . I assure you that a most divine experience awaits."

She laughed. "I'm sure it does, but I—"

"Go ahead, Nell," I said quickly. "Trapper will see me upstairs. There's no need for you to turn in this early."

"Perhaps you would care to join us," Mr. Lambert asked politely, but without his former exuberance.

"No, thank you . . . I'm quite tired." I gave Nell a knowing nod and excused myself. Some things never change, I thought during the quiet elevator ride upward, smiling to myself. Nell would always find gentlemen friends to bring that sparkle to her eye. Who was to say that her outgoing, lascivious friendliness should be curbed? She dealt out as much happiness as her generous nature soaked up for itself.

A sudden weariness put a droop to my shoulders as I walked down the carpeted hallway to my room. I handed my key to Trapper and he was unlocking the door when I suddenly changed my mind. An impulsive idea caused my fatigue to suddenly disperse like frost before a morning sun. "I think I'll go up to Mr. Langston's suite and see how he's feeling."

I sent my skirts whirling and, without waiting for Trapper, I hurried up the curved staircase to the floor above, recalling that day in the rain when I had gone to his suite. As before, the improprieties of such a visit seemed of little importance.

It was not Chang who answered, but Ty himself. When he saw who it was, his face lost its weary lines and he smiled broadly. There was no lack of warmth or welcome as he exclaimed, "Tara . . . you must be a mind reader." He glanced past me to Trapper, lingering a discreet distance from the door, and nodded to him as he motioned me in. "It's all right, Trapper . . . I'll see Miss Townsend safely back to her room . . . you can sign off for the night."

"Yes, sir." His grin was broad as he lightly touched his leather hat in a kind of salute.

Ty closed the door, and my eyes instantly went to his bandaged arm. "How are you?"

"Fine."

"Shouldn't you have it in a sling or something?"

"Did you come here to nurse me, or give me the pleasure of your company?" he teased.

"Both, I guess."

"I assure you I don't need nursing."

"Then, perhaps I'd better go," I countered solemnly, but there was no conviction in my tone and my shining eyes probably gave me away.

His grin was mocking. "Let's talk about it . . . over supper." He took my arm and guided me into the sitting room. I saw then that a table for two had been set in front of the windows.

Had he planned on inviting someone else . . . had I intruded? I was suddenly embarrassed. "I really shouldn't stay . . ."

"Shouldn't you?" He stood so close that his warm breath bathed my face and a spicy, masculine scent reached my nostrils. I knew then that he was freshly shaven, and I suddenly became aware of his casual attire. A velvet lounging jacket covered a white shirt open at the neck, showing soft curls of dark hair on his chest. Soft, beige nankeen trousers encased his legs, slightly wrinkled, as if he had been lying down when my knock summoned him. He let one hand run lightly along my arm. "Chang would be disappointed," he said softly. "How could I explain your sudden departure without enjoying the meal he's prepared for us?"

"I didn't know I'd been invited."

"My attention was diverted before I could issue the invitation. Believe me, I was waiting for your return from the theater, hoping you would accept. Will you have dinner with me, Miss Townsend?"

His formal tone was a mockery to the sexual tension leaping between us. Our eyes were fastened by an indefinable pull that kept us gazing at one another. His hand on my arm fused a fiery warmth at the point of contact of his flesh and mine.

Was I foolish enough to believe I could enjoy an intimate after-theater supper with him and then remove myself from the physical attraction that made me want to forget everything but the joy of being in his company? "I would be delighted to have supper with you." My voice was thin and slightly breathless.

"Thank you." He gave a mock bow and guided me to the table. Covered tureens sat on silver stands with candle flames keeping warmth radiating through the dishes. Tantalizing odors of shrimp simmering in lobster bisque mingled with mysterious spices in golden rice and small peas. He lifted each lid with a dramatic flourish, and we drew in the heavenly smells.

"Shall we . . . ?"

I nodded, suddenly ravenous.

He pulled out a small Victorian chair for me and deftly, with one hand, poured white wine into crystal goblets. As he handed me mine, he sat down and asked, "Would you mind doing the honors?" He handed me his plate.

"Of course." I played the part of a gracious hostess and served us. His eyes kept bathing my face as we ate, and I found myself chattering foolishly. The world was far removed and all the pent-up tensions and frustrations that had plagued me simply wafted away as we laughed and gazed at each other.

"Remember the day you flung your challenge at me?" he asked with an amused chuckle as we ate. "You actually dared me to prove my ability to make you a good actress. As I watched you tonight with Dana, I was able to get a different perspective of your performance and evaluate my success as your tutor. I must confess that playing Romeo to your Juliet was a unique experience for me, Tara, my love. In spite of my years in the theater I was less than detached when I played your lover." I knew he was berating himself for allowing such a thing to happen. His hand suddenly reached out and covered mine. "You must know that the energy we generated together was more than two actors executing their roles. You felt it, didn't you?"

"Yes . . . it was harder tonight."

"Because you were really acting. Look at me, Tara. Do you know what I'm saying? You're an actress, a magnetic, commanding presence that draws an audience into believing the words that come from your mouth. They live and die with you. I saw it happen tonight." He picked up his goblet and touched it with mine. "To my new leading lady."

At one time I would have reveled in his words.

They defied all the things I had believed about myself—that my talent had been finished with my childhood popularity, that I could only expect to let others rise in the profession, that I should be content to handle only walk-on parts. Why then this sickening emptiness? *I didn't want to be one of his leading ladies.*

The food in my mouth lost its zest. Had Ty arranged this dinner so he could critique my performance? I felt betrayed and angry. When did his professional life and his personal one begin and end? Were they so intertwined, he didn't know the difference? I laid down my fork, lowering my gaze so he wouldn't see the red coals beginning to simmer there in a black pool of heartache.

"What's the matter? You did what you set out to do. You convinced me and everybody else that you are a talented actress, far above the Rafferty Players." His face clouded. "I think that's what's eating at Farley, and maybe, Budd, too."

"That's not true!" I flashed. "We have always shared each other's successes. There's nothing petty or mean about any of them. If you think so little of them, why did you hire the Rafferty Players in the first place?"

"I needed someone like Budd, and I hoped he would extend his natural talent in a legitimate theater. I gave him an inflated salary for the parts he was playing because I reckoned that he would be one to incur heavy fines, and I wanted him to have something left to live on. Farley is just adequate for secondary supporting roles and is a hanger-on actor—never growing, never extending himself."

"How can you say that?"

"It's true. He took up with Booth because he likes to be at the edges of somebody else's limelight." He poured himself another glass of wine. Mine remained untouched.

"He's a very nice, sensitive person . . ."

"Most inadequate people are," he said bluntly, "and they know how to make shackles out of love and friendship, even that of a small child's. I know what he's been doing to you. I can imagine what his reaction was when you told him you were moving out."

"Farley didn't mean to stab you," I said with as much conviction as I could. "It was an accident."

"Perhaps," he said with infuriating calmness. "We'll never know, will we? Unless he pursues some further vengeful course."

"Farley's not like that." Tears welled up in my eyes because I knew Ty spoke the truth and he had hit a sensitive chord. I could not hide my distress.

In one quick movement he was on his feet, pulling me into his arms. He pressed his cheek against mine and his mouth nuzzled my ear with light kisses. "Tara, darling, please . . . I don't want to say things that hurt you, but it has to be done."

"You're cold and heartless. You attack the only family I've ever had and try to make a prisoner out of me . . ."

"To protect you! Your childish loyalty is dangerous."

"Not as dangerous as falling in love with a man who only thinks of me as a theatrical asset." There, I'd said it. "Now, let me go . . ." My body trembled with sobs. "All you care about are your leading ladies—and I don't want to be one of them."

His chest heaved, and I knew he was laughing at me. "Tara, darling . . . you are delightful." Deep chuckles rippled in his throat. "Don't you know that you far surpass any role I give you to play?"

"Don't patronize me."

"I'm not. Really, I'm not."

"Yes, you are. Bragging about how good an actress you've made me—" I choked.

He sobered. "I didn't want to do it, if you remember. I tried my best not to create this kind of conflict between us. You persuaded me that this is what you really wanted."

"Well, I don't. I wish I'd never set foot on that stage."

"And what were all those months of hard work about?"

"I only did that because . . ." I faltered and let his arms tighten around me.

"Because you love me?" he finished gently.

I nodded, and he tipped up my chin. "Then why are we wasting time arguing about things that don't matter?"

I didn't have an answer, but his descending lips didn't leave air for one anyway. His kisses were like the infusion of a drug into my system. All rational thought gave way to pure sensation. Already the moment was passed when I could summon resistance against the hunger that his caresses engendered. The words of passion we had spoken on stage had brought us even beyond this moment and since I had already known him fully, there was no turning back.

"Tara . . . Tara, my darling," he whispered as he nuzzled my neck and let his rampant kisses find their way to my soft, parted lips. He gently tugged at my mouth, pulling its softness into his, working it, tasting it, and let his tongue make darting quests that sent tingling fire through my veins. I crossed my arms around his neck and pressed my swelling breasts against his firm chest. He was my own true Romeo. There was no other world but this one we shared. No lines to be said, no pretenses. The leaping warmth between us created a wordless dialogue more perfect than any that had been spoken or penned.

Our clothes fell away in his private chamber and he cosseted my nakedness in the warmth of his embrace. For a moment we stood by the bed in the darkened room, our nude bodies intertwined like some Greek statue depicting the power of love. Filtered moonlight through lace curtains laid a patina of ivory softness upon his virile masculinity and my soft yielding body as we melted together in a passionate embrace.

It was the most perfect moment of my life. Nell was right in saying I was not the type for dalliance. From the moment his eyes had captured mine I had wanted this man . . . and him only. I had fallen irrevocably in love, and only then had I felt the demanding rise of desire. His hands and lips roved over my responsive body, building a sweet ache that made me gasp in torment and passion.

He lifted me up in his arms and with tender kisses upon my lips laid me on the coverlet. We did not cover our nakedness as he made love to me this time. Delighting in the revealed beauty of each other, we touched, tenderly kissed, stroked, and murmured endearments. My hands traced the hard contours of his body and an urging beyond anything I had ever experienced brought his tantalizing length upon me. I was no longer hesitant to express my delight in the welcoming thrust that blended us together. He took me slowly, gently, with excruciating delight. My hands pressed against his back, gasping a passion-laced cry of indescribable fullness as love, passion, and desire melted into an exploding sensation.

The bliss of union remained even as we descended from the peak of passion and lay satiated in each other's embrace. He held me close, his bandaged hand resting softly on my breast as my fingers laced the dark, soft matting on his chest. We have removed ourselves from the world and nothing could touch us.

I smiled and nestled against him, content and spent. *No other Juliet had loved her Romeo more fully.*

12

Nell peeked in my room when she came in at about dawn and I feigned sleep. Floating on the delicious aftermath of lovemaking, I hugged myself. I had never felt so gloriously alive. Ty had promised to have a late breakfast with me before we went to the theater. My mind reveled in the knowledge that he loved me . . . me, Tara Townsend! I muffled my delight in my pillow, for I wanted to sing and shout it for all to hear . . . Tyrone Langston loved me! Dreams of never-ending happiness overtook me as I slipped away for a few hours of renewing sleep.

When I arose and dressed I was completely refreshed, and Nell commented on my high spirits. Fortunately, she was wound up in her new conquest and dominated the conversation, reciting the great laurels of Willy Lambert. When Ty knocked on the door to take me to breakfast she was still dressed in a morning wrapper and had rag curlers in her hair. Horrified, she scooted out of sight and I told her I would meet her at the theater.

Ty drew me into his arms for a quick kiss in the corridor.

"Where's Trapper?" I gasped, looking around furtively.

He laughed. "I told him I would be seeing you to the theater this morning. He'll meet us there."

"I don't like having him dog my footsteps," I complained.

"I know." His eyes lingered on my face with a lover's touch. "But I'm not taking any chances. It's either me or Trapper, or Nell and Mrs. Faraday nearby all the time, until . . ."

I refused to let my buoyant spirits feel the weight of that unfinished sentence. With my senses saturated with his presence, I had little inclination to think about anything but the wondrous enchantment of being with him. His debonair good looks were only increased by the warm, smoldering glint in his eyes and the soft contour of his lips as he smiled at me. His impeccably tailored smoke-gray jacket fitted smoothly over his shoulders and tapered downward to hug his hard, smooth hips and abdomen. Unabashedly, I followed the lines of his close-fitting attire with my adoring eyes and then, as sudden heat rose in my face, I averted my gaze. A few hours ago I had traced the contours of that tantalizing masculinity with my hands and the knowledge brought a new tingling to secret crevices of my body. The light chuckle he gave told me he had read my thoughts completely. I floated along on his arm, contented and happy, with every sensory bud exploding at the slightest casual touch of his flesh against mine.

In the hotel dining room he ordered a breakfast that

kept the staff serving us for nearly an hour. I wondered if love excited the appetite as well as the passions. I asked Ty about it, and he threw back his head and laughed. "I'm sure I don't know." Then he sobered and squeezed my hand under the table. "You are a delight, m'love. Your freshness, curiosity, and wonder . . . I find you enchanting."

"I've never been in love before."

"I know. That's what makes you all the more precious, and I'm going to make certain that nothing happens to you. We had best think about today's rehearsal. I'm going to let Dana handle the performance again tonight. My arm is still giving me some pain . . . too much activity last night, perhaps." He grinned.

"I'm sorry . . ."

"Are you really?" he teased, but there was a serious questioning in the depths of his eyes.

"No." I blushed, for I knew what he was really asking.

He seemed relieved. In the privacy of the carriage he held me close again. My lips clung to his like a honeybee drinking nectar. My wanton behavior embarrassed me, but I wanted to touch him, gaze at him, and memorize every curve and plane of his face. My eyes had truly been anointed with a love potion as in Shakespeare's delightful *Midsummer Night's Dream*. When I suggested that he choose it for our next production so I could play Helena opposite his Lysander, I expected him to laugh and say something facetious. Instead he became quite solemn. "I don't think it wise to parade our love so blatantly . . . I mean, for the moment we should exercise some constraint around others."

"Are you . . . ashamed . . . ?"

"No, of course not, but perhaps it's our relationship

that is making someone act in this insane way. An open romance between us . . . well, it might stimulate more insanity. I've been wondering if someone is trying to get to me through you."

"That's what Nell thinks," I confessed, "but who would be jealous enough to harm me . . . Lila, perhaps?" I prodded shamefully, wanting to know if there had ever been anything romantic between them.

"No, I don't think so, but I confess, darling, I don't understand any of this . . . Maureen . . . Jessie . . . that crazy note! I just want to try and keep things under some kind of control. We have to be careful—and discreet—at least for a little while. That means you're going to have to subdue that lover's glow and pretend that last night never happened."

"I see." I withdrew from his embrace and sat stiffly, staring unseeing out the window. I didn't believe him! If he really loved me, he would be ready to declare it to the world. There was something more to all of this than he was telling me. He had spoken of love, but not marriage. Had similar plans made by Maureen gone awry? Had he lied to me about being the one Maureen had intended to marry? Nothing he had said indicated any promises for the future. My heavenly bliss had a mocking ring to it.

"Please, try to understand, my love."

"I understand." I blinked rapidly and kept my face turned away as I alighted from the carriage.

"We'll talk this through after tonight's performance," he promised. "Trust me."

I nodded, but I knew that the first rosy glow of falling in love was over.

We entered through the front doors and separated in the lobby. Ty went upstairs to his office while I continued on through the theater to the backstage area. We were a little early, but I could hear the sounds of scenery being moved about. I thought I heard voices that sounded like Budd and Billy talking together. Budd had not turned up for last night's performance. I wondered if he was still drinking. I wasn't up to finding out, and no doubt Mrs. Faraday was waiting for me in my dressing room.

Foolish tears burned hotly and threatened to spill down my cheeks as I made my way downstairs and down the hall to my private dressing room. Ty's attitude had made our love affair a tawdry, cheap thing, and I suddenly felt mortified about what had happened. Nell had warned me and I hadn't listened. I had added my name to Ty's theatrical and amorous bill of leading ladies.

Sniffing, I put an arrogant tilt to my head as I passed Lila's dressing room. The door was closed and I didn't hear any sounds coming from it. Thank heavens . . . I didn't want to face her supercilious, all-knowing glare.

As I went through the open door of my dressing room, I saw that Mrs. Faraday hadn't arrived yet. I was glad to have a few minutes to compose myself. A day that had started on wings had plummeted downward like leaded weights. I slumped down on a padded stool in front of my mirror. It was then that I saw it!

A rag doll sat facing me on the counter amid my makeup. Its blond head dangled grotesquely. My wide eyes fastened in horror upon the cord tied viciously around its neck. A note was pinned to its breast: ''Beware . . . Enter the Villain!''

At that instant the door to my dressing room slammed shut. Even as I leapt, startled, from my stool, an odor of kerosene invaded my nostrils. Before I could reach the doorknob, a fiery river of flames poured under the crack and ran toward me. The ignited fuel leaped in red-orange tongues.

My cries became choked gasps. I screamed and lunged backward as my full skirts swung treacherously near the approaching flames. In horror I watched the burning liquid running across the floor, greedily leaping at hanging costumes and dry timbers. In a moment the room would be a fiery inferno!

Blinded by the thickening swirls of black smoke, I covered my face and screamed, "Help! Help!"

A steamer trunk shoved into the corner was the only refuge out of the pool of encroaching flames. I scrambled up on it, frantically pulling the full folds of my dress and petticoat around me. A whirling sea of black smoke and flame rose to meet me. I clasped my hands over my mouth and nose, coughing and screaming with strangled breaths. Already a searing heat encased my bare skin. My lungs burned even as I tried to yell for help. Crackling flames, popping wood, and falling charred cloth roared, and a lack of oxygen engulfed me. I felt myself blacking out.

In desperation, I let out one piercing scream as a final effort. I felt myself slumping downward as a rush of air touched my face. A coat went over my head and rough hands half dragged, half carried me through the inferno. A few steps down the corridor, the coat was jerked off. Hovering over me was not the face I expected. "Cal . . . Cal . . ." I sobbed as his slight face and cap of curly hair wavered into focus.

Ty rushed up behind us. "My God!" he swore as he saw the flames leaping out of my dressing room. In a swift movement he had me up in his arms. I closed my eyes and let myself sink against him as the three of us fled down the long corridor to the staircase.

The moment we reached the top of the stairs Nell was at my side, still in her bonnet and cape, indicating she had just arrived.

"Get her out of here," ordered Ty, setting me down. His bandaged arm was showing a crimson stain as blood flowed from his wound. "Is there anyone else downstairs?"

"No." Cal coughed. "The green room's empty!"

Lila suddenly appeared. "You're bleeding." She pointed hysterically to Ty's bloodied bandage. He pushed her away. "Get out of here, all of you! The whole building may go!"

As we left through the stage door, someone took my arm and I looked up into Farley's lean face. "For Godsakes, what happened? Are you hurt?" His hazel eyes swept over my sooty face, loose hair, tear-smudged cheeks, and the bonnet dangling down my back. His concern was like a lifeline pulling me out of shock. I stammered, sobbed, and whimpered. "A fire . . . in my dressing room . . . Cal . . . came . . . and got me out!"

"Get away from the building, both of you." He darted back inside.

A few moments later a red steam engine pulled by four horses clanged to a stop in front of the theater. The firemen who poured off were volunteers but well trained. Even though station houses were like clubs, with rooms outfitted with billiard tables, libraries, and bars, the business of fire fighting was very competitive among the various brigades. I was relieved to see their efficiency with valves, pumps, buckets, hoses, and other firefighting gear.

Nell wanted to take me to the hotel, but I couldn't leave. If the Imperial was going up in flames, I had to be there to see it. I had forgotten my own anguish. "Please . . . please, save it," I prayed, knowing that not only this building but others clustered around it, and perhaps the whole town, could be in peril, as it had been in three disastrous fires already. I could only sob my relief when word came that the fire was out. The floor of the stage above my dressing room had been gutted and the private dressing rooms were destroyed, as well as a costume and storage room at that end of the hall, but, miraculously, the building had been saved.

I agreed to leave as shock made me tremble so violently that my teeth chattered. Back in our hotel rooms Nell fussed over me as she stripped off my singed clothes and ran a deep, warm bath for my grimy body. She washed my long hair and vowed there would be no scent of smoke left in it by the time she had worked perfumed soap through it and rinsed it in lemon water. I couldn't have been less concerned about the scent of my hair, but I let her towel it and brush it as if nothing else was more important at that moment. And all the time I gazed unseeing into the vanity mirror.

Someone had deliberately tried to kill me! Who? And why? There could be no doubt about it now . . . all speculation that someone was playing a cruel joke had been proved false. If Cal hadn't come, I would have lost my life in that burning dressing room. I shivered like someone suddenly taken with palsy.

"There now," Nell soothed. "You get into bed. I'll get you some hot tea. You forget all about what happened. It's over now."

But that was the horror of it all . . . it wasn't over. *Enter the Villain.*

When and where?

"Now tell me exactly what happened." Ty's eyes searched mine across the same secluded corner table of the hotel dining room where we had had breakfast an eternity ago. Purplish shadows hung in dark crescents under his eyes and weariness made deep lines around his mouth as he endeavored to smile at me. "You're sure you're all right?" He was exhausted from the day's turmoil, but had insisted upon taking me downstairs for dinner. "Why wouldn't you let Nell call the doctor?" he scolded. "My God, when I think what could have happened . . . !"

"I'm fine . . . really I am." My afternoon nap had refreshed me and with my usual resiliency, I had been able to detach myself somewhat from the horrid events.

"Do you feel like telling me what happened?" His eyebrows matted in concern.

I found my voice even and amazingly calm as I related going down to the dressing room and finding the doll and note. "The door slammed shut and before I could even reach it flaming kerosene began running under the door, forcing me back into the corner."

"Then someone was waiting for you . . ."

"I guess so, but how did they know I would be alone? Mrs. Faraday . . . "

"That's what brought me backstage," said Ty. "When I left you in the lobby I went upstairs to my office. She was there, holding a note she had received. She demanded to know why she was being dismissed."

"Dismissed?"

He nodded, his hand tightening on the stem of his glass. "Someone signed my name to a note telling her not to report to the theater, that she had been relieved of her duties. Thank God she was made of stern stuff and came in to find out why. In a terrifying flash I knew that you were unprotected, that you would be alone in your dressing room. I flew through the theater shouting your name and bolted down the steps two at a time. I got there just as Cal was pulling you out of the flaming room. If he hadn't been there . . ." His haggard expression deepened, and I knew he was blaming himself for what had happened.

"Don't think about it!" I reached over and touched his good hand. "I'm fine. You did what you could to protect me . . . in spite of my protests."

"Did you see anyone at all lurking backstage or in the hall downstairs?"

"No. I heard some voices backstage as I went down and thought one might be Budd's . . ."

"Budd? No one's seen him around the theater."

"Are you sure? I could have sworn he was laughing with Billy . . . but I didn't really see anyone. I wasn't feeling very sociable so I went on downstairs. Lila's door was closed as I passed, and I wondered if she was already there."

"No, she was upstairs when the fire began. Our arsonist could have been waiting in her dressing room for you to pass, ready to pour the fuel and light it."

"It could have happened that way. But who—?"

"Just about anybody . . . that's the problem. Farley, Dana, Lila, Billy, and Nell all met us at the top of the stairs. Any one of them could have set it and raced upstairs, or someone like Budd, who wasn't visible . . ."

"Budd would never harm me! Nor Farley either!"

"But they might want to burn down my theater."

"No!"

"Your loyalty is touching," he said wearily, "but twisted things happen to people we think we know . . . and for reasons we can only guess. It's almost impossible for a rational mind to understand an irrational one. And that's the problem we have here. We are trying to come at it in some logical sequence while some demented mind is adding it up differently."

"What can we do?"

"Well, it's going to take a few weeks to repair the fire damage. We'll be closed as long as a month or six weeks."

"But what about the company?" It might not be a major concern for Ty not to have an income for that length of time, but no money, no savings, and no work to tide the performers over until productions began again could be a real hardship.

"I've been thinking about it," he granted. "There's a small theater in Sacramento that I've been thinking about leasing. I could take most of the company up there for a short run. We could do some light melodramas, repeat some of the productions we've done here."

"That would be wonderful!" My eyes must have lit up for he laughed and shook his head.

"You are amazing, Tara, my love. Most females would be languishing in bed after such an ordeal and here you are, clapping your hands about going on the road."

"But that's been my life. Change is not a change for me, it's the norm. I love moving on to the next show in a different town, with a different audience. It'll be like old times for the Rafferty Players."

"I wasn't thinking about taking *all* the Rafferty Players."

"Then I'm not going, either!" I set my chin.

"Don't be childish. You know that Budd is fast becoming a drunken derelict."

"And needs a change of scenery. You seem to forget that his wife was pushed downstairs to her death."

"We don't know that."

The time had come to tell him about the impression I had that night of someone lingering in the shadows.

"My God, why didn't you say something?" He took

my hand and held it tightly.

"It seemed wiser not to voice my suspicions. Jessie didn't fall down those stairs. I think she found that lavaliere in someone's possession and had to be silenced. She was dragged out on that landing and thrown down the steps to her death. I know it! And so does Budd! How can you expect him to come to work in surroundings that keep his loss festering? If we move on to Sacramento, he might be able to conquer the demon that's riding him."

"I'm sorry for him—I wish to God none of this had happened—but I'm not running a convalescent home for free-loading actors."

"Budd is not a free-loader! You don't know him the way I do. All those years he worked harder than any of us and kept us all in jobs. You've admitted that he was the one you really hired; the rest of us were thrown in with the deal."

"That's true, but things have changed. Only you and Nell are worth a space in the company."

"Well, you'd better make space for Budd and Farley or you'll have two more empty places, Nell's and mine."

"All right. Budd and Farley can come along with the rest of the company," he said grudgingly, and then his eyes softened. "You continue to amaze me. Aren't you concerned for your own precious skin?"

"Of course I am. I'm not a complete fool! But I'm not going to sacrifice honest people who have my real interests at heart."

"And what name would you leave off that list?"

"I . . . I don't know."

"And that, my dear Tara, is the crux of the matter! You can't trust anyone."

I knew he was right. Behind some mask lurked a demented mind. "Not even you?" I said lightly, but in dead seriousness.

"Not even me . . . but not for the reasons you might think." The corner of his mouth quirked. "Especially when I get you aboard the *Athena*."

"We're going on that lovely boat?" I couldn't believe it! Another fantasy was coming true. My spirits began to rise like soft mist after a black storm.

We talked about the delights of the 250 navigable miles of the Sacramento River. Many of the early camps, Marysville, Knight's Landing, Poker Bend, Dry Slough, and Twenty-Mile Island, still remained, inhabited by hardy pioneers who had given up the search for gold for commerce. He entertained me with stories about some of the early trade on the river, and I knew that if the theater was his first love, the river was his second.

When he kissed me good night in front of my door my head was filled with sights and wonders that he promised to show me.

Nell was less than enthusiastic about trooping on the road again. She complained that she was getting too old for that sort of thing, even if we were traveling in the deluxe accommodations of a fashionable riverboat. She had begun to plant her roots in San Francisco, she said, forgetting that she had been pleading with me to leave the Imperial a few nights ago. She didn't like the way Langston was making all the decisions for the company without talking it over with anyone. She grumbled and flounced and tossed her head in a rebellious fashion—until she learned that her Willy was coming too.

He smiled broadly with a lewd twinkle in his eyes. "Mr. Langston's given me permission to handle the gambling tables in the Gentlemen's Saloon. The little trip will be most refreshing."

I laughed to see how quickly my redheaded Nell

sang a different melody. The excursion would do us all good; it would be like old times, the Rafferty Players on the circuit again. "We must take our best party dresses," she said with a lilt in her voice. I hid my smiles as we packed, shopped, and waited for Ty to complete all the arrangements.

I clung to a reassuring conviction that all the recent pain and tension would be left behind. Only in recurring nightmares of fires, poisoned vials, and plunging rapiers did the truth hover on the edge of my awareness, mocking my feeble pretenses. An uneasy premonition settled darkly on my shoulders.

We were taking the villain with us!

13

Preparations for our overnight trip and stay in Sacramento were enormous, and I scarcely saw Ty in the frantic days that preceded our departure. The afternoon of the *Athena*'s sailing, I stood on the passenger's deck with Budd, Nell, and Farley and watched roustabouts fill her cargo deck with props, trunks, and other theatrical equipment needed to put the newly leased Emerald Theater into operation. Budd and Farley seemed to be more like their old selves, and I knew the change was going to be good for all of us. As we laughed and talked and pointed out sights on the river, it seemed like old times again, as if the Rafferty Players were preparing for a new engagement—this time in style!

A weathered ferry boat with scars of hard use gave a shrill toot as she left her berth and headed for growing settlements across the bay. She wore the name *New World* on her bow and her decks were crowded with derby-hatted men, husky laborers, miners in work clothes, coolies in oriental garb, and women passengers with children and babies wrapped against the chill of the water. Some of them waved as the boat clanged past the fashionable *Athena*, rocking it in its churning wake.

"She's an old boat, the *New World*," said Budd, noting an excited expression as my eyes followed her.

I knew a story was coming.

"They say her captain stole her when she was berthed in New York Harbor over fifteen years ago, sailed her out from under the nose of everybody, brought her around the horn," Budd told us. "It's a sad tale they told of a yellow fever epidemic, deputies and soldiers waiting to take her the minute she set to shore in Nicaragua, but she fooled 'em all . . . steamed into San Francisco Bay like a victorious frigate, she did! Been here ever since." He shook his head sadly. "And would ye be looking at her now! A decrepit old ferry. 'Tis enough to make a strong heart weep."

At that moment Ty came into view on the wharf and instantly my attention centered on this man who dominated my senses. He strode over to a pile of waiting cargo, directing Cal's attention to something that needed special handling. Copper glints in his dark brown hair caught the light under the rim of a low crown hat and a burnished glow made his face appear lightly tanned in the late afternoon sun. A smooth, long coat spanned his shoulders and hung open over a waistcoat in darker shades of wood tones. As he stooped down to examine a crate, tailored nankeen trousers molded the muscular lines and sinews of his legs above shiny black boots. His fashionable attire could not disguise or diminish the vision of his naked body that had been forever etched in the deepest recesses of my mind. A memory of soft bronze hair curling upon his chest and plunging downward to a firm, flat abdomen brought a flash of hunger leaping as I viewed his striking figure. His hard buttocks flexed as he stooped and lifted the crate from one pile to another and a flush eased upon my throat as I recalled their tightening under my pulsating fingers. His long, hard legs moved with masculine grace, and I marveled that they had been heatedly entwined with mine. My eyes must have been feasting greedily on his every move for I suddenly felt Nell stiffen beside me.

"Let's go see what's happening in the Social Hall," said Nell, quickly, taking my arm.

My reluctance to leave the railing must have been evident, for Farley said shortly, "I believe I'll head for the Gentlemen's Saloon and have a drink."

"And a good idea it is too." Budd brightened. "We'll be seeing you ladies later."

"At dinner, perhaps?" Farley suggested, looking directly at me.

Even though Ty had not said anything about dining with me, I wasn't going to commit myself to Farley's company. I pretended I didn't know what he was asking and Nell, bless her heart, gave a casual wave of her hand. "The boat's not that big. We'll be seeing you."

Farley looked from one of us to the other and his lean face tightened. He knew exactly what was happening—we had other escorts in mind. He turned away abruptly with Budd at his heels.

I said something about feeling guilty and Nell waved it away with a merry toss of her head. "Don't be foolish. After a few beers neither of them will remember we're aboard. Come on, let's take a peek around . . . see what we can see." She winked knowingly.

I looked back at the wharf and saw that Ty had disappeared so I willingly went with her. We sauntered along the deck until we found a door marked by a bronze, engraved plaque: SOCIAL HALL. We lifted our skirts and stepped over the raised threshold into a long room, framed on two sides by large windows, offering a panoramic view of the bay. Easy chairs and sofas were scattered about, as well as small tables for refreshments or a game of whist. Seated about in chattering groups were various members of the Langston Players. I heard my name and was startled when I saw Dana waving for us to join him and Lila. They were sitting at a table near a window, apparently enjoying a four o'clock tea. I hesitated. I wondered why Dana wanted us to intrude upon the twosome.

Nell looked around, obviously trying to catch sight of her new admirer. The stocky, flamboyant figure of Willy Lambert was not in evidence. Disappointed, she followed me to Dana's table and gave Lila a broad smile that was not returned. In fact, Lila's expression was almost a grimace, as if our presence had brought on a sudden attack of some feminine complaint.

Nonplussed, Nell returned the actress' pained expression with a look of concern. "My goodness, Lila, you look positively peeked . . . don't tell me you don't like the water? You surely can't be seasick already. We've not cast off yet." She gave an amused titter.

"I am a very good sea traveler," she said curtly, "and I *was* enjoying myself." The inference was clear that her displeasure came from our company.

Dana cleared his throat, obviously not wanting to be caught in the middle of these female thrusts. "How are you, Tara? I haven't seen you since the fire. What a shame to have something like that happen. No one seems to know exactly how it got started."

I know he had invited us over to find out how much I knew about the fire. With a quirk of stubbornness, I pretended I didn't know he was asking for information and gave him a vacant nod.

"Carelessness, pure and simple," snapped Lila in the silence, as if her opinion on the matter was a definitive answer. "You know how those backstage grips are . . . always leaving paint sitting around . . . this time it was kerosene. No doubt one of them set it off with a pipe or cigarette."

Was her explanation a little too pat? It seemed to me it flowed as if it had been rehearsed.

Lila tossed her handkerchief, wafting a sickening gardenia scent in the air. "I shudder to think that but for a few minutes I would have been in my dressing room when it happened."

"Yes, that would have been a shame," responded Nell almost too sweetly.

"It's unfortunate that Ty decided it was best to close up the Imperial," Dana commented, searching my face as if waiting for some significant comment.

I kept the vacant smile on my face.

"I don't see why he couldn't have given us a little time off," Lila said, glaring at me. "Instead of forcing us to perform in some backwater theater."

Her criticism of Ty dissolved my passive attitude. "I understand that the Emerald is a very nice, small theater," I countered.

"Well, you heard wrong!" She glared. "Dana was just telling me its name is the only elegant thing about the place. The stage is reported to be so small that no respectable play can be performed there. No wonder Ty is scheduling some crude melodramas. I don't see why he's dragging all of us along. There are plenty in the company to handle that kind of program."

We all knew she thought only Shakespearean productions were up to her caliber as an actress. Undoubtedly, she was heartsick that the fire had closed the theater before she could star in *Camille*. Whatever her personal feelings toward me were, I knew she would not have ruined her chances at this great role by trying to trap me in a burning room. I felt guilty about my earlier suspicions, and a flicker of pity softened my reply. "I'm sorry, Lila, that the fire postponed *Camille*."

Her narrow nostrils flared, and I could almost see her teeth bared.

Dana touched her with a restraining gesture and said quickly, "I guess you didn't know, Tara . . . Ty canceled *Camille* the day before the fire."

"He canceled *Camille*?" I echoed, my eyes round. "But why?"

A hard expression settled on his face and his blue eyes suddenly flashed like honed steel as they stabbed me. "Who knows? He just told Lila he had changed his mind about letting her star in it."

"Don't pretend you didn't know," Lila hissed, her chiseled features hard under taut skin as she glared at me. "We're not blind . . . everyone knows what's going on! You and your cheap, harlot tricks! You talked Ty into giving the part to you, didn't you? No need to act the innocent! You're just like Maureen, trying to get your hooks in him since the first day he signed you up."

"That's not true!"

She snorted. "You're just a new plaything for him. Once the novelty wears off . . ." Her smile was lewd. "How long do you think he'll be entertained by a scheming little twit who—"

Suddenly the silver teapot went over. Lila screamed and leaped to her feet. Her rose merino gown was drenched with hot tea that must have seeped through all the layers of ribboned undergarments to her skin.

"Oh, I'm sorry . . . what a clumsy thing . . . did I scald you with that hot tea?" Nell was a flutter of concern. She grabbed a napkin and tried to wipe at the actress' dripping skirts.

Lila shoved her hand away. "Don't touch me—you —you—" She choked on a word that sounded like *trollop*.

"I'll see you to your cabin, Lila." Dana took her arm, and the glance he gave us as they left should have withered us on the spot.

I was stunned, as if I had received a swift, hard blow to the middle. Two waiters hovered around us with concerned expressions on their faces. "We had an accident," said Nell easily. "We'll need fresh table service and another pot of tea . . ."

Her voice barely penetrated the black maelstrom that Lila's words had left in my mind. *Ty had taken the part of Camille away from her—the day before the fire! She thought it was my doing.* All moisture left my throat and mouth. I looked at Nell with a sickened feeling in my stomach. "She could have done it," I croaked. "She could have been in her dressing room, waiting for me to come down . . ."

"She's got the personality for it," Nell agreed. "A witch if I ever saw one, but I find it hard to believe she'd choose that way to vent her anger. Pretty drastic measures, if you ask me. If every leading lady burned down a theater when she didn't get a role, we'd all be out of work!"

"She hates me . . ."

"You're a real threat to her and she knows it."

"It's not my fault. I didn't know anything about . . . about Ty taking *Camille* away from her."

"I know you didn't. Can't help but wonder why he

221

did it." She gave me one of her candid, no-nonsense looks. "What's happened between you and our handsome director?"

"What do you mean?" I parried.

"You're not fooling me with that innocent flutter of your eyelids. You've been in his bed, haven't you?"

I didn't answer.

"You know what I'm asking?"

I nodded.

"All right, let's hear it, have you . . . or haven't you?"

"Yes."

"God in heaven. I knew it, but I didn't want to believe it."

"I love him, Nell . . . and he loves me."

"And where's the sound of a wedding march, may I ask?"

"We have to wait . . . he's thinking of my safety . . ."

"Let me tell you something, girl, when you ring the bell before you go to church more often than not you never get there. Tarry, Tarry, I wanted more for you than that."

"All I want is Ty . . . any way I can get him."

She sighed. "Well, there's little I can say to that. It's a man's world, all right. I'll never land Willy Lambert, for the same reason, you'll never become Mrs. Tyrone Langston. Course, I never cared about settling down to anything permanent . . . but you're different. You're going to be hankering after this one fellow the rest of your life, just like your ma did after your pa. I remember when he was courtin' her. She was acting the same lovesick fool as you . . ."

"But my father married her."

"Yep, he did that, but I couldn't help wondering if it was a spot in the troupe that he was really wanting.

I don't aim to speak ill of the dead, but I don't want you to be living with any idea that a golden halo circled your pa's head. Your mother was never well after that trip through Panama—but that never slowed him down none . . . know what I mean?''

I knew what she meant; I had already gathered as much from Farley. He used to assure me that he wouldn't ever desert me the way my father had . . . going off on an adventure that got him drowned.

Nell talked to me as frankly as she ever had, but it had little effect on me. I didn't care what she said . . . I was in love and that's all that mattered. We finally drank our tea in silence and then I excused myself and said I was going to our cabin to rest.

Nell nodded and I left her sitting there. Usually there were several men hanging around to catch her attention, but today her full chin dipped at a forlorn angle and there was a decided slump to her plump shoulders. Her merry, inviting eyes did not float around the room but were cast downward. I hoped Willy would come along and brighten her up.

I had just made it to the door of our cabin when I heard my name. ''Tara . . . wait up!''

I spun around at the voice. The world brightened like sun spears through dark clouds. Ty reached my side just as the lines on the *Athena* were tossed free and the gallant lady began to move. ''Come on.'' He grabbed my arm. ''Let's watch her from the bow.'' A shrill whistle alerted passengers and crew that we were under way.

All my heavy spirits left with the lightness of the gulls darting and soaring over the water. I forgot about Lila and everyone else as I moved beside him with his possessive hand cupping my elbow. A swooping breeze tugged at the brim of my bonnet and lifted curls about my face as we stood at the bow and watched the craft cut through the water, spilling a white ribbon of foam on each side.

Ty laughed and eased his arm around my waist. He pointed out landmarks on the receding shoreline. The long ferry building looked less formidable at this distance, and the wharves appeared to be small wooden stalls. Only twenty years ago San Francisco had been a collection of tents and shacks. Now Telegraph Hill rose triumphant over a myriad collection of gaily colored houses and buildings, roads and parks, docks and beaches. There was an air of paternal pride as Ty swung his sun-burnished face in every direction as the panorama that was San Francisco spread before us. His eyes were bright as dark pebbles under clear water. "She's the most fantastic city in the world," he breathed.

How could I dispute it? Happiness leaped around me like a palatable entity, making my breath tremulous and sending shivers of delight wriggling up my spine. Across the bay the sun was getting ready to add a dramatic flare to the whole scene by splashing brilliant pinks and oranges across the water as it bowed its departure. There are some moments that are like colors caught in a prism and they remain long after the light has faded. Standing there, sharing and filling our senses with land, water, sky, and air was one of those moments. I knew the memory would never really die . . . that in some ways I would always be there, leaning against the freshening breeze, sharing an exquisite sensual and mystic communion. He must have felt it too for his arm tightened around my waist, as if I were somehow a part of the wondrous moment.

And then it was over. The world intruded. We turned away from the railing just as Cal came up the steps from the cargo deck. He handed Ty some papers. "I checked everything off. No doubt we forgot something, but it can come up on the next load." He looked tired as he pulled out his tobacco bag and began to roll a cigarette. "Next time you decide to move a whole theater, count me out!"

Ty laughed and slapped him on the back affectionately. "Don't worry, my friend. I've had more than one regret about leasing the Emerald. God only knows what we'll find when we get there. We may have to rebuild the whole thing . . . it's not been used for five years."

"I think I'm jumping overboard right now. Want to join me, Tara? Let this crazy fool go on alone," said Cal.

"I guess I'm just as crazy as he is," I confessed. "I think it's going to be exciting."

"No accounting for tastes . . . well, I'm going to enjoy myself tonight because I have a feeling there's no rest for the wicked once we get to Sacramento." Cal's slight figure disappeared through the crowd.

"I'll be forever grateful that Cal was close enough to hear your cries and bring you out of that burning room. To think I might have lost you . . ."

"Don't think about it. I try not to." I didn't want to admit to the recurring nightmare that filled my nostrils with remembered smoke and brought me lurching up in my bed, sweat beaded on my brow. "What's Cal's background?" I asked, wanting to change the subject. "Have you known him a long time?"

"Four or five years . . . I found him in a sailors' dump on the waterfront, playing the piano for drinks. He had jumped ship, after joining the navy when his wife ran off with some other fellow."

"What a shame."

"I don't think he's ever really gotten over her.

Anyway, I watched him several nights hunched over a rickety old piano. Even though he was bleary-eyed with cheap wine, there was magic in his fumbling fingers. Decided he might be worth sobering up. It ended up that I offered him a job at the Golden Nugget. He used to drop out of sight now and again and drink himself senseless, but I couldn't fault him for that. Not after what happened to him with a bunch of crude sailors who took a liking to his slender body and pleasing face. The things that happened to him are not for the ears of ladies. That's what makes him a loner.''

''He does have an air of sadness about him.''

Ty sighed. ''He may be right, you know. It's pure idiocy trying to launch a new theater at this time. Maybe I should have just closed down for a couple of months and taken a vacation.''

''When was the last time you had one?''

''A vacation? You mean like sleeping late and lying around in the sun?'' He laughed. ''Not since the first summer I arrived here, nearly broke. I had time then, before I started making money. Ironic, isn't it? Leisure time belongs to the unemployed. I started a little gambling parlor on Market Street and that was the beginning . . . next the Golden Nugget, a dozen investments, and finally the Imperial . . .''

''And now the Emerald.''

He sighed. ''What a fool! Let's chuck it all and take a trip to the Orient instead.''

''On this boat? Aren't we headed in the wrong direction?''

''Details . . . always details.''

''Ty—?'' I hesitated.

''Yes. What is it? You look as if you're about to ask me something quite ponderous. I can always tell, you know. Your eyes change to a peculiar shade of French

226

blue when you're deep in thought. And when you're angry they change into an arctic gray, with no soft tints at all. They're dark now, so you must not be displeased . . . but worried."

"I am. It's about Lila."

"All right. What about Lila?"

"Did you take the Camille part away from her?"

"Yes."

"But why? You knew that she wouldn't like being pushed aside while I played Juliet. Wasn't Camille a kind of compensation?"

"Yes, that was my thinking all right when I gave her the part, but it didn't work out. I told her I had decided against doing the play."

"But she thinks I talked you out of giving her the part."

"Nonsense!"

"It's not nonsense. She accused me of all sorts of things. You must have known how she would react. Why did you do it?"

"Because she was terrible in spite of all our work . . . she just couldn't get a handle on the role. She wasn't right for the part, pure and simple. I knew the play would die on stage before Camille did." He grinned, as if the whole matter was something to be amused about.

"And you told her the day before the fire . . . ?" I pressed.

"Yes, but what does that have to do with anything? You don't think that she—?" I had the satisfaction of seeing the grin fade from his face, replaced by a stunned expression.

"I think she was angry enough, yes, but whether she did or not, I don't know."

"No, not Lila. She might get someone else to do it for her . . ."

"Like Dana?" I asked before I had time to consider the question. That's the weakness of fear, I thought, it makes everyone suspect.

He laughed then. "Dana would be more likely to set fire to himself, before he'd burn down any stage! Your imagination is really running away with you."

"Maybe he has a personal vendetta," I insisted stubbornly. "He's bound to have some kind of life outside the theater."

"What are you getting at?" Ty had sobered.

"If I had the answers, I wouldn't be badgering you about this!" I countered. "You know these people better than I do."

"Apparently not. You are presenting some valid insights that I may have missed. I'll talk to Lila, explain why you would be more suitable for the role."

"No! I'm not doing *Camille*. Not after what she said!"

His face clouded, and I could hear stormy rumbling through his even words. "I am the director of the company. I say who plays what part! Jealousy between two women has no place in determining the kind of production I present to the public. If you are better for a certain role, you'll get it!"

"But don't you see how it looks?"

"Tara, darling." He softened his tone. "I've tried my best to stay away from you because I know how it looks. I didn't want you to become a tidbit for theater gossip but—" The timbre of his voice softened. "I couldn't keep from loving you. You don't know how hard this has been for me."

Protests died in my throat. Ty would never let any personal relationship affect the quality of the Imperial Players. The decisions he made were for professional reasons, and if he thought I would be a better Camille than Lila, that's all that mattered. I had to trust his judgment.

"That's better," he said, his fingertips playing lightly along my cheeks. "I prefer that soft, luminous shade of blue in your eyes." A twist of suppressed passion was visible in the smoky depths of his caressing gaze. He dropped his hand from my face, but the physical contact was still there, radiating between us. A myriad of sensations flowed like the surging tide of deep waters; awakened desires, pulsating vibrations, bold demands that almost had us leaning into each other. My lips had shamelessly parted, as if waiting for his kiss. The press of people moving around the *Athena*'s deck had no importance for me. He was the one who had to maintain a mien of decorum between us.

"I'd better let you go," he said softly in a voice thick and passion-laced, "before I sweep you up in my arms and we disappear into your cabin for the rest of the trip."

"Will I see you later?"

"Of course. I intend to show you how lovely the river is in the moonlight." His lingering eyes promised much more. "Oh, I forgot to tell you, Captain Whitney had asked us to join him for dinner, and I graciously accepted for both of us."

"You're very sure of yourself. Maybe I have another engagement," I teased.

"Have you?"

"No."

"That's what I thought," he said with infuriating conceit.

14

When Ty and I entered the dining room we were
seated at a small table for four with Captain Whitney
and another one of his officers, a quiet, thin man in
his thirties who left the conversation in the hands of
his captain and gave his attention to the five-course
dinner that was served to us.

I found Captain Whitney to be a gregarious person,
schooled in the art of drawing people out, and was
content to listen to him and Ty talk about river
commerce and reminisce about the early days. There
had been excitement and tragedy as competing riverboats fired up their boilers and raced up and down the
Sacramento River. They said that at one time there
were so many vessels on the river that the price of
passage fell from twelve dollars to ten cents as
competitors vied for the river trade in a price war.
Bad feelings remained . . . and the recent incident that
had inflicted damage upon the *Athena* had been

motivated by revenge. The captain gave credit to men like Ty, who formed the California Navigation Company to stabilize transportation on this vital river.

"The Sacramento's not like some of the rivers I've known," Captain Whitney said with a wry grin. "Now take the muddy Colorado . . . you can't go a hundred yards without getting hung up on a sand bar! And the U.S. government thought they were going to make a navigable river out of her." He laughed. "They'd done better to sink their money in a mud hole. I had enough of that river in short order and headed west in 1851, along with all the others."

In response to a question about my family, I told the captain some of the things Nell had passed on to me about their trip to San Francisco. "My parents came by the Isthmus route about that time. They crowded into a Panama steamer handling twice the number of passengers it should have. I guess the conditions in makeshift sleeping quarters and crowded decks were not to be believed. After they arrived at the squalid village of Chagres they were poled up a river in native boats . . . then on mules back to Panama City. Nell said that they had to wait almost six months to get passage on a boat up the west coast to San Francisco at the cost of two hundred dollars a person. If they hadn't been able to put on entertainment for the crowds waiting for passage, they never could have afforded to get out of that horrid place. They were determined to get here at any cost."

"Now I know where your stubbornness comes from," said Ty with a warm glint softening his eyes. "I'm glad they made it."

"It's a miracle they survived all the disease, filth, and poor food," the captain agreed.

"My mother didn't . . . I mean, she contracted some

disease that she was never able to throw off. After I was born her strength steadily slipped away."

The captain nodded sympathetically. "I've heard a good many sad tales . . . everybody willing to suffer what they must to reach the goldfields and become overnight millionaires. And you, Ty? What adventures did you have before arriving at the City by the Bay?"

"Not many, I'm afraid. I came overland and decided to make my fortune off the good luck of others."

"It's worked out very well for you."

"Yes. Who could want more out of life than this?" He picked up his wineglass and smiled at me over its rim. "I've found my treasure." He gave me a knowing grin as his gaze bathed the soft skin of my face, neck, and the swelling fullness above my gown.

I tried to acknowledge the compliment without blushing like a lovesick fool.

During the meal I looked around the room and saw that Nell was at a table with her dapper gambler, Willy. Occasionally, her rich laughter floated above the clicking table service and rumble of voices. Once, my traveling gaze caught Dana and Lila sitting in a corner, and I looked away quickly. Budd and Farley were not to be seen, and I felt a tinge of guilt for refusing to accept Farley's obvious invitation for dinner. Then Ty reached over and touched my hand, and I was glad I hadn't sacrificed a moment of my lover's company.

"Would you like to take a turn on the deck?" he asked, a lazy grin curving those mobile lips. "The river is lovely this time of evening."

I nodded, and we made our polite amenities to the captain and his officer. With his hand sending fiery sparkles through me, Ty guided me across the room toward the open doors. Nell gave me a bold wink as we passed. I could sense eyes boring into my back with the stab of an ice pick and felt that everyone in the room was watching our departure.

I shivered.

"Are you cold?" Ty asked solicitously.

"No," I said quickly, but gathered the folds of a soft wool shawl over my shoulders. "It's a lovely evening." A soft light played on the water, moving and changing like a liquid sculpture. The sky was like an inverted bowl, glazed in deep tones of indigo and starlight.

"Let's go up on the hurricane deck where the captain has his quarters . . . more privacy."

"Are we allowed up there?"

"Oh, I think so, one of the privileges of ownership, I imagine." He took my arm possessively and guided me up a staircase and along a narrow deck to the stern of the boat behind the wheelhouse structure. With his arm around my waist, we stood together at the railing and gazed across the river, rippling translucent in the moonlight and bringing starlight down into its depths. The sound of dipping and emptying paddle buckets made a harmonious, lulling counterpoint to swishing waters lapping against the boat's hull. Like a gentle, soft bosom, the deep Sacramento cradled the craft and its deep green skirt rippled to gentle banks lined with willows and cottonwoods. Night sounds were different than those of the city . . . hushed, unhurried, echoing, and soothing. Somewhere on the bank a night bird's trill floated across the water. A mesmerizing white wake rippled away from the boat like foaming ribbons. A soft breeze from the movement of the boat pressed against us and I lifted my face to it, delighting in its freshness. My spirits reached out in quiet harmony to the blending of earth, water, and sky.

"That's what I like about you," Ty said softly, watching my face. "You open up your senses— willingly, eagerly—you don't worry about the wind mussing your hair or pretending that everything is too gauche to be enjoyed."

I laughed softly, "I guess all my pretenses at being worldly have been a little ridiculous."

"Don't try to be anything but what you are, m'love." He turned me gently away from the railing. "You know, of course, I didn't want to get involved. . . . I tried to keep a professional distance between us. If you'd been a *grande dame* I could have resisted you. But you were so fresh, so innocent." He chuckled. "And so exasperating." He lifted my hand and brushed his lips against my skin, like the stroking of a velvet petal. "I didn't know whether to spank you or love you."

"I'm glad you decided on the latter," I said breathlessly. His nearness was spinning all rational thought out of control. He drew me into the circle of his arms, his hands caressing me as one lovingly cupped the fullness of a breast. Instantly a hard nipple pushed up against the lace of my camisole and a responding fullness surged through my body. Mellow moonlight caught the firm-fleshed sweep of his cheek and chin like an artist's stroke. Desire flamed between us like a torch. His half-lidded, smoldering gaze clung to mine. "It's never been like this for me before . . . you have to believe that. There have been other women, but none like you."

At that moment I did not care how many lovers he had taken. His mouth lowered to mine and his tongue lightly flickered on my waiting lips, tasting, working, teasing them until they parted. His kisses and embrace suffused my body with instant warmth.

Even if I had wanted to control my responses, I would have failed. Remembered ecstasies betrayed a hungering need. His kisses roved away from my mouth to trail down the smooth curve of my neck. The erotic caressing of his fingertips sent desire cruising rampant through me. My shawl fell unheeded to the deck.

I raised my arms so they could encircle his neck and wantonly threaded my fingers into his hair. His hands molded the curve of my back and waist, as if sculpting them with each loving caress.

Somewhere on the fringes of awareness I heard footsteps on the stairs. A stiffening of Ty's body told me he had heard them too. He eased my arms down just as two figures emerged at the top of the staircase. There was no time to step back into the shadows as they approached us along the narrow deck.

"Oh, there you are," said Captain Whitney in an apologetic tone. "I told Mr. Calabrese you might be up here, enjoying the night air."

"Yes, we were." There was an edge of censure in Ty's reply.

Cal said quickly, "I'm sorry, Ty . . . it seems some entertainment has been planned and they're holding everything up. I was looking for you when the captain said you might be up here. They won't start without you."

"Why not? I fail to see why my presence is necessary."

The captain cleared his throat. "Well, the fact of the matter is, Mr. Langston, I have promised someone that you would be in the audience tonight . . . a kind of informal audition . . . as a favor to me, really. You see, one of them is my nephew, and a very talented young man . . . puts on a good show . . ."

I could feel Ty's anger mounting at this imposition,

so I said quickly, "It might be fun to be entertained ourselves for a change." I gave a light laugh, which I hoped would ease the situation. "It's been a long time since I've been in the audience."

"I don't conduct theater business on someone else's whim, Captain." Ty said in a frosty tone.

"I realize that but . . . I thought . . . well, as a personal favor to me . . ." He went on apologizing and pleading until Ty cut him off.

"All right, I suppose under the circumstances we can see what your young man has to offer . . . if Tara is agreeable."

I smiled my consent and took a few steps away from the railing, hoping the night shadows hid my flushed face. Someone touched my arm. I turned around, expecting it to be Ty. It was Cal, holding out my shawl. "I believe you dropped this."

"Yes, thank you," I responded and, with as much poise as I could manage, swung it over my shoulders. From his expression I knew Cal had no doubts that it wasn't a look at the scenery that he had interrupted.

When we entered the Social Room I saw that it had been changed into a kind of dance hall with a raised platform at one end. A trio of musicians were playing a lively tune and the center of the room was filled with couples dancing. At our entrance a signal was given to cut the number short, and before we had reached a table at the front of the room the musicians were already vacating the platform.

The captain's nephew was a slight, freckled-faced young man wearing a derby, striped jacket, and forest-green pants. With a flushed face and thatches of wheat-colored hair falling down on his forehead, he played the banjo and bellowed some ditties that bordered on saloon fare. He looked like a hayseed just arrived from Iowa. The young man was terribly nervous and it took him several minutes to settle down, but after a couple of numbers his energetic and youthful charm dominated the unpolished, rough routines. I laughed and clapped, for he reminded me a lot of the Rafferty Players in the early years of traveling around the gold camp circuit.

Captain Whitney clung to every expression that flickered across Ty's face as he watched the young man's act. The captain was obviously relieved by something Ty whispered to him at the end of the performance, and I guessed Ty had told him to send his nephew around to see him when we got back from Sacramento. He'd probably start him out at the Golden Nugget, the way he had Cal.

I thought the show was over, but, in fact, it turned out to be just beginning. An empty stage was an invitation to the entertainers collected on the boat and before long an impromptu show was underway. Cal was hustled to the piano and familiar songs and dances, juggling acts, and joke routines were presented by some of the Langston Players. Encouraged by her new gentleman admirer, Nell perched on top of the piano while Cal accompanied her in an amusing English ditty about a girl who left the farm and found city life to her liking.

Ty's good humor had been restored and he laughed and clapped with the rest of us. He was the one who walked over to Budd, sitting morosely in a corner, and persuaded him to offer his Irish vagabond routine. I saw a remembered sparkle come back to Budd's craggy face as he brought the audience to the floor with laughter. It was the old Budd who was up there, a few beers under his belt, to be sure, but an animation in his face that hadn't been there for a long time. He motioned for Farley to join him on stage, and the two of them did an old routine that had been in mothballs for years. I had seen it hundreds of times, but tonight it had a special meaning . . . things were as they used to be. When Budd and Farley and Nell insisted that I join them in an old sailor's jig and song that we had retired years ago I tried to refuse, but Ty said, laughing, "Go on! It's a party! Don't be a spoil-sport."

"All right . . . but your turn's next!"

Cal helped me up on stage and nodded when we asked if he knew "A Sailor's Life For Me." Budd and Nell carried the lyrics and Farley and I executed the dance routine in pretty good order. At least our generous audience clapped enthusiastically when we finished.

"Now, it's your turn," I told Ty as Farley returned me to the table, breathless and with my face flushed.

"No . . ." He shook his head.

"Poor sport . . . poor sport," I chided.

The crowd took up the chant and forced a reluctant Ty on the stage.

I wondered what he would do. The frolicking mood of the evening did not allow for any serious Shakespearean soliloquies. Could Ty play the ham with the rest of us?

I needn't have worried. He whispered something to Cal and then asked to borrow a derby from the captain's nephew. He tipped the hat at a rakish angle over one eye. The piano began to bounce as Cal pounded out the strains of Daniel Emmett's brand-new tune, "Dixie." Ty improvised a very competent soft-shoe dance as he moved across the stage with flowing, loose-jointed movements. It was a different Tyrone Langston that we were seeing. The audience roared and clapped and started singing the lyrics of the song, "Lookaway . . . lookaway . . . lookaway, Dixieland." They wouldn't let him off. Ty had to do two choruses before they would let him go.

No one wanted to follow that act, so they cleared back the furniture and urged the musicians back. Ty led me out onto the dance floor and the evening took on a crystal glow that shimmered, vibrated, and encased me in a whirl of happiness.

"You were very good," I murmured as Ty swirled me in a graceful rhythm to a lovely waltz. "I didn't know you were a dancer."

"I'm not. I used to watch our field hands dance and sing and I'd mimic them. I was surprised my feet remembered what to do. It's been a long time."

"I know what you mean. I wasn't sure I knew a single step of that sailor's dance." I laughed. "This is a wonderful party."

"I suppose so," he granted, but his grin told me he was remembering how rudely we had been interrupted. "I guess the evening's young . . . and I'm sure I can remember where we left off." His warm gaze brought back the breathless ecstasy I had felt in his arms. The night was ahead of us with its promise of love. He gave a sudden twirl on the dance floor and I felt his lips lightly brush my forehead. "That's on account," he whispered.

When we returned to our table Captain Whitney stood up, bowed, and asked me for the next dance. If I had refused and stayed at the table, the evening would have kept its glow; the dark forces threatening me would have been kept at bay. For a little while longer I would have been insulated from the ugliness that mocked my happiness . . . but I smiled and said, "I would be delighted."

The captain was surprisingly agile on his feet. As we danced a two-step he asked me if I thought Ty had been impressed with his nephew. Not wanting to put Ty in a bind I responded that I was sure Ty would help him if he could.

"Nice fellow, Mr. Langston," agreed the captain happily. "It's like old times having a party like this aboard. Let's see, it was a year ago April or May that he took a party up to Sacramento. That lovely Miss Cole was with him then . . . yes, I remember watching them dance on this very floor."

The music suddenly became a loud discord vibrating in my ears. "He was here . . . with Maureen . . . ?"

"Aye, Maureen Cole . . . what a terrible thing . . . her killed like that. I was in port the day they dragged her body out of the water." He shook his head. "Sad, sad . . . her so young . . . and in her condition." He leaned forward and said privately in my ear, "She was pregnant, you know."

I must have stumbled, for suddenly his arm tightened around my waist and he held me up as I gave a strangled gasp. "Are you sure?"

"Positive . . . I sent the ship's doctor over to see if he could help and he came back and said she was nearly three months along. If that cord hadn't been around her neck, it would have seemed a suicide, for sure . . . her not married and all."

Maureen was carrying someone's child!

"Are you all right, Miss Townsend? You look rather peaked. I do believe all this excitement has worn you out."

"Yes . . . yes . . . I feel quite tired." I couldn't go back and face Ty. *The lovely Miss Cole was with him then.* "Would . . . would you see me to my cabin?"

"My pleasure."

Fortunately, we were close to the outside door. I did not look back as we left. The captain made polite conversation as we walked to my cabin, but I didn't hear a word he said.

Maureen was here . . . on this boat in May . . . and dead in August . . . with someone's baby in her womb.

"Are you all right, Miss Townsend?"

My stomach twisted in a spasm. I mumbled something and took a deep breath to still a rising nausea.

"Shall I send someone to you?"

"No, no! I'll be fine." We had reached the door of my cabin. "Thank you," I murmured and fled inside.

I leaned against the closed door and shut my eyes. Earlier in the evening Ty had said there had been other women, but had assured me I was different. And yet a mocking laughter in my ears taunted me that the same horrifying pattern was there.

15

Ty knocked on my door a little while later. When I
didn't answer the soft concern in his voice changed to
brittle anger. I stifled the impulse to call him back as
he stomped away. There were too many things I had
to think through before I saw him. I knew myself well
enough by now to admit that I was incapable of
rational, unemotional thought when I was with him.
My love for him colored everything he said . . . and I
foolishly believed and trusted him in the face of all
evidence. It was only when I was alone that his
answers seemed vague and twisted. No, I could not
fall into his arms as if the past was to be shoved aside
and forgotten.

Someone did not want me to forget. At every turn I
was faced with a pattern that was Maureen Cole's.
Was there an evil force directing my steps? Had I
assumed an unwittingly role that had been
diabolically orchestrated once before? *Had we fallen in*

love with the same man?

I wrestled with these questions through a fitful night. My eyes were puffed with tears and, at breakfast the next morning, the question was still twisting at my insides. Nell had not come back to the cabin all night, so I entered the dining room alone. I saw Ty at once, at the same table we had had that first day when he had taken me for a ride in his carriage. There was no use running away. There were things that had to be said. I knew he had been waiting for me when he pressed a napkin to his lips and stood up. I steeled myself to say a pleasant "Good morning" while avoiding a direct look into those fathomless, dark eyes as I sat down.

"I trust you are feeling better this morning?"

"Yes."

"The malady came on you suddenly."

I nodded.

"So suddenly, you left the party without a word."

"I'm sorry," I mumbled.

"So am I," he answered curtly, "for I found out from Captain Whitney what the conversation had been when this *indisposition* overtook you. I also was able to surmise the cursory route of your thinking. Your refusal to answer my knock made your conclusions quite evident."

I was not going to let him put me on the defensive. "Did you know that Maureen was . . . pregnant?"

"Yes."

"Why . . . why didn't you say something about it?"

"Why? Such a tragedy is best forgotten. And you didn't even know Maureen."

"No, but—" I faltered.

"Why don't you say it? Your behavior has made it quite evident. You think I was the father of her child."

244

"I . . . I don't know . . . what to think. You were here with her just about the time that she . . ."

"I see. Guilty, just like that!" His jaw tightened and his smile was forced and narrow. "My dear, even a condemned man usually has the chance to say a few words before he's hung."

"I don't want to believe it," I said quickly.

He gave a short laugh. "But my reputation cannot be denied . . . is that it? You, of all people, know how entranced I become with my Juliets. I bring them to my hotel suite and seduce them!" The words were cruel and bitter.

I couldn't respond to his fury.

He stood up. "Well, I think we can consider this conversation at an end. Any discussion of the past would only confirm your fears that I have dallied with your affections, unscrupulous rogue that I am. How could you be expected to believe a word that flows out of my deceitful mouth?" He cut off my stammering protest. "We'll be in Sacramento in a few hours and there will be enough professional challenges waiting to overshadow our personal affairs. When we return to San Francisco . . ." He let the sentence hang ominiously.

"Ty—?" I could not keep the anguish out of my voice. He had lashed out at me for my lack of trust and loyalty, but he had not said one thing to deny any similar romantic involvement with Maureen. I watched him stride angrily out of the room and I knew that any chance to narrow the chasm between us was gone.

I had been to Sacramento countless times with the Rafferty Players when we traveled the mining camp circuit, but I had never seen it from the river. We had always come overland with our horses, mules, and

245

wagon. As I stood at the railing I could see how widely the city had spread around the confluence of the Sacramento and American rivers. A variety of buildings housed banks, haberdasheries, stables, saloons, and the Emerald Theater. Hotels and mercantile stores sprawled along the Embarcadero, which was the low land west of Sutter's Fort chosen for a landing on the Sacramento. Several impressive structures had been built on piles to save them from flooding. A sprawling business district had been laid out for several blocks bordered by Front Street along the river.

Not unlike San Francisco, there was a bawdy gaiety along Sacramento's boardwalks and cobbled streets as gamblers, roustabouts, and libertine women rubbed shoulders with merchants, bankers, and the prosperous elite. The days when it had been a Spanish land grant deeded to John Augustus Sutter were gone. The day the Mormon's workman found gold while building a new mill brought Sutter disaster instead of riches. As the cry of *gold* reverberated across the nation, '49ers sprawled all over his land and stayed to build a town.

As we neared the dock I saw a crowd of cheering, waving people waiting to meet the *Athena* as she eased into her berth. Apparently news of the new opening of the Emerald Theater had been received enthusiastically and a committee of city personages stepped forward to greet Ty Langston as he and the captain went down the gangplank. A band began to play, and we saw carriages and hacks lined up to take us to our hotel.

"Wowee!" laughed Nell. "Now ain't this something! To think of all the times we sneaked in and out of town by the back door."

Even Farley had a grin on his lean face. "I wonder if

that mule trader will recognize us and want his money back. That cranky old jackass I pushed off on him might have gotten him a little riled."

"Remember back when we played the Eagle." Budd chuckled. "What a makeshift joint that was . . . the sides were canvas . . ."

"The stage made out of scrap lumber and old crates . . ."

"And the audience sat on rough boards set right on the ground . . ."

"Them were the days. . . ."

"Well, boys, you can have 'em." Nell laughed, tossing her head like a filly feeling a touch of spring. Her romantic interlude on the boat had left her cheeks flushed with the indefinable air of a loved woman. "No more plantin' my backside on a mule. Lead me to the carriages. I'm aiming to take my proper place in society."

Her high spirits were infectious. My weighted spirits lifted. Old ties united the four of us again as we crowded into a well-sprung carriage with all our belongings. If Jessie had been there, she would have scoffed at such extravagance. The Ebner Hotel was only a couple blocks away . . . imagine riding that short distance when two good legs would take you there without any muss or expense!

The Ebner was a provincial establishment compared to San Francisco's elegant hotels, but it was certainly up the scale from what we had been used to during our stays in the city. I could remember horrid sleeping rooms with lumpy mattresses for beds. Those rooms had been stifling hot in summer; if you opened the windows, you invited swarms of mosquitoes off the river sloughs; all the walls were thin enough to allow snores from the adjoining room to punctuate bawdy laughter and swearing on the street below. Oh, yes, the Ebner was a cut above all that. Clean, freshly painted rooms with high ceilings and polished woodwork were modest but pleasant.

My third floor room was large and spacious, furnished with dark furniture, polished and shiny and brightened by a braided rug that still retained its myriad of fresh colors. I was grateful Ty had arranged for me to have a private room—with Nell across the hall—and a shared bathroom for only four rooms. How quickly I had become used to luxurious accommodations.

I was both disappointed and relieved to learn that Ty would not be staying at the Ebner but at the Brandon House, closer to the Emerald on Second Street. Since I hadn't seen Dana, Cal, and Lila, I wondered if they were staying there also. It was obvious that one hotel could not house all the people Ty had brought with him. Why, then, did I feel somehow set apart from everyone? He had been so concerned about protecting me in San Francisco. Did he think we had left the danger there? My resentment at his casual dismissal of my well-being was misplaced because when I left my third floor room to go down to the lobby, I sensed someone behind me. Apprehension made me swing around furtively.

Trapper touched his hat in greeting. A smile whitened lips between his black beard and mustache. His presence was reassuring. Ty had brought him along to be my watchdog. This knowledge sent a bewildering mixture of relief, wonder, and new anxiety through me. The implication was obvious. Ty did not think the danger was over.

In the days that followed I was grateful I did not have time to sink into the quagmire of my own feelings, for Ty refused to relate to me on any personal level. It was my fault; I knew that. My reaction had been purely emotional . . . and it was too late to look at the matter rationally. He had been hurt by my lack of faith in his integrity and I was still harboring too many unanswered questions. Fortunately, we immediately swung into an exhausting schedule that allowed little time for anything but hours of demanding work and blessed sleep.

Ty was determined to hammer a production together in less than two weeks' time. He had chosen a melodrama, *Plight of the Damsel*. The play had two strong female roles, the ingenue and the villainess sister of Sir Bascombe, a cad who pursues the pure heroine and is thwarted at every turn by the hero. When the cast was posted I saw that Dana and I were to play opposite each other as hero and heroine; Ty was taking the part of Sir Bascombe, with Lila as his villainess accomplice. I don't know what he said to soothe her, but Lila seemed satisfied that the role had more depth than playing the insipid heroine.

The Emerald Theater was small, crowded, inadequate, and in every way a contrast to the facilities that the Imperial had offered. There was no green room, only shared dressing rooms for each sex; a seamstress' room that was scarcely more than a closet, with nails pounded on the wall to hold costumes. There was no need for Mrs. Faraday's company. I was never alone. We all were cramped, like scurrying ants trying to pass each other in narrow halls and crowded aisles.

It was too late to make any of the renovations that Ty had planned when he leased the Emerald. I think he realized that trying to open it without proper planning had been a foolish move. Now he seemed to have a diabolical determination that we had to present the most professional production possible to make up for his judgment. He had never been so demanding and dogged; he never showed any qualms about doing a scene over and over again, insisting that we move about the stage at a near run. "Get a handle on it . . . faster . . . faster . . ."

Budd and Nell had been given character roles that provided comic relief, so important in an overly sentimental melodrama. The timing of their antics had to be exact in order to be funny, and Ty was relentless, banging his cane furiously. "No . . . No . . . can't you see what you're doing . . . slowing down the whole scene pulls it apart. Nell, you've got to be ready to swing that broom the minute he walks through the door. It's only funny if it's unexpected!"

Farley's role was that of the hero's friend, whose appearance and dialogue on stage was mainly confined to reporting what was happening offstage. It was scarcely more than a walk-on, walk-off part, and I knew Farley was angry and frustrated that he hadn't been given a bigger role. His lean face was set in a perpetual glower, and I tried my best to make light of the slight, but I knew that Ty had placed the last proverbial straw upon Farley's back. He was like tinder waiting for a spark to ignite.

No one escaped the whip of the taskmaster. Cal hunched over his piano keys night and day, scoring as Ty directed. Every gasp on stage had to be accented by a response from the piano . . . thumping chords accompanied fights and quarrels . . . soft, lyrical music echoed soft words of romance. Without the *melo* part of the *drama*, the play was flat. Every change Ty made on stage had to be reflected in a new musical score—and the changes were constant!

It was little consolation that Ty was working as hard as any of us. He had to carry his role on stage as well as direct, but his taskmaster tactics built up resentment and friction against him and among the cast. Instead of working together, petty jealousies were magnified. Lila seemed to delight in giving a miscue when I was on stage so that it would look like my fault when I took the dialogue and went in the wrong direction . . . or she feigned a move that made my response premature and crude. When Ty raked me for such amateur performances, a slight smile hovered on her pursed lips. Her malice was barely contained under her smooth, white skin, ready to spew out at any opportunity.

Dana made it obvious to everyone that he thought the play entirely beneath his skills and he executed his part with a condescending ease that shamed the rest of us. As the handsome, blond Roland, he made a perfect hero and foil to Ty as the dark, lecherous Sir Bascombe. I watched the two of them on stage and my heart quickened at the skill with which they fed lines, picked up cues, dominated the stage, and propelled the kind of energetic force that Ty was always searching for. They were good and evil, black and white, and yet always projecting subtle shades of gray that gave each character dimension. I knew Ty was trying to achieve the same thing between Lila and me, but the same level of performance eluded us. I feared that in this production of *The Plight of the Damsel* we were merely players and not actors.

In spite of Billy's protests that it could never be done, the sets were ready in time; various scene changes were organized to eliminate as much confusion as possible. Finally all the nail hooks were filled with costumes, ready and waiting for our dress rehearsal. As they were handed out, and we discarded our working clothes for the garb of our characters, I experienced my usual fluttering excitement. From childhood I had delighted in this make-believe world, and a stirring of innocent joy was still in me.

Nell smoothed the lace collar of my simple white dress and then tied the streamers of my pink bonnet. ''There now, love, if you don't look like a white cake with pink frosting, my poor old eyes are deceiving me.'' She squinted and we laughed, for she was dressed as a gaudy woman servant with grayish hair showing under a rakish day cap. Maybe we were giddy with fatigue, for we took one look at Budd and started laughing. Budd's bold plaid pants, red suspenders, and puce shirt struck us as hilarious. Even Farley in his simple pants and tunic laughed with us when we gathered on stage for Ty's final approval.

''Would you look at that?'' I followed Nell's eyes as Lila moved out of the wings to join the gathering for our costume call.

Her costume was black velvet, with a high, fanlike collar that flared behind her slim neck. Jet-black hair was pulled tightly away from her face and her eyebrows were drawn almost to an oriental slant. Heavy, blackened eyelashes gave her lids a sinister, half-closed look. Her narrow, long nose, rigid mouth, and expression of hauteur and disdain took on a miasma of evil in that costume. Then Ty joined her. Heavy makeup accentuated his deep-set eyes, making them black coals ringed with white. His hair was arched back from his forehead and held with heavy hair oil. A black cape and suit was relieved only by a gold chain strung across his vest. He made a perfect match with Lila. ''Good casting, I'd say,'' hissed Nell. She knew that things were strained between us and she was openly delighted. She made no bones about insinuating that his attention had moved elsewhere.

As our director made his way down the line,

looking at each costume with a critical eye, my breathing became more shallow. A wardrobe seamstress hovered near him, nodding and making notes about his remarks or suggestions. We all knew that costumes, like everything else, had to come up to his standard of excellence. When he reached me I moistened my lips nervously and waited.

"How does it feel?" he asked, his eyes traveling downward from the lace collar to the pink bows caught in the flounces of my skirt. "Can you move easily in that much fullness?"

"Yes, it's fine."

"Turn around. Again . . . faster! All right, it gives a nice teasing view of your ankles. The audience will enjoy that."

I stiffened, and then saw a teasing glint in those black eyes and felt myself relaxing in spite of his sinister visage. "Maybe it'll take their minds off my mistakes."

"I didn't think we were planning on having any of those. We've worked hard. We'll put on a good performance."

It did not matter that we were in a provincial theater, its facilities crude and inadequate, and that only common people starved for entertainment would be in the audience. Ty Langston would present his Players as if they were opening in their New York debut. How could he know that all his efforts were for naught? That another drama beyond his control would be acted out on a lighted stage—the threats real and the dangers of life and death more than just glitter and paint?

16

As the arriving theater patrons took their seats, an echoing rumble that was a mixture of muffled footsteps, suppressed laughter, muted chatter, and rattling programs floated backstage. A five-minute call brought us from the dressing rooms in a quiet flurry to take our proper positions in the narrow wings.

At that point Cal took his place at the piano on the raised dias. He must have bowed, for the audience clapped loudly, eager for the entertainment to begin. This boisterous reception was reassuring. It was the right kind of audience to enjoy our melodramatic play.

Cal's nimble fingers bounced over the keys in a gay medley of piano tunes that soon had the audience tapping their feet. This warm-up show was an important one, and Cal was superb at it. I took a peek through a slit in the crimson curtain and saw him with a derby set rakishly on one side, wearing a red-and-black-striped vest over a white frilly shirt and black pants. He sat with his back to the audience as his lithe figure moved rhythmically on his small piano stool.

Then the notes of his last ballad faded away. The audience clapped and then waited. That hushed moment of pure anticipation as the curtains began to part was one that always took my stomach in a downward, sickening plunge. Sweaty hands smoothed my skirt for the last time, touched my ribboned hair, and caught my lower lip in a grimace of pure fear. I was wearing a pinafore over my white dress for my first scene and I nervously felt in the pocket for the handkerchief I needed.

The minute my fingers touched the crispness of paper, cold dread made me draw it out. I knew what it was. It would have been better if I had left the folded paper in my pocket. Boldly printed letters seared my breathless gaze. "The stage is set . . . your death awaits . . . Enter the Villain!"

At that moment a welcoming roar from the audience stifled my audible cry as Sir Bascombe and his sister, Regina, made their entrance from opposite wings. Immediately, Ty and Lila swept the audience into the drama of good and evil. Terror I had never known before made that open stage a yawning abyss waiting for me, and I knew there was no escape.

As I stood in the wings the familiar dialogue of the play floated over me unheard. Sir Bascombe and Regina have just learned that the demure, innocent Angelique is really the true heir to their father's fortune and stands in their way of inheriting. They plot against me, drawing Sir Bascombe's dastardly and lecherous character and Regina's cruel and spiteful jealousy.

When I heard my cue I couldn't move. The note crumpled in my hand distorted reality. Somebody gave me a shove and I lurched forward. Master that he was, Ty paraphrased my cue so there wasn't a drop in the action, but his eyes blazed at me. He was furious! Lila's mouth quivered in a smirk and her obvious delight jerked me out of my near collapse. *Maybe she had planted the note out of viciousness . . . wanting to destroy my performance.* Anger came to my rescue, but there was an honest tremor in my voice when I pleaded against being sent away to a hunting lodge where danger awaited me.

As always, the force of Ty's theatrical powers overwhelmed me. In my bewilderment his harsh grip on my arm was real. His threats of ravishment brought an honest lurching of my heart into my throat, for there was nothing of the devoted lover about him. Lila laughed with apparent true mirth as I pleaded against his advances, as if my words were underscored with something more than the words of a script.

Dana's entrance as the hero whose noble nature would protect me from Sir Bascombe's evil plans met with loud clapping and cheering. I was grateful for his smooth, professional delivery, which carried me along. The rest of that act was a blurred nightmare, and I wondered if the audience could tell that I truly feared for my life when swords and knives came anywhere near me.

There was little time between acts, but I tried to find Ty as soon as my appearance had been changed to resemble a captive maiden, prisoner in a sinister hunting lodge. I knew he was in the opposite wing, and I would have to make my way behind the backdrop in order to see him. Nell and Budd were in the next scene as the drunken, bawdy caretakers; I had less than five minutes to navigate the clutter of para-phernalia backstage. As I moved in the darkened, narrow space, I prayed I wouldn't knock over anything and ruin the action on stage. The darkened backstage tunnel seemed endless. There was only diffuse light to guide my steps around the shadowy mounds and stacks of clutter. Then, above the rollicking dialogue on stage, I heard breathing and felt hot air on my neck.

In the dark shadows a thick arm reached out and grabbed me, jerking me back into the caverns of waiting scenery. A cry lurched into my throat, but a hand covered my mouth. "Quiet!" hissed the voice.

It was a wonder I didn't strike out and hit the back-drop, but even in that moment of panic I recognized the voice.

"For the love of Mary, watcha doing back here, lass?" Billy whispered in my ear. "Another step and ye'd have sent a dozen pails tumbling."

Relief made me lean my head against his. "I have to speak to Ty . . ." I croaked.

On the other side of the backdrop, inches away, we could hear Nell and Budd and the punctuation of laughter as the audience responded to their comic antics. The loud chords of Cal's accompaniment and the frolicking notes matching the humorous buffoonery muffled our words.

"He'll skin you alive for being out of position."

"I know, but I have to see him . . . now!" That trite phrase about life and death seemed horribly ominous.

"You'd better be watching where ye put yer feet." He took my sweaty hand and, inch by inch, threaded through a maze of props, stealthily, carefully, and with agonizing slowness. I could tell from the dialogue that the comic scene was over—Ty was on next!

The minute we reached the other side of the stage I bolted away from Billy. Ty was waiting in the front wing, ready to make his entrance. I frantically grabbed his arm. "Ty . . ."

He swung around at my cracked whisper. "What the hell—"

"What shall I do? I got another . . ."

He cut off my words. "For God's sake, Tara! Not now!"

I reached in my pocket to bring out the note, but it was too late! Before I could hand it to him the cue for his entrance brought him out on stage, only a split second late to Cal's accompanying chords.

I stared after him, stilling the impulse to follow him out on the stage and make him listen to me. But my training was too strong. Nothing must interrupt the show!

There was nothing to be done now. A surge of dispair brought tears into my eyes. I had less than two minutes to make it through the dark labyrinth backstage to my position in the opposite wing. Fortunately, Billy grabbed my hand again and we made the return trip with him leading me like a blind person behind the backdrop that shielded us from the audience. Inches away, separated by a thin drop of canvas, I could hear Ty's voice and the hushed waiting of the audience as the melodramatic plot evolved. For a moment I considered kicking over every blasted beer bucket backstage.

Hot tears swelled up. Damn the play! Why couldn't Ty have listened to me? Nothing else mattered to him . . . not me . . . not anybody. He wouldn't veer one particle from the rehearsed script. No matter what happened he would carry through so the audience would not know something was amiss . . . a madman could kill me onstage and Ty would never let the audience down by disrupting the play.

I made it to the other side with only seconds to spare. The next scene was a romantic one, and my performance was listless and wooden. I could feel Dana's anger building as we went through our embraces and vows of love. As soon as we were off stage he exploded. "What are you trying to do out there? Make me look like a bungling lover!"

"I'm sorry, I—"

"Sorry! Just who do you think you are? All your subtle tricks . . . trying to put us all down as actors."

"That's not true!"

"Isn't it! You persuaded Ty to play Romeo instead of me and you've shut Lila out of *Camille* by cozing up to him. You want every performance to be given to you! To hell with the rest of us."

"No . . . please . . . !"

"I understand perfectly . . . you're trying to make me look like some goddamn amateur! You better watch yourself in this last act." His expression was as threatening as his tone. "By God, they're going to see a play they will remember!"

I closed my eyes, but there were no tears, only pain. The instinct to bolt was there. Later I wondered what kept me moving toward disaster with such fatalistic surrender. I prepared for the climactic scene with slow, lethargic movements. Dana's caustic lashing had left me wounded and defeated. Even Nell's chatter and helping hands could not dispel the sense of disaster that had settled upon me.

"Don't know what's happening to everybody. Nobody's acting normal," she said with her usual perception. "What's the matter, Tarry, you're as life-less as a doll stuffed with straw, and I had to break up a fight between Budd and Farley backstage . . . like two stray cats, they were. Don't know what set them off. Lordy, I wish this thing was over . . . thank God, only one scene to go.''

One scene to go. In my mind I accepted a presentiment that it was too late now to stop the forces of destruction that battered against me. Unlike the melodrama we were enacting on stage, I could tell that there was no promise of morality in the events to follow; no rewards for virtue and punishment for evil. From the first moment I had slipped Maureen's cape upon my shoulders the script had been written and now . . . enter the villain.

The action of the last scene was set in a bedroom of the hunting lodge where Sir Bascombe and Regina prepare to kill the innocent heroine.

I took my place. As the curtain parted, battle shouts and the clash of swords came from offstage. To the mounting chords of Cal's accompaniment, I rushed from my small bed to center stage.

In a frantic soliloquy, I expounded on the siege my brave hero had laid upon the lodge in order to thwart Sir Bascombe's evil intentions. I told the audience that at that very moment my beloved was struggling at the edge of the forest, fighting to reach my side.

Nell picked up her cue as the frowsy, grin-laced caretaker who has befriended the heroine. She entered from stage left at a near run, waving her fat arms and wailing about the dangers besetting the heroine. With dramatic delivery, Nell milked laughter from the audience with her frenzied antics and wailing laments.

More sounds of fighting and thunderous music.

At a frantic rate Cal pounded out the rising crescendos on his piano keys. Nell rushed to the window to describe the scene. ''Alas . . . alas . . . Sir Bascombe's men have triumphed. They have overcome your beloved, m'lady . . . taken him

prisoner!'' Chord! Chord! She turned to comfort me.
The audience booed on cue as the malevolent Regina
made her entrance. Lila's voice rose in triumph as she
announced that the hero had been taken to the
dungeon!

Lila and I played out our lines in rhythm as the
melodramatic action and dialogue mounted, and I
could almost hear Ty breathe a sigh of relief.

Then he made his entrance amid hisses and jeers
from the audience, swishing his villain's cape.
Fortissimo, thundering melody.

''Be gone, old woman,'' he commanded Nell, who
made her protests with comical intensity but was
routed from the bedroom at the tip of Ty's rapier.

''It is time, my lovely.'' He leered at me as he pulled
me up from my suppliant position and jerked me to
him. The audience's appetite was whetted by his
leering visage. ''One kiss . . . and then you die!''

Cheers and applause rose to a level akin to mob
scenes where the satanical villains became black
heroes. Ty's ability to hold and mold an audience
response was evident at that moment. They wanted
him to have his way with the heroine. He kissed me
with the force of an uncaring rapist, and I felt a trickle
of blood where his hard mouth had pressed against
mine. He was Sir Bascombe and I was fighting for my
life against him! I could tell he was pleased with my
delivery as he tore a cord from the draperies and
bound my hands behind my back.

I struggled and pleaded as Sir Bascombe carried me
to stage center. The audience screamed and booed.
Cal pounded out the rising crescendo as Sir Bascombe
placed me on a stool and put the hangman's noose
around my neck. His leering visage held little
resemblance to the lover who had caressed me and
led me to the heights of passion. My wide-eyed stare

brought an expression into his eyes that I could not read.

"No . . . please," I pleaded, but the words were soft, for his ears alone.

He seemed to drop his role for a split second as his gaze swept mine, but at that instant Lila jumped a cue. She prematurely pulled his lines and drew him stage right. Without faltering from her miscue, he made a speech to the audience amid boos and hisses and then gave a diabolical laugh that was Dana's cue to appear at the window.

Dana leaped on stage with a triumphant cry. A bedraggled but still handsome hero was greeted enthusiastically by the audience.

Chord! Chord! Shouts and cheers. To the delight of the jeering spectators, rapiers were drawn with a flourish as Sir Bascombe and the hero, Dana, faced each other. Thundering chords vibrated from Cal's piano as the frantic music accompanied the duel. The two men moved back and forth across the stage, plunging and retreating with thrusts and parries.

It was their scene. I only had to make silent, frantic gestures with my body. It was going to be over in a matter of seconds, when the hero would fight his way to me and cut the rope in a gallant sweep. In some detached part of my mind I thought that my fears were foolish, unfounded. The note had been intended to throw me off stride. The scene was going well. Ty would be pleased. He would say the show was alive with energy!

At the moment I decided that the note had been a malicious trick I lowered my eyes with thankfulness. Then I saw it! Tied around one leg of the stool on which I stood was a strong wire. It ran unobtrusively in front of the footlights across to stage left. I followed it with horror. *One tug and the stool would go out from under me!* My neck would be snapped in a real hanging in front of the unsuspecting, cheering audience!

My eyes flew to the wings. Farley was standing there watching my every movement.

"No!"

At that moment the script called for Dana to be flung down at the bottom of the stool, giving him a chance to emote in heroic tones, "Faith, my true love, he shall not lay his hands upon thy loveliness. I shall fight him to the death."

I was supposed to gaze at him in adoration and make entreaties for his safety. Instead, I gasped frantically, "Untie me! Untie me!" My frantic cry stepped upon his last line and withheld the cue for his next speech.

A look of pure malevolence swept into his eyes *He thought I was trying to destroy his performance.* "No! No," I cried. "Please!"

But he cut off my cry and lurched away. With his powerful voice, he launched into his next speech to Sir Bascombe.

"Help . . . do something!" I screamed.

My ad lib pleas blended with a script calling for my frantic entreaties to be freed. Ty had talked a great deal about the professional actor being able to hold a scene together by setting up new lines, jumping cues, and incorporating unexpected happenings so that an audience could never be quite certain what was spontaneous and what was not. Dana showed his competence as he took the audience with him. He had warned me that he wasn't going to let me break up his scene.

A madly racing crescendo brought my eyes frantically to the wings again. Farley was gone! No one stood there to tug on the fatal wire. Bewildered, my eye began to trace the wire again and I saw something I had missed before. It did not go as far as the wings! The wire trailed offstage—to the dais.

Cal's black eyes were fixed upon my ashen face with a crazed intensity. Triumphant music exploded under his fingers. A cigarette dangling from his lips was a dagger point of light. He smiled, a crooked, sadistic twist as if he had been waiting for this moment since that first day he had offered me Maureen's clothes. I did not know why—or how—but recognition was there. *The stage was set—Enter the Villain!*

He had been toying with me, pulling me into this web of madness. He laughed.

I let out a piercing scream. But the energy that had been unleashed on stage drowned out my frantic plea. My cry was absorbed in the clamoring cheers of the audience. As if on cue, Cal leaned down and pulled on the wire running to the base of the piano.

I felt the stool go out from under me.

The noose instantly tightened. A band of fire encircled my throat, but I did not fall!

At the last second Ty swung around in my direction and his strong arms were suddenly there! He held me securely and jerked the hangman's noose from my throat.

The audience went wild, clapping and jeering. The piano music broke off in a discord. I heard a muffled shot . . . and Cal fell from the stool with a gun in his hand. He had brought down the final curtain upon his drama.

The confusion around me had little importance as Ty's hands caressed me and his lips murmured in my ear. "My darling . . . I'm sorry . . . my precious darling . . . please forgive me . . ." He cradled me in his arms and I knew that neither foolish pride nor

misunderstandings would ever make me leave them
again.

17

If Cal had not revealed his twisted, crazed mind in his dying confession, I doubt that I would have ever been convinced that he had murdered Maureen and Jessie and been the villain who set fire to my dressing room and jerked the stool out from under my feet. As the pieces fell into place there were taunting misgivings. If only I had not doubted Ty . . . and if only he had been honest with me . . . if only we had known. But all these regrets had to be laid to rest.

Ty hired a buggy and we took a long ride along the river, talking, touching, kissing, sighing, and even crying as we sought to untangle the chords of treachery and revenge woven into an evil pattern.

Although Ty had known something of the horrible trauma Cal had endured aboard ship at the hands of vile sailors who had abused and assaulted him, he had not realized it had left such a festering madness. There had been no indication in his quiet, solitary manner that his abuse had been twisted as a vendetta against his unfaithful wife, whom he had left because she had been carrying another man's child. He had signed on a ship, only to be brutally misused. The trauma had been twisted in his mind against his unfaithful wife, Maureen and then me. A photograph found in his belongings showed his wife to be blonde, slender, and with petite features akin to mine and Maureen's.

"But I didn't know there had been anything romantic between Cal and Maureen," I protested, still trying to bring the horror into some kind of sane perspective.

"There wasn't . . . at least not until her situation made her reach out for help. You see, it was Dana who was the father of her child, not Cal nor . . ." He gave me a disappointed look that I deserved. "Nor me."

"Dana!"

"Maureen was very attractive to men, and Dana had been briefly enamored of her. She made the mistake of thinking that his single-minded dedication to his art was only because he hadn't found anyone he really loved. Whether or not she planned to trap him into marriage I don't know, but when she became pregnant he refused to acknowledge or accept any responsibility in the situation. That's when she turned to me, demanding that I marry her to save her good name. Our brief romantic relationship had ended nearly a year before when I signed her up for the Imperial. I didn't even know who she had been seeing."

"That's what the fight was about the day she left?"

"Right. She wouldn't tell me who the father was, but she hinted that he was someone outside the theater, so when she left I assumed she must have decided to marry him after all. She refused my offer of financial help, called me every dirty name that she could think of, and swore she'd never darken my doorstep again."

"That's why you were surprised that first day . . . in the green room . . . when you thought it was her instead of me."

He nodded. "I was startled and relieved and glad of a chance to erase the angry words between us. I thought maybe she had changed her mind about letting me help her."

"That's why you were disappointed to see me instead of her. And I thought—"

"I know what you thought, darling. Once you get an idea in that stubborn head of yours you won't let go."

"I'm sorry." He forgave me with a lingering kiss. "I had no idea that she turned to Cal for help," I said, settling my head against his shoulder. "He must have given her a present at one time."

"The lavaliere."

"Right, and he must have taken it off her the night he killed her. In his twisted mind she was another unfaithful woman carrying another man's child and expecting him to marry her."

"Jessie must have found the necklace in his things . . ."

I nodded, remembering Jessie's scrounging habits. "Or seen it in his hands . . . and he had to kill her to silence her. He was the one in the shadows of the theater that night," I said, and shivered involuntarily.

Ty tightened his arm around me. "After Cal threw her down the steps he must have raced down after her, intent on getting the necklace, but he didn't have time. Maybe he was getting ready to give it to you, the way he had the clothes. He might have thought in the beginning that you liked him.''

"But I did. I mean, I liked Cal very much . . .''

"But not in the way he wanted. When he saw you and me falling in love the twist of madness must have come back and centered on you.''

"But he saved me from the fire . . .''

"I've thought about that,'' said Ty. "He was the one who sent the note to Mrs. Faraday. When I came running through the theater, shouting your name, he must have been on the stairs with no place to go but back down. He was trapped at the scene of the crime. The only way he could prove he was innocent of setting the fire was to go back and pretend he had heard your cry.''

"So he saved me . . .''

"Thank God.'' His lips lingered on my cheek and I felt his warm breath caressing my skin.

"I never once suspected him and all the time he was the one writing those vicious notes and planning that diabolical hanging in front of the audience.'' I choked with the horror of remembrance.

"I'll never forgive myself for not listening to you on that stage. My pride was smarting because you didn't trust me. I couldn't understand why you didn't believe me. I knew that Maureen had not meant anything to me.''

I gave a weak laugh. "And I tried so hard to step into her shoes. I didn't think you would even notice me unless I wore her clothes and pretended to be like her in every way possible.''

"You precious ninny. I've told you before, it was that impish face peering around Budd that first day and that foolhardy scamp scurrying up and down a rope ladder that caught my heartstrings and wouldn't let me go.'' He bent his head and his mouth worked gently upon my lips, tugging, pressing, welding a passionate contact that brought my arms around his neck. "You could never be anybody else," he whispered, "and I intend to keep you always and forever for myself." He tilted my chin gently with his hand and searched my face. "Could you put up with my arrogant, demanding ways . . . Mrs. Tyrone Langston in private and my leading lady on stage?"

"No, I could never do that." The finality in my tone was unmistakable.

"Why . . . why not?" A sudden torment leaped into his eyes.

A secret smile softened my words. "I've told you before that I don't want to be one of your leading ladies. I have no intention of making the theater my whole life. I'm interested in one role only." My eyes gave me away.

He smiled in obvious relief, but his tone was quite solemn as he took my hand. "Will you consent, Miss Townsend, to sign a lifetime contract as my wife?" he asked in that deep, resonant voice that sent trills up my back. I gave him an answering kiss. Then I murmured, "How pleased Nell will be."

"Will Lambert's making sounds like he's about to offer his own nuptial proposal. Do you think Nell will accept?"

"Yes, I think she's ready to settle down, especially with someone as exciting as Willy. And since Farley and Budd . . ." my voice faltered.

"Have given notice and taken jobs with a new company in Virginia City," Ty finished. "Don't look back, Tara. There's too much happiness ahead for us."

I smiled agreement, blinking back a sudden fullness in my eyes.

"That's settled then. I suggest we stop this dallying

and talk to Captain Whitney about doing the honors. We'll take our time getting back to San Francisco, give everyone in the company a brief respite with pay." With a light flick of his whip he sent the horse trotting back along the river to Sacramento. "I hope you aren't one of those brides who needs six months to assemble a trousseau."

"I don't think I'm going to have much need for clothes on our honeymoon," I said with a wanton smile.

The promising glint in his deep-set eyes told me I was right.